It's Not Like It's a Secret

It Must Be Love

GRACE J. CROY

*To all those who read my books and encourage me to keep going,
even when I want to give up.*

Chapter One

AVERY

The longer the doctor takes to return to the exam room, the more I perspire through the thin hospital gown. I've become a watering system of sweat, with rivers running down my back. A stream streaks from my hairline and across my cheek. With all the humidity my body is putting out, my beach waved hair is wilting.

My thoughts spiral back to the last time I sat panicking in an exam room. I was seven and my older sister decided she would make me a basketball star. I was tall for my age, and besides height, there wasn't much else to the sport, right? She took me out to the driveway, and without warning, threw a basketball at my face to see how I would respond. I didn't. The ball broke my nose and gave me two black eyes.

Mom took at least a hundred pictures and scrapbooked a fifteen-page spread of the catastrophe. The first few photos are of me bawling, blood gushing from my nose, into my mouth, and down the front of my Phineas and Ferb T-shirt. The next page shows the rush to the ER. I'm still crying, but I have a bloody kitchen towel and a frozen bag of peas covering most of my face.

In the last picture, I'm standing in the hallway of the hospital just before we leave for home. My bandaged nose looks like a beak, and mottled, purple bruises surround my eyes. From then on, Dad called me his Little Owl. It would've been sweet if it wasn't so ironic. There is nothing little about me.

I haven't touched a basketball since the tragedy, not even for gym class, much to the disappointment of every coach from middle school through college. Instead, I joined the cross-country team, a sport that promised to never throw balls at my face.

The doctor's knock brings me back to the present. She enters wearing a big smile. My nerves settle because her expression lets me believe there's no serious problem with my health. My relief lasts as long as the silence. When she begins speaking, I find out that everything is worse than I could ever imagine. All I can think about is the long-ago basketball fiasco, the shock of that awful orange ball hitting me, and the pain and panic that followed.

My hand shakes as I reach up and rub the bridge of my nose.

"What did you say?" I ask.

The doctor's still smiling, not at all annoyed at having to repeat herself. "I want you to come back for an ultrasound as soon as possible."

"No, before that."

She tilts her head and purses her lips. "You're pregnant?"

My hand drops to my lap. I squeeze my eyes closed, wishing it was enough to shut out this conversation. "That isn't possible."

"Obviously it is possible because you're pregnant."

She needs to stop saying that word. "I can't be."

"It does explain your heartburn, nausea, and recent weight gain."

And my boobs. They're so tender. I swear they've doubled in size. A lot of men are eye-level with my neck, and I don't need to give them any more reason to look down instead of up.

There must be another explanation because I am not... you know, the p-word.

"Lay back and let me do a pelvic examination."

This gets better and better.

I obediently unstick myself from the paper and lay down on the table. I don't know what I expected when I came in today with a list of complaints. Cancer. Celiac disease. Polio. But this diagnosis isn't an option.

I wait for the doctor to say, "*Oops, I guess I made a mistake.*" It doesn't happen. Instead, she says, "Based on your hCG levels and your measurements, I'd say you're about nineteen weeks along. Does that line up with your last menstruation?"

I have no idea. My periods have always been erratic, and I don't pay much attention. But the last time I saw my ex, The Liar, was almost five months ago, so the timing would line up...except that I am *not* carrying his Mini-Me.

"Your baby is about the size of a mango," the doctor says in a chit-chatty voice. "Next week a grape fruit."

That sounds delightful. Whose great idea was it to

determine the size of a fetus by comparing it to food? The doctor drones on with useless bits of information, but I can't process what she's saying. My problem must be wheat. I'll stop eating gluten, and that will make me feel less tired and irritable.

After the exam, I dress slowly. My white button-up blouse is snug but at least there aren't any gaps, and I just manage to zip up my blue pencil skirt. Using the compact from my purse, I check my make-up, then put my long hair into a ponytail. Now that my armor is in place, my confidence increases. As I leave the exam room, I shove everything that just transpired into a corner of my brain where it can hang out with memories of The Liar. I have no need to remember.

I leave with a bottle of prenatal vitamins, an information packet on pregnancy, and an appointment for an ultrasound next Monday. I imagine the doctor feeling sheepish when she discovers her mistake because I am definitely not pregnant. If I were, that would make me just like my sister.

I am not my sister.

By THE TIME I PULL INTO THE PARKING LOT OF BALDWIN-Dickson Pencil Company, the heat of the morning has settled into my bones. Ladybug's AC can't seem to cut through the hazy heat. I should rename her Slow Cooker. I pat her dash, repentant. No need to give her any cause to give out on me now. I place the blame where it belongs: the Tucson, Arizona sun in early August.

My phone beeps with a text just as I exit my car.

TAMRA: What did the dr say?

Of course, my best friend has to text me while I'm still feeling shaky from the ordeal. My visit rears up and wants to make itself known, but I beat it back into its corner.

AVERY: Celiac. I'll call you tonight and give you all the details. It's pretty funny so be prepared to laugh until you pee

TAMRA: giving up bread is no laughing matter!

Which makes me laugh. When I realize I'm rubbing my nose, I force my feet toward the building. Oh, man. It's only Tuesday, and I'm ready for the weekend. I love my job, but right now I want a nap. To get through the day, I'll do what I'm good at: focus on the immediate future and banish everything else. I have six hours until quitting time. I can handle six hours.

I let myself in through the staff entrance with my keycard. I usually love the first big sniff I get of cut wood, but today it's the AC that makes me happiest. It blows against my damp skin, and I shiver with relief. If I wasn't already late, I might stand under the vent for an hour before going up to the third floor, where all the hot air goes to live.

Around the corner, I see Mary from HR with some guy, probably a new hire, waiting for the elevator. I can't handle Mary right now. I take a step back, hoping to slip into the stairwell before she sees me, but no luck. My size-eleven flats squeak against the linoleum before I can hide.

"Avery!" she calls out. "Come meet our new factory employee!"

I reluctantly step forward and shake the man's hand. I peg him at five feet, nine inches. He's one of those guys where his attention goes down before heading slowly up—

and up—to my face. Some men have the decency to blush when they realize I've caught them introducing themselves to my chest before my eyes. He's not one of them. His grin grows.

"Paul," he says with awe, as if he can't believe my height. Or maybe my cup size.

"Avery."

"I'm so glad I found you!" Mary says. "I'm trying to get the final count for the company picnic next weekend. You didn't RSVP, but I put you down anyway. I was wondering if you were bringing any family? Or a date?"

Not only do I find her enthusiasm exhausting and her sickly-sweet falsetto voice irritating, but she's also the company Gossip Girl. If she finds out any interesting information, within ten minutes, so does everyone else. I try to avoid her like I do karaoke, cranberry juice, and bootcut jeans.

"Sorry, but I won't be able to attend." I try to soften my rebuff with a smile, but my cheeks feel stiff. Probably the mixture of foundation and sweat, now dried by the AC into a salty, lumpy mask.

The elevator arrives, and I slip inside. Mary and Paul follow.

"The picnic is a great way to get to know the other employees outside of the accounting department. You should come."

My smile remains as I shake my head. "No, thank you."

I should attend to show company pride, but I cannot bear to watch Sandra Baldwin, the owner's daughter, flirt with Theo, who is my best friend and coworker. The idea of

6

it makes me feel sick. And, well, socializing isn't a talent I possess.

Gossip Girl plows forward, ignoring my silence. "Can I set you up with my brother for the picnic? You never know when you'll meet your soulmate."

Mary's a petite five feet, four inches. Her brother might be taller, but I'd bet my pristine Louboutin heels he isn't taller than me. I already walk through life feeling like an anomaly because of my height, I'd hate feeling like one on a date. Especially if I'm to have an audience—like every employee at BD. No, thank you.

I shake my head. "That won't be necessary, since I won't be attending."

Just as the elevator stops on the third floor, Paul blurts out, "How tall *are* you?"

I get that question a lot, but usually from kids. Paul looks at me with unabashed curiosity. It isn't like it's a secret, so I answer as I exit, rounding down a half-inch.

"Five feet, fourteen inches."

I get perverse satisfaction at the wrinkles around his eyes as he tries to do the math.

Gossip Girl leads him to the right toward HR, but not before saying, "Let me know if you change your mind about my brother."

Not going to happen.

I go left toward the accounting department which consists of a nook off the main hallway, large enough for three desks, two that face each other and a third that runs along the side of the first two. No partitions. No door. Even the copy machine across the hall has its own four walls and a door. Yes, I'm jealous of an office appliance.

The other two accountants don't look up as I plop down into my squeaky chair and bang my drawer open to stash my purse. We're all familiar with interruptions.

I log into my workstation, and a second later a message pops up at the bottom of the screen. I glance up and see Theo looking back at me over the top of his computer.

THEO: How was the dentist?

So yes, I lied to work about my appointment for no other reason than I didn't want to get into the particulars of my symptoms. Of celiac disease.

AVERY: no cavities

THEO: You missed Bob's sister. He forgot his lunch and she brought it to the office.

I look out of the corner of my eye toward Bob. He's a bald, portly man who moved in with his older sister five years ago when his wife died. He says little and counts down to his retirement on a calendar on his desk. Only six hundred, thirty-nine days to go.

The front of his desk butts up against the side of Theo's and mine. I believe his sole goal each day is to ignore us as much as possible. We help him by messaging each other instead of talking out loud.

AVERY: Dang it! I can't believe I missed her again.

THEO: she brought me brownies

Theo lifts a plastic container so I can see it, then slides it across our desks. I lift the lid and the heavenly scent slaps my face. I'm starving. I lift one out and take a bite. It's cakey on the outside, fudgy on the inside, and just a bit chewy. Perfection in a two-inch square of butter, sugar, and chocolate.

I've heard a lot about Bob's sister from Theo over the

eleven months we've worked together, but I have yet to actually meet her. He once said she's the closest thing he's ever had to a grandma. I could use a grandma in my life.

THEO: You'll meet her at the company picnic.

Theo assumes I'm attending the picnic, and I have yet to tell him otherwise. Meeting Bob's sister is a better reason to attend than the one Gossip Girl gave me earlier.

AVERY: Mary just tried to set me up with her brother for the picnic

Theo's grin spreads as our eyes meet over our monitors again.

THEO: Did you know they're twins?

I snort in laughter and earn the side-eye from Bob. Right, we're supposed to be working. I take one more brownie before passing them back to Theo.

Besides Tamra, Theo is the only other person who makes me feel normal. Not a sideshow or an anomaly or a social project, because I'm not only Tall Girl, I'm *Shy* Tall Girl. Awkward, squared.

On my first day here, after my new hire orientation, Mary brought me to this desk and introduced me to my two accounting coworkers. At the time, my heart galloped when Theo stood and I had to look *up* to meet his beautiful green eyes. He's around six feet, five inches. A rarity in my experience. He reached out for a handshake, and his hand completely enveloped mine. I was officially smitten.

Theo insisted Mary allow him to give me a tour of the building, and she reluctantly released me from her clutches. I got the impression that I wasn't the only one who found Theo's deep voice hypnotic. He showed me the factory and production lines, then took me to lunch at a diner down the road, which I affectionately nicknamed The Pit.

For those first few days, I daydreamed about him in a way that was not platonic. He was so friendly, I actually believed something might happen between us. I soon realized the way he treated me wasn't special. He was kind to everyone. Thinking I would be anything to him other than a colleague was ridiculous.

Especially after I met his girlfriend, now ex-girlfriend, a perfect specimen of womankind: Sandra Baldwin, The Model, daughter to the co-owner of the company. I realized what kind of girl he was attracted to: willowy, five-feet, eight-inch redheads with small hands who wore flowing dresses and high heels.

They broke up in the middle of March, and The Liar and I the following week. We were both left with broken hearts and empty schedules, and one night he asked if I wanted to go to a movie. A few nights later we went on a hike. Now, we hang out after work almost every day. Our friendship developed so quickly that he was a best friend before I realized we'd left coworker territory.

Still, we will only ever be friends. After Sandra, he was very vocal about not dating a coworker. There are quite a few women here who have tried to grab his attention and change his mind. I will not to be one of them. Why ruin a good friendship with kissing?

Nowadays, I appreciate Theo's friendship for what it is and don't allow my dreams to get past my morning alarm.

A sigh escapes.

THEO: You ok?

As if I would admit I have yet to perfect my ability to ignore my more-than-friend feelings for him.

AVERY: It's this heat. It saps my life force

THEO: It's cooler in the mountains. Want to drive the scenic byway tonight after work? We can pick up sandwiches on the way and have a picnic at the top

A few weeks ago we'd talked about all the things that tourists come to Tucson to do and that we'd never done. On my list was the scenic byway up to Mount Lemmon. He remembered.

AVERY: Yes!

THEO: I'll swing by your place at six?

AVERY: Perfect.

I love my Tucson life. I love my job working with numbers and formulas. The freedom I enjoy in my own apartment. The variety of restaurants and other entertainment. I especially love my friendship with Theo. I want none of it to change. Ever.

I spend the afternoon lost in Number Land, barely taking notice of the hours passing. Hardly remembering my doctor's appointment or the upcoming ultrasound. I definitely don't remember my celiac disease when Theo offers me another brownie as we head out to our cars at the end of the day.

Chapter Two

AVERY

IT'S BEEN ALMOST A WEEK SINCE MY DIAGNOSIS AND I HAVEN'T yet managed to go two days in a row without eating gluten in something. Which accounts for why I'm especially bloated and gassy today. If I hadn't skipped my ultrasound appointment this morning, the technician probably would've been able to see the gas bubbles on the screen.

Ugh. That isn't where I want my thoughts, and I do my best to get into the thick of Number Land and ignore my discomfort.

Taylor Swift begins to sing, but I don't pay any attention until Bob pokes my arm with a three-foot-long pencil, the kind we sell to souvenir shops across the country. He brandishes it like a sword and points to my phone. By the time I pick it up, my mom's left a voicemail.

"Avery, your uncle surprised us with tickets to a show and dinner in the city Wednesday night for our anniversary. We're

heading up tomorrow and want to take you out to dinner. You can show us your apartment and drive us past your office. Call me when you can and we'll firm up the details."

My parents cannot find out about last week's doctor's visit. Panic makes it difficult for my lungs to expand. The air is thick and hot, like trying to breathe through a coffee straw.

I vaguely hear Theo saying my name, asking me questions, but the static playing in my ears keeps me from understanding. Afraid I might pass out, or worse, throw up, I flee to the women's bathroom and barricade myself in a stall.

The band of my bra digs into my ribs, so I unhook it and when my chest is able to expand without restraint, I suck in air while I lean my forehead against the cool metal of the door. I can't allow myself to think, or I might collapse into a sobbing mess. I fill my mind with thoughts of my toes, then tighten the little piggies, and release. I do the same with my calves, then my knees, working my way up my body, one muscle at a time. I've just reached my shoulders when the bathroom door squeaks open.

"Avery?"

Theo.

"What are you doing in the women's bathroom?" Thankfully, my voice sounds calm.

"Technically, I'm not standing in the women's bathroom, merely leaning in. Are you okay?"

"I'm fine."

"Since you almost plowed into Mr. Baldwin on your rush to the bathroom, you'll understand why I don't believe you."

I almost ran into the co-owner of the company? Humiliation burns me from the inside out. Hopefully,

Gossip Girl didn't see, or the whole building will know and start guessing at my state of mind.

Reluctantly, I hook my bra back into place. As much as I hate bra shopping, I have to admit the time has come. I smooth my blouse over my stomach and can't ignore the little pooch I've gained over the last week. The panic begins to rise again, but I remind myself that one of the symptoms of celiac is bloating. Everything is okay. I'm okay. My parents will never find out my doctor is an idiot.

When I exit the bathroom, Theo's waiting just outside with his hands in his pockets, brow furrowed. His gaze takes in every detail of my face. I smile.

"Who was the call from?" he asks.

I shrug, hoping to appear nonchalant. "My mom. She and my dad are coming to visit for a few days." My voice cracks on the last word, and I clear my throat, upping the wattage of my smile.

Theo isn't buying my performance. "I'm taking you to The Pit, and you can tell me all about it."

"There's nothing to tell," I say, but I sound unsure even to my own ears. I glance at the clock on the wall. "We still have twenty minutes before quitting time."

"You're here early every morning. It'll be fine. Grab your stuff and let's go."

I'll take any excuse to spend time with Theo, but there really is nothing to explain.

THE PIT IS ONLY AN EIGHT-MINUTE WALK, BUT IT'S STILL sweltering outside so Theo drives. I love his Nissan Rogue because I fit comfortably inside without having to contort my body. His AC works so much better than mine, and I'm comfortably cool, even though his dash says it's 98 degrees outside. When I've saved up enough to replace Ladybug, I will definitely get a compact SUV.

We beat the rush to The Pit, and Theo takes a booth in the back. The lighting is poor, the furniture dark brown, and the walls are plastered with old travel posters from exotic locations. I love it. It may look dim and worn out, but the staff is friendly, and the food is amazing.

Theo leans back in the booth, his hands on the table top. One of the things I appreciate about The Pit is how wide the tables are. We can sit across from each other, even slouch, and not knock knees. It's the little things that make me happy.

My favorite waiter shows up with ice water and silverware rolled in napkins. "The usual?"

Nearby, the door to the kitchen swings open, and I hear the sizzle of the grill and smell greasy food. I swallow a wave of nausea. No loaded mac n' cheese for me today. Actually, everything sounds awful at the moment except for one thing.

"I'll have a slice of chocolate cake and vanilla ice cream."

I'll recommit to no gluten tomorrow.

Our waiter doesn't balk at my order, but Theo blinks at me a few times. I don't usually eat dessert for dinner.

"Bacon burger and fries," he says.

Once the waiter leaves, Theo turns his attention back to me. I feel him study my face, but I keep my focus on the poster of Fiji on the wall as I sip my water.

"Your parents are coming to visit," he says. "I thought you got along with them?"

"I do."

"So why the panic?"

Because it's hard to keep secrets from my parents when they're staring at me across a table instead of talking on the phone from 130 miles away. "It's just not a good week for a visit."

"Why not?"

I shrug.

When Theo laughs, I glare at him, indignant. "What's so funny?"

"I have never met anyone who guards their personal life as tightly as you do. You can trust me, you know."

"I do."

I share more with him than he realizes, more than I do anyone else except for my bestie Tamra, who also lives 130 miles away. Still, I do struggle to open up, even to him.

Theo leans closer. "Just know that I'm here for you, okay?"

The white noise of conversation hums around us, making me feel as if we're alone. His words, mixed with the intensity of his stare, makes my heart race. His goodness and honesty open my mouth.

"I have an older sister. Alison." Savage Al, though I never called her that to her face, or she would have become even more predatory.

He tries to hide his surprise. "Okay."

I've mentioned my parents and their alfalfa farm many times, but never my sister. I run my finger over the condensation that drips along the side of my water glass to avoid his gaze.

"She and I have never gotten along. She's what you might

call a rebel. In high school, she got pregnant. Once Gavin was born, she disappeared."

"I thought Gavin was your brother?"

His confusion is justified because I pretend he is my brother. I'm happier pretending Savage Al doesn't exist. I sigh and resign myself to acknowledging the truth.

"No, he's my nephew."

The waiter brings our food, which gives me a few minutes to collect myself. The ice cream is exactly what I need. It's unusually hot in here tonight.

"So you and Alison don't get along?"

I haven't spoken to her for ten years, but yeah, we don't get along.

"Growing up, I did everything to be different from her. I studied hard in school. I never touched alcohol. Never stayed out past curfew. I followed all our parents' rules. I never lied to them."

At least not while I lived in their home. The lies of omission only started when I moved to Tucson last year.

"My hard work paid off," I say. "I've accomplished what Alison didn't. I earned a scholarship, graduated with honors, and now work in a career that I love. I'm proud that I'm nothing like my sister, and so are my parents."

Theo's forehead creases at my speech. I suppose my relationship with Savage Al would appear odd to someone like Theo who gets along with his family so well.

"Is Alison coming with your parents tomorrow?"

"No." I shake my head at the idea of Savage Al in a car with my parents for two hours. None of them would survive. "We haven't heard from her in years. I have no idea where she is now."

"Then what does Alison have to do with your parents visiting?"

Theo is a patient guy, but I can tell my round-about way of explaining is driving him crazy. His concern for me is written all over his face. I trust him more than almost anyone else. So why is it so hard for me to speak openly about my relationship with my parents?

I drop my spoon on my plate and try to explain.

"I'm the perfect daughter. I'm the one who doesn't make mistakes. I'm the daughter that makes my parents proud. When they come tomorrow, what if they don't like the life I've built in Tucson? What if they're disappointed in me?"

I'm struggling to breathe again. The doctor's words from last week break out of their prison and march across my thoughts. What she said cannot be true, but the possibility that my parents will associate me with Savage Al has me freaking out.

I must look as horrible as I feel because Theo leaves his side of the booth and moves to mine. He wraps his arm around my shoulders, pulls me into his chest, and rubs my back. He smells like sunshine and woods and something that is uniquely him. I hold on tightly.

"Avery, it's okay. I'm here. Just tell me how to help."

I burrow my face into his shoulder, taking comfort in his touch. If only I could take Theo with me everywhere so that I would always feel this safe. My thoughts twist down a serpentine path and I wonder... I can't take him everywhere, but could I at least take him to one dinner with my parents?

Chapter Three

THEO

I TEND TO FIND MYSELF IN THE ROLE OF A COMFORTER PRETTY regularly. There must be something about me that screams, *I'm here to help! Tell me everything that troubles you!* I don't mind, in fact, I like being useful.

But to have Avery lean on me for comfort is a surprise. She has a tough exterior she shows to the world, and though we've become best friends over the past few months, she's still extremely independent and keeps a lot to herself. Watching her fall apart twice in one day is troubling.

Also troubling is how my brain short circuits as I hold her. I've hugged her many times, but this feels completely different. Definitely not a good time to notice how perfectly she fits into my arms, or how all of her soft curves mold to my side. The fruity scent of her shampoo fills my head, and now I crave a big bowl of strawberries with whipped cream.

Avery pulls away too soon and looks up at me, her

expression hopeful. Her makeup is smudged under her eyes which gives her a fragile appearance.

She is the most beautiful woman I have ever known.

"My parents want to take me to dinner tomorrow." Her hand grips my wrist tightly, painfully. "Will you come with us? It won't be so terrible if you're there."

None of this makes sense to me, and I go back to what she said before. "Why wouldn't your parents be proud of you? You've built an incredible life here."

Avery sits up straight and puts back up her composed exterior with her lips turned down on the edges just a bit and her eyes clear. Her perfect, outer persona. She looks calm and composed, but she's rubbing her nose, so I know she's not. "You won't go with me?"

"I didn't say that. I'll go if you want me to."

"Thank you."

I move to the other side of the table and take another bite of my burger. She eats small spoonfuls of half-melted ice cream.

"When's your interview?" she asks, breaking the silence and effectively changing the subject.

I know that if I push her to explain about her parents' visit, she'll retreat farther, so I let the topic slide without further comment, even if I am worried. And if I'm honest with myself, disappointed she doesn't trust me enough to fully explain her fear.

"Wednesday morning, eight o'clock," I answer between bites.

She knows exactly when my interview is, as we've talked about it quite often over the past few months since the Chief Financial Officer at Baldwin-Dickson announced his retirement. Our small pencil company is expanding next spring, so not only would it be a promotion now, it would be another promotion next year as we move to our new building, enlarge our distribution, and hire more employees.

"Nervous?"

"Me? Nervous? Not at all." I wink to hide the fact that I am. "I'm prepared for the interview, and I'm sure the best applicant will win. And I'm obviously the best applicant."

She laughs, and the sound skitters across my skin, raising goosebumps. I always feel like I won a prize when I earn a laugh from her.

"I can't argue with that. Mr. Dickson is your biggest fan. I bet the job is yours."

I hope so. I want this promotion so bad it's what I dream about at night. I want the title, the pay increase, the sizable yearly bonuses, more responsibilities, and varied challenges beyond accounts receivable.

The only downside will be leaving Avery in the accounting office. We'll still have instant messaging, but that won't be the same as seeing her over the top of my computer monitor every day.

"Want to practice some more?" she asks.

For the next half hour, Avery throws interview questions at me. I recite back the answers I've practiced until they're memorized, though I hope they don't sound rehearsed on Wednesday morning. I've worked for Baldwin-Dickson for two years, and they know my talent and work ethic. I'm hoping it'll help get me past the first interview and on to the second.

We're in my car, and I'm about to push the ignition

button when Avery lays her hand on my wrist. I still. Her expression is once again serious.

"I didn't have a dentist appointment last week. I went to the doctor for a check-up. I haven't been feeling well. I have celiac disease."

My mind goes back to the cake she just demolished. And the burritos we had for lunch on Saturday. Then the sandwiches we took up to Mount Lemmon last Monday. She doesn't seem to be taking the diagnosis too seriously. Before I can ask how she feels, she continues.

"The doctor doesn't think it's celiac, though it obviously is. She had some crazy idea that I...um."

She waves her hand over her stomach.

When I say nothing, she continues. "She's totally mistaken, but she thinks that I'm..." She creates an imaginary bulge over her stomach, her fingers splayed out.

"Bloated?" I tease.

Her eyes roll, and she shakes her head, then repeats the movement. Whatever the doctor said, it has to be something huge, because I've never seen Avery panic before today. Or play charades instead of speaking in succinct sentences.

I have no idea what she's pantomiming until she brings her arms together and starts rocking them like she's holding a baby.

She's pregnant.

I'm sure my shock is evident on my face. "Tyler's the father?"

Her lips pinch, and her eyes narrow. "As I said, the doctor's making things up. She looked like she graduated high school yesterday. She has no idea what she's talking about."

I'm sure even an inexperienced doctor can figure out if someone is pregnant. Don't you just pee on a stick? I sit with this information for a minute. Avery is pregnant. I don't know how I feel about this. Does it matter? It's not really my concern except as a friend.

"What does Tyler think?"

She bites her lip. "I sort of lied to you when Tyler and I broke up. We didn't break up so much as he ghosted me. *Poof.* Just disappeared. I haven't spoken to him since, and I never will again."

He *ghosted* her? I'm a lover and not a fighter, but if I ever see Tyler again, I'll have no compunction against punching him in the face.

"So, you'll come with me to dinner tomorrow?"

"Yes. If you're sure you want me, I'll come."

She swallows as if it's painful to do so, and blinks rapidly. Anxiety is showing through the cracks in her demeanor. "I need a buffer, a distraction, from me."

It doesn't feel great to only be needed as a distraction, but I understand the situation better now. I want to reach out and pull her into my arms to offer her support and comfort. The memory of how it felt when she melted into me an hour earlier keeps me where I am. Instead, I put the car in reverse and pull out of the parking lot.

"I never told my mom about Tyler," she says softly. "I've never lied to her before, but I was afraid she'd think I was getting distracted from my career if I told her about him." Her voice cracks again, and my fists tighten on the steering wheel. "When he disappeared, I was glad I hadn't mentioned him. But now, what if she sees me and *assumes* I'm pregnant? I'm so bloated all the time."

Avery has only ever spoken of her parents with love and respect, so this sudden fear of them doesn't make sense to me. "They'll understand."

She nods her head, and her ponytail swings back and forth. "Yes. I'll make sure they understand that I've been stressed about work. And ate a lot of bread. When Alison was pregnant, she had morning sickness for months. I haven't. My symptoms match celiac, not pregnancy. I need my parents to understand."

I don't believe anything I say will change her mind, so I don't try. I'll wait until after I meet her parents to figure out how to help her deal with this situation.

"Anything you need, just let me know," I say.

She reaches out and lays her hand over mine on the wheel. Gives it a squeeze. "Thank you."

She turns up the radio, conversation over, and she sings along to Maroon Five until I drop her back at her car.

———

When I reach home, I don't go inside immediately, but sit on the gliding bench on my front porch. I can't believe that Tyler treated Avery so badly. I only met him once, quite by accident, before Sandra and I broke up. We went on a date to a movie and ran into Avery and him doing likewise. In our two-minute conversation, he didn't make a good impression. He's the type of guy who thinks he's the big man on campus long after he's left the schoolyard. He kept looking around to see who was looking at him, unaware that the only person who should matter was the woman holding his hand. He gave Sandra more attention than he gave Avery.

24

I was glad when they broke up because she deserves so much better than him. No—they didn't break up. He used her for what he wanted and then he *abandoned* her.

Now that my need to protect Avery has been triggered, it's hard to think of anything but her. I force myself to focus on the scene before me.

The sun is setting behind the foothills. The temperature has dropped a few degrees, and it's almost pleasant outside. My neighbor is throwing a baseball with his son. Another neighbor walks past with her dog, and we wave to each other. A slight breeze brushes past, helping to cool my temper.

I love this view. I used the money from my parents' life insurance policy for the down payment, and I believe they would approve. I think of them all the time. The way they kissed every morning before Dad left for work. Mom dancing around the kitchen as she packed my lunch for school. Movie nights on the weekend and cartoons on Saturday mornings. It's been twenty-one years, but I still miss them. This house makes me feel like they're close. The only thing that would make my house feel more like a home is if I had someone to share it with. Someone besides my roommate, Aaron.

Unbidden, my thoughts fill with Avery again. The way she felt in my arms. The anguish and fear in her eyes at the thought of seeing her parents alone. Tyler.

The desire to protect and help Avery won't surprise my older sister, Michelle. She thinks my propensity to help the downtrodden (her words, not mine) is my greatest strength, but also my potential downfall. Every time I start dating a girl, she cautions me to not fall for her just because my hero instinct has been activated. I love Michelle, but she has the annoying habit of pretending she's a psychologist and psychoanalyzes me at every opportunity.

Still, with Michelle's warning ringing in my head, I thought I'd made a good decision dating Sandra. She didn't need a hero. There was nothing for me to rescue her from. Even then, things didn't work between us. No, after our breakup, I needed someone to rescue me. That someone ended up being Avery. We hang out a few nights a week and go to the gym together on Saturday mornings. I want to spend all my time with her, and sometimes I wonder what it would be like to kiss her.

I banish that thought to outer darkness. Not going to happen.

Sure, she's curvy and tall, with slender, shapely legs and shiny, long, brown hair that mesmerizes me. No matter where she goes, she attracts the attention of everyone she passes. She thinks it's because she's tall, and that's part of it, but it's also because she's gorgeous.

But no, no dating. She's the most competent person I know, but right now she does need a hero. At least someone to help her through the next few months with her pregnancy. A pregnancy that she is not handling well. When she accepts her situation, she'll need a friend. That's my role.

Besides, she's my coworker. When I lived in Phoenix a few years ago, I dated a coworker. A week after I proposed and she said yes, she broke up with me because *she just didn't love me in that way.* Finding myself alone in my feelings hollowed me out. I'd never felt so rejected. I couldn't see her every day at the office and still function, so I quit and moved back to Tucson to be closer to family.

When I met Sandra, I didn't stick to my resolve to stay away from coworkers because she wasn't technically a coworker. Huge mistake. As the boss's daughter, she might as well be my coworker. After she broke us up, I was once again alone. Sandra regularly visits her dad at work so I see her more than I'd like, but this time I didn't quit. Baldwin-Dickson is a great company to work for, but if I'm honest, Avery is a big reason why I stayed.

With where my thoughts are going tonight, I catalog the other reasons why I can't ask Avery out on a date.

She's never given off any vibe that she wants more than friendship. I don't want to ruin what we have by being greedy for more.

She doesn't confide easily and guards her thoughts and life zealously. Almost like she's a human vault protecting precious secrets behind lock and key. That makes me nervous. Sandra and I dated for a year, and she kept things back from me that led to our break up. I don't want to travel that road again just to find myself alone at the end for the third time.

Then, in her fifty-year plan, children don't enter until she's thirty. I get it, she's only twenty-three, but I wanted to get married and start a family by the time I was twenty-five. I'm twenty-eight.

I strike this last reason from my list since she's having a baby and her plan to wait until thirty no longer fits. Then add a new reason: she's having her ex-boyfriend's baby.

No matter how incompatible Avery and I are in the romance arena, she's one of my best friends. She keeps most people at a distance, but over the last few months, I've gotten to know the person behind the tough exterior. I like that person a lot.

A bark comes from inside the house, bringing me back to the present. My boxer, Gigi, must've noticed my car pulling up and has waited patiently for me to come inside. Until now.

I'm careful as I open the door so that she doesn't slip out. She's Houdini escaping the house and yard, and I don't want to make it easy for her by letting her bolt out the front door.

She jumps up on me and tries to lick my face as I bend down to scratch her ears. Only when I kneel does she calm enough to allow me to give her the body rubs she loves so much.

My cat, Oscar the Grouch, comes out of the office to the right of the hall and rubs his whiskers against my ankle. When I reach to pet his head, he runs away. Even after a year, he's still skittish.

"I took Gigi for a walk about an hour ago," Aaron calls from the living room.

I walk past the office and the hallway that leads to the bedrooms and go to the back of the house where the kitchen and living room are located. Gigi's nails tap against the tile floor behind me. Even with her earlier walk, I'll take her into the backyard and throw the ball with her for a while.

Aaron's sitting on the couch playing *Splinter Cell* on the big screen. His mom mentioned recently that she hates facial hair, and now he's working on growing a full beard. It still catches me off guard every time I see him.

"Where were you?" he asks. "We were supposed to clean out the garage tonight."

Oh right, Aaron wanted to set up weights in the garage,

but it's full of unpacked boxes. Part of my inheritance from my parents, taking up garage space because Michelle didn't want to store them any longer. I'm not sure what's in most of them, and I promised to clean them out so he could set up his home gym.

"Sorry, man, I forgot."

"No worries." His words are punctuated by the gunfire from his game. "I figured you were out with Avery. How's she doing? Haven't seen her in a few weeks."

I grab a bottle of water from the fridge and collapse on the couch. "She's good." Not really, but she probably doesn't want Aaron knowing the particulars.

Gigi jumps up next to me and lays her head on my lap. Oscar's on the back of the couch and sniffs my head, then bats around my hair. It's his favorite pastime and sometimes it even feels like a head massage.

"Chloe wants to double on Saturday. You free?"

Aaron's girlfriend has tried to set me up innumerable times over the last few months, and for the first time, I'm ready to accept. Aaron and I have been friends since third grade, but I want a wife, not a roommate. And to get a wife, I have to get back into the dating game and find the woman that won't skip out on me. An image of Avery enters my head once more, but like I've told myself so many times, I am not going there.

"Sure," I say. "Let Chloe set me up."

"Really?" He turns away from the game and his character gets sniped.

Chapter Four

AVERY

I'M DEEP INTO THE FOREST OF NUMBER LAND ON TUESDAY when my phone chirps out an alarm at 4:45 as a reminder to leave work on time. For dinner. With my parents. Just breathe.

I called Mom last night after Theo dropped me back at my car, and we made plans to meet at a chain restaurant downtown, close to their hotel since Dad hates driving in the city. When I asked if I could bring a friend, she was quick to say she'd love to meet any friend of mine. I've never been what you might call social, but Mom's enthusiasm was a little much.

I then called Tamra to commiserate with her about my parents' visit. She didn't disappoint with her sympathy, but I'm pretty sure she's on the side of my doctor when it comes to my misdiagnosis. Probably because she can't accept my celiac prognosis. She loves her bread almost as much as she loves Twizzlers. Still, I've felt unbalanced since hanging up with her.

I send a quick IM to Theo.

AVERY: leave in ten minutes?

His eyes crinkle as he smiles, and my stomach does a little flip.

THEO: Yep

There have been short-lived rumors that we're dating since he broke up with Sandra. I'm nervous that people will see us leave together tonight and make assumptions again. Which is stupid. We hang out almost every night and leave work at the same time each day. I guess going to dinner with my parents just feels different, and I'm afraid someone will pick up on that. I brush the apprehension away. I have more important things to worry about.

AVERY: Meet you at the elevator?

He gives me a thumbs up. I grab my purse and head to the bathroom where I run my fingers through my hair, fluffing the waves. Hand tremors make it difficult to reapply my lipstick, but I manage without getting any on my teeth. My mouth is dry and my pits sweat for absolutely no reason. I'm fine. Everything is fine.

I'm even more fine when Gossip Girl enters the bathroom as I smooth out the skirt of my navy blue jersey dress.

"You look nice!" She sidles in close as if we're best buds and I'm about to spill all my secrets. "Do you have a date?"

"No." I pack up my make-up and slip out of the door.

Theo's coming out of the men's bathroom. His smile steals my breath.

"Ready?"

Lies have never come easily, but I try anyway. "Yep."

Whatever my expression is, it makes Theo laugh. "Everything will be great. You'll see."

We walk toward the elevator but don't get far before The Model comes around the corner and almost knocks into us. When she sees Theo, her expression brightens. A flash of jealousy drives a spike through my heart.

As the owner's daughter, she's always visiting her dad at the office. The last few weeks she's stopped by to chat with Theo. I think she wants to win him back. I'm sure she will, eventually. Perfect women like her always get the best men. The inevitability depresses me. Theo and I won't have the same friendship after they start dating again.

"Theo!" Her voice is melodious, and she says his name like it's the beginning of a song. "I've been looking for you. You weren't at your desk."

Theo tugs absently on his tie. "Sandra. Hey. I'm on my way out. Did you need something right now?"

"Yeah, it's kind of urgent." Only then does The Model notice me. "Hi, Avery. How are you?"

It stings that there's no jealousy in her tone. She doesn't see me as competition for her ex-boyfriend's affections. It reminds me that I'm not.

"We really need to get going," Theo says to her. "Can I call you tomorrow?"

"Nope, I need you now."

She loops her arm through his and pulls him back the way we've just come. He mouths, "Sorry," but still allows himself to be taken. They stop far enough away that I can't hear what they're saying, and I slide a step closer. Nope, still too far away.

I don't call Sandra The Model because she should be on the runway, but because she is the type of woman that all women everywhere aspire to. She owns her own business, is a certified yoga instructor who teaches classes at a local studio every morning, and has a book coming out at the end of the year on entrepreneurship. She's gorgeous, has impeccable style, and never looks tired. Sweat would not dare glisten her forehead. I'm even envious that she can get away with wearing three-inch heels. Mine sit in my closet, dearly loved, but unworn, because I'm too afraid to add any extra inches to my height.

I close my eyes against the next thought that enters my mind, but it doesn't help. The words march across my eyelids. *The Model is the type of woman my mom would love as a daughter.* Instead, she got Savage Al and Shy Tall Girl. I'm nervous enough as it is about tonight, I don't need The Model reminding me how much I lack. Not right now.

I make a wish that she will disappear, somewhere wonderful like Maui, but when I open my eyes, she's still standing next to Theo.

His shoulders are hiked up to his ears, and his beautiful smile has disappeared. He says something that makes The Model flinch. I wish I had a spy gadget handy so I could figure out what's going on.

Gossip Girl comes out of the bathroom while they're still talking, but neither Sandra nor Theo notice. She walks slowly away, down the hall opposite from where I'm standing, then stops abruptly and looks past them to me. Her eyes widen, as does her smile. I hope whatever they're talking about isn't personal, because after this it won't be private.

Theo strides toward me, his eyebrows low, and lips pinched. I look over his shoulder at Sandra. She looks defeated, almost as if she's about to cry. Theo grabs my hand and pulls me toward the stairs. Soon we're outside and at his Rogue. He opens the passenger door for me, and slams it shut before walking around to his own door. He pulls out of the lot fast enough that his tires screech. I can't remember ever seeing him this worked up before.

"What did she want to talk to you about?" I ask.

"She asked me to go with her to a dinner with clients."

The light turns red, and he slams on his brakes. His right arm comes out and lands just under my bust. As if that would protect me better than my seatbelt, but I love that he cares. His eyes go down to my stomach.

"Sorry. I shouldn't drive carelessly with...precious cargo."

I have no idea what he's talking about. "It's okay."

He lets out a deep breath, and when the light turns green, he proceeds at a normal speed. Why did Sandra have to show up just as we were leaving to fill my head with doubt and put Theo in a bad mood? I need him to be happy and charming to take the attention off of me tonight.

I go back to what he said before. "Sandra asking you to go out tonight made you angry?"

His shoulders sag. "Not angry. More annoyed. Why does she expect me to change my plans at the last minute because she needs me? She broke up with me."

"I'll be okay if you want to go with her." At least I hope I'll be okay. I'm doing my best to stamp down any thoughts that might lead me to believe otherwise.

"Nope." He shakes his head. "I don't owe her anything."

I still don't know the particulars of their break-up. I never asked about Sandra after they parted ways because I never wanted to tell him about The Liar disappearing. If Theo wanted to tell me, he would, but he never has.

"What did you tell her just before we left? It really upset her."

"I don't know why. I just said I already had plans to go to dinner with you and your parents."

I inhale from the shock and choke on my own spit. "She's totally going to assume we're dating if you put it that way. Meeting my parents?"

Theo looks confused for half a second until he realizes the same thing and starts to laugh. "Oh, that's perfect."

I don't find the situation funny. "What if she tells her dad? He'll assume we're dating."

He's still laughing. "Sandra won't tell anyone. But maybe if she thinks we're dating she'll stop coming by my desk to talk."

I'm not so sure, but at least he's in a better mood as we pull into the restaurant parking lot. Not me. My panic revs up. Theo opens my door and holds out his hand. I realize I'm rubbing the bridge of my nose which is irritating. My mom will totally guess something is up with me if I do that during dinner.

The hostess leads us to a table where my parents wait. They're studying the menu, and it isn't until our shadows cross the table that they look up. Mom is smiling as her head lifts, but as soon as she sees Theo, it falters. I realize too late that when I mentioned a friend, she assumed a girl, not a boy.

"This is my *friend,* Theo," I say quickly, my voice quivering just a little. I swallow down my nerves and act as natural as possible. "Theo, these are my parents, Kate and Jim Morgan."

They stand. Dad gives Theo a handshake. "Nice to meet you."

Dad's about my height, just a half-inch taller. When he pulls me into a hug, the scent of alfalfa overwhelms me and brings tears to my eyes. I miss the farm. I lean over and hug my mom. I make it a quick hug so she doesn't notice my bloating. When she doesn't comment on my weight gain, I relax. She's five-eight, a perfectly respectable height for a woman, but she's as tough as ten men. I don't know how Dad's gargantuan growth gene overwhelmed her overall stronger ones.

Theo holds out my chair and we all sit down. Mom's across from me, and our knees knock before we resituate, my knees pointing one way and hers the other. It's a familiar maneuver and it only takes a second.

Mom lifts her hand to get the waiter's attention, and he comes right over.

Once we've ordered, I make sure to steer the conversation toward the farm. Dad can talk about cotton and alfalfa for hours. He does so until our meals arrive. My first bite of chicken fettuccine hits my tongue and settles easily in my stomach. An unfamiliar feeling of optimism begins to grow. My parents suspect nothing. Dad and Theo converse easily. This might just become an enjoyable way to spend the evening.

When Dad stops talking to take a breath, Mom interjects. She points her fork between me and Theo. "How did you two meet?"

Or not so enjoyable.

Theo tugs on his tie and glances over at me. Is he disappointed that I've never mentioned him to my parents? He's my best friend in Tucson, after all. I catch Mom's narrowed eyes. This is why I never mentioned him. Because she wouldn't believe that he was *only* a friend.

Theo answers when I don't. "We work together. We're both accountants at Baldwin-Dickson."

"How long have you worked there?" she asks him.

"Two years. I worked in Phoenix for a few years after graduating from Arizona State, but moved back here since this is where my family is."

"You've been an accountant for a while?" Mom is in her inquisition mode, which can be frightening, especially to someone who isn't familiar with her.

I widen my eyes at Dad, hoping he'll stop Mom, but he looks interested in the answer and doesn't notice my discomfort. Or decides to ignore it.

"Six years," Theo answers.

"Why are you at the pencil company?" Mom's all but forgotten her meal. "It's not a very prestigious situation. A good stepping stone if you're just beginning, like Avery, but you're a seasoned accountant. Can't you get a better job?"

"Mom!" She has a tendency to be blunt, but she doesn't have to be rude. I know it's because she thinks we're dating and is intent on finding his every flaw. Sometimes I wish she were like Tamra's mom, who makes everyone feel like family, even grumpy Mr. Erikson who throws rocks at anyone who steps on his property.

Theo shakes off his surprise quickly. "Um...yeah, I guess you could see it like that. This was the first job I found when I decided to move back, but I'm happy and haven't wanted to leave. Not only that, but Baldwin-Dickson is expanding quickly. It isn't such a little business anymore. The Chief Financial Officer position is open, and I have a good chance of getting it."

Mom's head swings toward me, her lips set in a frown. I was so worried about her noticing my stomach, that I didn't have a brain cell free to devote to worrying about her finding out about the job opening. A hot flush burns my cheeks. I wish Theo wasn't here to witness my mom turn into Zealous Mama.

"Avery," she says, her voice accusatory. "You didn't tell me about this job opening. I'm sure you applied. You would be perfect for the job."

"No, I wouldn't."

"Don't sell yourself short. You are a smart, driven woman, and they would be lucky to have you."

Mom is a farmer. She married a farmer. Her parents were farmers. She has never stepped into an accounting office in her life, nor does she understand what I do, but she believes she knows best. This never irritated me until I moved out of her house and had some experience in the world.

"I don't have the needed experience to apply for the position." I hope I can make her understand, enough to let the subject drop, at least for now. She'll circle back to it next time we talk on the phone. "I've been working in the profession for less than a year. The minimum they were looking for was five years."

Mom's shaking her head before I finish. "You should apply for everything that comes open. That way your bosses know that you're serious about moving up the ladder. Or at the very least, that you want more responsibility."

What she doesn't understand, probably because I've never told her, is that I don't want to move up the ladder. I want to manage numbers, not people. I want to spend my time working with spreadsheets, not in meetings. But Mom has big plans for me to take over the world, so someday soon I'll have to pick up my feet and start the climb. Just not yet.

"Chief Financial Officer sounds impressive," Mom continues. "I'm sure it's a hefty raise."

It's Dad who finally saves me from this torture. "Theo, you say you have family here in Tucson?"

"Yeah. My parents and sisters live in Tanque Verde up in the foothills."

Mom whistles. "That's a swanky neighborhood."

None of us comment on that.

"How many sisters do you have?"

"Four. Stella turned twenty last week. Naomi started at college this week. Kitty's sixteen, and Monroe's twelve."

He tells them funny anecdotes about his youngest sister, who is an absolute firecracker, but probably just to keep them from asking more probing questions about his family. He doesn't like to talk about it, but Theo's parents died in a car accident when he was eight. His older sister, Michelle, was in her early twenties at the time and raised him. With strangers, he calls her his mom, and his brother-in-law Steve, dad. Stella, Naomi, Kitty, and Monroe are his nieces but they're more like younger sisters so that's how he talks about them. I've never met his family, but I've always been a little envious of the good relationship they share as siblings.

My parents have tortured Theo for long enough so I ask, "Will you tell us about Gavin?"

Gavin is a topic that Mom can talk about for hours, but

she doesn't take the bait. Instead, she says simply, "He'd like you to come visit. We all would."

Guilt swamps me. I know he wants me to visit because I talk to him on the phone a few times a week. Still, I've been making up excuses and haven't been home since Christmas. The Liar and I met in January and with his work schedule, we only saw each other on the weekends. After he disappeared, I was too depressed to pretend otherwise and needed to avoid Mom. Then Saturdays became Theo days. We go to the gym together and then lunch afterward. It's my favorite day of the week.

I've been selfish. Further proof that I can't make good decisions on my own. I need to visit home.

"I'll come visit this weekend," I say around the lump in my throat.

Mom nods, happy with my answer, but then she points between me and Theo again. "Are you two dating?"

I drop my fork, and it clatters to the table. "What? Mom. We're just friends."

Mom doesn't believe me. She's so sure that some boy is going to come along and change my plans for the future. Since I was a little girl, she told me I shouldn't seriously date until I'm in my late twenties. Children could wait until my thirties. *Live your life for you*, she repeated over and over again.

"I was wondering the same thing." Dad leans back in his chair, arms crossed over his chest, but he has a wide smile stretched across his sun-tanned cheeks. He looks at me with pride. He probably can't understand why guys aren't falling all over themselves trying to get my attention.

I didn't think through how Theo coming along with me

tonight would appear to my parents, which was stupid. All through middle school, high school, and college, I never had a good friend that was a boy, much less a boyfriend. Now I bring a man to dinner? We must be dating!

The longer the silence stretches, the more they believe I have a secret boyfriend. This is sort of the truth, except the secret is an *ex*-boyfriend, and it isn't Theo. My stomach rolls.

I do the only thing I can think to do: I flee.

Chapter Five

AVERY

I'm out of my chair and across the dining room in seconds, honed in on the women's bathroom. Even so, I'm not fast enough. Mom follows me. I'm sure she'd follow me into a stall if there was one empty, so I guess I'm glad that they're full. She can have her say, then I can hide out for a few minutes.

We stand along the wall, and I pretend I'm not scared and overwhelmed and frustrated. I want to ask why she doesn't trust me, but I already know the answer: Savage Al stole all the trust she had, leaving her bankrupt.

"Avery." Her voice is fierce but soft. "Tell me the truth. Are you dating that boy?"

He's a man, not a boy, and his name is Theo. He's the best person I know, and I'm lucky to have him as a friend. Please don't scare him off.

"No."

"Remember the plan. You don't want to settle down until you're twenty-eight, at the earliest. Thirty would be better. And—"

A hand dryer comes on and effectively drowns out the rest of her words. A moment later a stall becomes empty, and I move quickly to claim it. My stomach is still rolling, and I lean over the toilet, my hands braced on either side of the stall. I don't know how long I stand there, but a tap on the door tells me it's been long enough.

"Avery? Are you ill?"

Can this day just end already?

I think about ignoring her, but she'll just become more insistent. Also, Theo is stuck with my dad. I can't abandon him after dragging him along to this family reunion in the first place.

Regretfully, I leave my sanctuary.

When we reach the table, our dishes have been cleared away and Dad has already paid the bill. Thank goodness. I escape out the front door with everyone following behind. A breeze cools my warm cheeks, and my stomach settles.

Mom comes up beside me and loops her arm through mine. "We wanted to see your apartment tonight."

"Can you visit a different night?" I'm practically begging. "I'm tired."

Theo stands on my other side, and I lean into him for support. Mom notices, but at this point, I don't have enough energy to care. She already believes we're dating anyway.

"No," she says decisively. "It has to be tonight. We have the play tomorrow, and we're leaving early Thursday morning."

I have no choice. "Okay." I struggle to make the best of

the situation. "I have some ice cream we can have for dessert."

She glances at my stomach but thankfully doesn't comment on the calorie load. Then she says something worse. "Theo, do you mind driving us all? Jim isn't a great night driver, especially in the city."

And now we're carpooling. Yippy.

THEO PARKS IN FRONT OF MY APARTMENT BUILDING, AND I lead them up the stairs to my second-floor door. My hands are shaking as I slip the key into the lock. I predict that Mom will look through every nook and cranny, ask questions, and offer opinions that I'm not strong enough to handle tonight.

Theo kept them occupied on the drive over by engaging them in a conversation about the city's entertainment options for tomorrow during the day. I think they've decided on a museum, but I didn't pay much attention. The worries in my head are too loud.

When I open the door, Mom's the first one inside. She has seen the apartment before, when she and Dad moved me down here. I didn't bring much, just my bed, a few boxes of kitchen stuff, and my clothes. I convinced Dad to let me purchase my own furniture, and he somehow convinced Mom. After they returned home, it was a treat to go shopping by myself and spend the money I'd saved without worrying about what Mom thought of the cost.

"Have a seat." I wave my hand toward the couch and armchair. By her pursed lips, I know this isn't the furniture she would have picked, but I don't regret the dusky blue color or the deep cushions. "I'll grab the ice cream."

Dad and Theo sit, but Mom goes around the small front room, which includes the kitchen, and looks at all the framed photos I hung of our farm. Next, she'll look in my cupboards and take a peek into the bathroom and the two bedrooms in the back. I ignore her and go to the freezer for cookie dough ice cream and grab the caramel sauce from the fridge. As I scoop, I let the sound of Theo's voice wash over me. He charmed my dad easily enough, though from the glances Mom throws my way she still isn't sold on the idea of me dating anyone seriously. After my experience with The Liar, I completely agree.

My stomach flutters as I put the ice cream back into the freezer. When I cross over to the couch with two bowls to give to the men, the feeling changes. It's as if a finger runs down my stomach from the inside, navel to pelvis. That wasn't bloating or nerves.

The bowls slip from my hands and clatter to the floor. Three sets of eyes stare at me. My breath hitches. I flee to my bedroom and slam the door behind me. I stand at the foot of my bed, my hands over my abdomen, unable to think further ahead than this very second.

"No, no, no, no," I mutter to myself.

There's a soft tap on the door. "Avery, it's Theo. You okay?"

When I don't answer, he walks in without an invitation. I'm lightheaded as I stumble a step in his direction. He catches me before I fall and encircles me in his arms. I lean into his chest.

"What's wrong?"

Everything that has happened since I met The Liar, each experience that I hid behind a mental brick wall, tumbles out. My memories build a picture that suddenly comes into focus. I can no longer deny the truth.

I'm twenty-three. I'm single. And...I'm pregnant.

"Avery, talk to me. What's wrong?"

I say, "I think I'm pregnant," just as my parents come into the room.

There are five long seconds where no one moves, except for the baby who continues to treat my uterus as a finger-painting canvas. We all stare at each other, confused, surprised, and frozen with disbelief.

Dad thaws first. His face contorts into a mask of fury.

"How could you?" he asks Theo.

Theo turns to face him. "I know you're upset—"

He doesn't get a chance to finish. Dad grabs him by his collar, pulls him away from me, and hits him in the face with his fist. Theo falls back against my bed.

I scream, horrified. I've never seen Dad hit anyone or speak with such anger, not even to Savage Al. I think he might be near tears.

Dad looks like he's about to hit Theo again, but now I step between them. It's Dad who stumbles back. He points a finger at Theo. "I expect you to take care of your obligations. I won't be raising another grandchild."

"Oh, Avery." Mom's supporting herself against the door frame while she cries. "How did you let this happen?"

My parents turn and leave my room as one. I follow them down the hall.

"Wait," I say. I'm not sure they hear me. If they do, they don't listen.

They're out the door and on the landing. Mom glances over her shoulder, heartbroken and weeping. Dad's fury has softened to disappointment, which is so much worse. I never wanted to see that expression aimed at me.

He closes the door.

I crack wide open.

Chapter Six

THEO

I'm squinting, my eye pounding in pain as I stumble into the kitchen. The front door slams shut and the next second Avery is weeping, wailing, almost screaming. Her arms are wrapped around her middle, and she bends over at the waist. When I reach out to her, afraid she might fall, she latches on to me and holds on tight. Eventually, her keening softens to a sob, but she doesn't stop crying. I can't even pretend to understand what just happened, but I hold her just as tightly as she holds me.

When Avery slumps against me, exhausted, I sweep her up into my arms and take her back to her bedroom, where I lay her on the bed. She rolls onto her side, her back to me, and curls into a ball. I grab the folded blanket near her feet and spread it over her, tucking it in around her body. I'm not sure what else to do, but I can't leave her, so I sit on the edge of the bed and rub her back. She doesn't push me away.

When her hiccupy sobs quiet and her breathing evens out, I think she's fallen asleep and slip out and shut the door behind me. The ice cream Avery dropped is a melted mess on the linoleum, with shoe marks tracking it to the door. I clean it up, wash the bowls, and wipe down the counters, all while planning my next move.

I call Aaron.

"Hey," he says on answering.

"Avery and her parents got in a fight so I'm going to stay over." I glance at the couch. It's more like a loveseat, and I can imagine how comfortable that will be tonight. "Can you bring me some clothes?"

"Dude, I thought she wasn't your girlfriend."

"She's not. But I can't abandon her."

"Is this your hero complex kicking in that Michelle is always going on about?"

"No. This is friendship." I try to think of a way to explain. An image of Avery enjoying her chicken fettuccine at dinner comes to mind. "Avery is like...fettuccine."

He chuckles. "Fettuccine?"

"Yeah. When I first met her, she was stiff and unbendable, like fettuccine noodles before they're cooked."

"Okay?"

"Then she dates this creep who breaks her heart, and I could tell that she was hurt, though she did a good job of hiding just how much. But she's strong and doesn't break." I'm pacing between the kitchen and living room as I talk, a total of six steps back and forth. Anger at Kate and Jim makes my neck and shoulder muscles tighten. "But now, her parents are really angry, and she just...turned into floppy noodles. All her strength boiled out of her."

"I think you should work on your metaphors."

"You're totally missing the point. You should have seen her. I don't know what to do. I don't know how to help. But I can't leave her."

"Then don't leave her. I'll bring you clothes."

"Thanks. My sweat pants are on the end of my bed. Slacks and a shirt for tomorrow."

"Don't you have your interview tomorrow?"

Crap. I do. I glance once more at the couch, wondering if I'll be able to sleep at all. Not that it matters, because I don't abandon friends. "My blue suit then? And the paisley tie on the back of my door. And a toothbrush."

"Sure thing. See you in a few."

After texting him Avery's address, I grab a bag of frozen blueberries from the freezer for my eye and collapse onto the couch with elbows on my knees. The cold feels good against my cheek as the memory of Avery falling apart replays in my head. The only other time I've witnessed such grief is the one clear memory I have of when my parents passed.

Dad died on impact when a driver ran a red light and t-boned their car. Mom hung on for a few days in the ICU. Michelle, her husband Steve, and I were with her when she stopped breathing. What I remember most is how Michelle wailed like Avery had earlier. It's a sound of inconsolable loss. But Avery's parents are still alive. How can they leave her over *this*?

A knock brings me out of my own head.

As soon as I open the door, Aaron asks, "What happened to your eye?"

He brought along Chloe, and though I like her, she does

have a tendency to be drawn to drama. There's plenty of drama at Avery's tonight, and I don't want to go into details. I block the door so they don't think they're invited in.

"I...hit myself," I answer.

"Riiiiight..." But he doesn't press.

He hands me a duffle and the hanger with my suit. Chloe reaches out to give me a hug, leans into me until I stumble back, then enters the apartment. Sneaky. I toss my stuff on the armchair and try to block her from going further.

"Anything we can do?" She looks around the tiny space. I'm not sure what she expects to see. Avery sick on the couch? "Did she just move in? There isn't much here."

"Everything's good. Thanks for bringing my stuff."

She isn't one to give up. "Your friend would probably appreciate the presence of a woman. I'm happy to stay."

"She's asleep right now."

"Come on," Aaron says, taking her by the hand. "Let's go back to our movie."

Aaron pulls a reluctant Chloe away, and I shut the door before she can come back inside. I yawn. It's been a long day, and I have a sleepless night to look forward to. I remove my jacket, shoes, and socks, but before I change into my sweats, I decide to check on Avery one more time.

The king-size bed takes up most of the small room, with just enough space along the wall for a dresser next to the closet. The light from the hallway falls across her body. She hasn't moved in the last hour. I'm about to return to the living room when Avery looks over her shoulder.

"I thought you left." Her voice is rough with tears.

"No. I'm sleeping on the couch tonight."

"You don't have to do that."

"Yeah, I do."

Silence. Then, "Okay." She reaches out her hand. "Will you sit with me for a few minutes?"

I leave the door open an inch and sit on the bed, leaning back against the headboard. She rolls over so that she's staring up at the ceiling with her arm flush against my leg. Her hair fans out across her pillow.

"I'm sorry. For everything."

Her voice is soft and rough from crying. Her expression guts me. I want to fix what just happened, but I'm not sure what happened.

"Sorry for dragging you to dinner with my parents. Leaving you with my dad when I ran to the bathroom." She gazes up at me and studies my eye. "I can't believe they think you're the father of...and he punched you."

I stiffen at the mention of her parents. I can understand they're upset and even Jim's punch, but I can't wrap my head around them leaving their daughter when she needs them the most. I brush a strand of hair from her forehead. "Don't be sorry. I'm glad I was here."

"It's all so humiliating. Not just my parents, but Tyler. The...pregnancy" She covers her face with both hands. "I thought I was smarter than this."

"Hey, don't beat yourself up. We all make mistakes."

"Not me. Not like this. I should never have moved to the city."

I pull her hands away from her face and sandwich them between my own. She looks up at me once again.

"Help me understand," I say. "Why are your parents so angry? Why can't you make mistakes? We've all been taken in by someone we thought we could trust. That doesn't mean you should've stayed on the farm. I know my life wouldn't be as great if you weren't a part of it."

Avery bites her lip to keep from smiling. In the dim light, I think I notice a tear track down the side of her face.

"Why are you so good to me?" she whispers.

"Because you're a good person."

She sighs as she shakes her head. "You want to understand why my Mom expects my perfection?"

"Yeah, I do."

"She married her high school sweetheart when she was eighteen. Farming was what she knew and all she thought she wanted until she took a few business classes at Eastern Arizona College. She loved college, she loved learning, she loved business, but only earned a certificate because by then she was pregnant with Alison and decided to stay home to raise her."

She pauses and we remain in silence for a minute. The AC kicks on, and I realize how hot I am. I loosen my tie.

"Four years after Alison, I came along. Since I was a toddler, Mom pushed me to excel at school. Earn a college education. Move to the city. Climb the ladder of corporate America. I need to reach my potential before I start a family or get sidetracked by a man. As her daughter, I need to do what she wasn't able to do because she became a mom first."

I try not to hate Kate. It may be impossible. "Just because you're having a baby doesn't mean you can't still do those things."

"A baby right now is not part of the plan, but it's more than that." Avery squeezes her eyes tight. "Mom has always had high expectations for me and Alison. Alison hated living up to them, hated school, hated the extracurriculars Mom insisted on, hated the house rules. The more Mom pressured her, the more Alison skipped school. Ignored curfew. Drank. One time she came home so stoned, I thought she wouldn't wake up. It was horrible."

I weave my fingers through hers. Squeeze.

"Her behavior got worse when she met this guy, Brad. She already hated us. Brad made her hate us more. She was only seventeen when she got pregnant. The fighting got worse. I hated being at home. I spent as much time as I could at my friend Tamra's house, but Mom never let me sleep over, and at night I'd lay in bed and listen to them scream at each other. I wished Alison would disappear." The tears start again and her voice cracks. "Those years left a scar on my family, and I promised that I would never make the same decisions she did."

She hiccups a sob. I have to hold her. I lay down on the bed and tuck my arm under her head. She leans into my shoulder.

"My wish did come true. Alison ran away with Brad and left Gavin behind. Gosh, I love that kid. I was thirteen when he was born, but I used to pretend he was mine." As she talks about her nephew, her sadness lifts a little. "He was better than any doll because he was real. Leaving him was the hardest part of moving to Tucson."

"But you came anyway?"

"It's ironic because Mom always told me I'd move to the city when I grew up, but when it came time for me to start applying to universities, she decided she didn't want me to leave. I think she was afraid of me messing up like Alison. I did an online program through Arizona State and lived at home. When I graduated, it was Dad who finally convinced her I was ready to go out on my own. But she was right. I can't be trusted not to mess up. I allowed a man to distract me, manipulate me, lie to me. And now I'm..." A sob slips out before she gains control. "I tried so hard to be the daughter she wants, and I still failed. I'm a failure. I'm just like Alison."

The more Avery tells me about Kate, the more disgusted I become. "You're not a failure. Not in any way. Having a baby does not make you your sister. You're twenty-three, not seventeen. You're self-sufficient, responsible, trustworthy. You will be a great mother."

"The way they looked at me before they left..." It's like she doesn't even hear me. "That's how they looked at Alison. I don't know if my mom will ever forgive me for screwing up like this."

I want to say her mom should love her daughter, no matter her mistakes. That her mom should support Avery in making her own decisions and not force her to live out her own dreams. There is nothing to be forgiven. I refrain from saying so, but I can't hold back completely.

"You've done everything your mom wants for your life. But what do *you* want for your life?"

"The same things. Our goals are aligned, they always have been." She pauses. "Or at least, I thought so until I moved here. Growing up, every aspect of my life was overseen by Mom, especially after Alison left. When I got here, I liked the taste of freedom too much. I was stupid, and now my whole life is ruined."

My anger knows no bounds. My head is pounding. My eye aches. I need to calm down before I say something stupid, so I change the subject. "You know my parents died when I was eight?"

Avery sniffles. "Yeah."

"I didn't know Michelle very well at the time. She's a lot older than me, she's a half-sister, and she lived hours away."

"I didn't know she was your half-sister."

"Yeah, her dad and mom divorced when she was a kid, then her mom married my dad and had me. When they died, Michelle was twenty-two, had been married a year, and was pregnant with my oldest niece, Stella. Into that situation, she took responsibility for her little, snotty brother. I didn't deal well with my parents leaving me. I threw temper tantrums and told her I hated her at least once a day. I completely ruined the plan she had for her life."

"Are you trying to comfort me?" More sniffles. "Because you're not succeeding."

Good to see her sense of humor hasn't completely left her.

"I'm trying to say that you and Michelle are the two strongest women I know. Her life plan changed, just like yours will need to. But you will pull through and succeed. I know it because I know you."

We don't talk for a long time. Avery's sniffles calm, then disappear completely. She leans up and kisses my cheek.

"Thank you," she whispers. "I wouldn't have survived tonight without you."

I decide to stay right where I am until she falls asleep. The loveseat can wait.

"I hope my parents made it back to the hotel okay."

I hope they have no idea how to use a car share service and have to walk the whole way.

Chapter Seven

AVERY

I WAKE SLOWLY, EVERY PART OF ME AWARE THAT THEO LAYS IN front of me, both of us curled onto our sides, facing the same direction. His woodsy scent, the weight of his body on the mattress, the warmth of his back against my forehead where I'm pressed against him—it makes me want to sleep forever.

Unfortunately, my bladder won't be ignored. I roll away from his warmth and stumble along the end of the bed until I get to the door. The hallway light is still on, and I squint against the brightness. I shut my bedroom door behind me and slip across the hall and into the bathroom with a stretch and a yawn. I slept better than I have in months.

The events of last night are skittering at the edges of my thoughts like monstrous shadows, but I don't shine any attention on them. I can't. Hiding among those shadows is a reality that I'm not ready to accept in the light of day. I just need to pee, then I can go back to bed. I have no idea what time it is, but I probably have a little more time to enjoy Theo's warmth before I have to get ready for work.

I'm washing my hands when the mango inside my stomach wriggles around. I gasp at the movement. It's disconcerting and too much reality this early in the morning. The shadows draw closer.

"Please stop," I whisper.

Mango doesn't listen and kicks me. Maybe it's a punch. Whatever it is, I'm sure it's payback for how much I hate him.

Except, I don't hate him. We're both victims of The Liar. It's The Liar I hate. I sink down to my knees as the truth I wanted to avoid this morning crashes around me.

I'm pregnant with The Liar's baby.

For months, I've buried away in the recesses of my memory every smile, every touch, every word The Liar ever spoke to me. I believed that soon enough I would erase every trace of him through sheer determination. But that's no longer a possibility because there's a part of him that's now a part of me. Forever.

Which isn't fair. My feelings build and build, creating a pressure that needs to be released. There's no way to hold it in, and I grab the bath towel from the hook and stuff it over my face. I scream and scream until my voice is raw and then I scream again.

All the things I tried to forget about The Liar rise up from their shallow graves and dance behind my eyelids. They're mocking me. Ridiculing my paltry efforts to move on from the most humiliating episode of my life: the time I fell in love with someone who only stuck around for as long as it took to get me to tumble into his bed.

I'm a pathetic cliché.

We met in line at the grocery store. It was late. There was only one lane open and the woman in front of me had a stack of coupons. The Liar struck up a conversation. He was funny and made me laugh. Though a few inches shorter than me, he didn't seem to care. Not once did he look at my boobs or my legs. We walked out of the store together, and when he asked for my phone number, I handed it over.

I'd lived in Tucson for four months and still gloried in the freedom I enjoyed living away from home. I ate what I wanted, went to bed when I felt like it, and gave my phone number to strangers. So rebellious, but in a safe way! Nothing like Alison. I never expected The Liar to actually call. No man had ever pursued me before. If my height didn't scare them off, then my no-nonsense facial expression did. But a week later, he did call and he asked me out.

Looking back now, I see myself as I was: a clueless, naive girl. He wooed me with dedicated attention, compliments, gifts, affection, and expensive dinners. Things I'd never had before. It didn't take long until I lived for his texts, daydreamed for the weekends, and molded myself into the type of woman he most desired.

When he had me completely addicted to him, he pulled away. Made me wait days between texts. Had a work meeting on the evening of a planned date. The more he distanced himself, the more I complied with his wishes. Until I finally gave him what he'd pushed for since the beginning: everything.

He used me. He manipulated me. And why? For what? The thrill of a conquest? To win a bet with a friend? I will never know, and I'm okay with that as long as I never see him again. No one has ever made me feel so small, so insignificant, so disposable. Which is impressive, as I lived with Savage Al for thirteen years, and she knew exactly what hurt me the most.

I'm not sure I would have survived The Liar's betrayal without Theo. Because of him, the last few months I've felt authentically me. I'm now smarter and stronger. No one will ever take advantage of me like that again. I've put The Liar firmly behind me—

—Except through a twisted turn of fate, he's become part of my future.

I'm having his baby. Another scream tears out of me, followed by a sob. I don't want to cry anymore, but I can't seem to stop.

What should I do?

I need a plan. I have no idea how to plan for a baby. I grew up believing that babies stole dreams and destroyed lives. How do I plan for that?

I need my mom to help me, but she's hurt and angry. What can I do to earn her forgiveness for messing up so badly? We talk on the phone regularly, but I'm sure she'll give me the silent treatment for at least a week until she comes to terms with what I've done. I can't wait that long.

I'll call her this afternoon and explain everything. Or at least, almost everything. Maybe The Liar can die at the end of my story. Yeah, like, he got hit by a bus last month just days before I was going to bring him to the farm and introduce him. That will explain his absence and take the heat off of Theo.

Who am I kidding? Mom won't pick up when I call.

Then I remember I promised to visit the farm this

weekend. She can't ignore me if I'm standing in front of her. Saturday is soon enough. I'll take her censure, her anger, then we'll sit down and plan an updated version of my future.

For now, I won't tell a soul about the situation. With some creative wardrobe decisions, I'm optimistic I can keep the baby a secret. This is good because I loathe being the object of gossip and BD is a hotbed for it. They'd all love such a story. I can already imagine the questions that would come: *Who's the father? When are you due? Is it a boy or a girl?* I wonder what they'd say if I answered, *It's a mango.*

Even that much of a plan calms me enough that my tears slow. I wipe my eyes and nose on the edge of the towel and sit back against the side of the tub. Everything will be fine. I have to believe this, or I'll never be able to leave the bathroom. It's not lost on me that bathrooms have become a refuge over the last few days. The disinfectant smell is really starting to grow on me. Like, literally. It's my new brand of perfume.

A knock at the door makes me jump. For a while there, I'd forgotten about Theo.

"Are you okay?" he asks.

That's a loaded question, and I don't have a ready answer.

"I...yes." My voice comes out as a croak. "Are you okay?"

Last night with my parents was horrible, but Theo was wonderful. He stayed with me, even after Dad hit him. He confided in me, encouraged me. His comfort last night, the way he accepted me and handled my hurts with a tender touch, means more than he will ever understand.

"Yeah, I'm good. I need to get ready for work."

What day is today? Wednesday. Something was happening on Wednesday. What was it? Theo's interview!

"Your interview! Are you late?"

"It's only six-thirty. My interview isn't until eight-thirty."

Relief washes over me. I jump up and have my hand on the knob before I recall that I probably look like a complete mess. Bedhead, morning breath, and red, puffy eyes. I don't want to terrify him.

"Go ahead and go home," I say without opening the door. "I'll see you at work."

"Are you sure you want to come in today? You could take a sick day."

And be left home alone with nothing but my memories and worries for the future? Um, no. The best thing for me is to get lost in Number Land.

"I'll be there. Good luck, Theo."

He taps on the door a few times as if he's thinking. "Thanks, Avery. See ya in a few."

I listen as he moves around the living room before the front door opens then closes.

A look in the small mirror over my vanity shows I look worse than I thought. I have major work to do in order to make my face presentable for the office. I refuse to show weakness to the masses, which means these puffy eyes have got to deflate.

OVERNIGHT, MY STOMACH GREW AN INCH. WHY IS THIS WEEK so mean to me? None of my fitted skirts fasten, and the stretchy maxi totally shows a pooch. The only dress that looks decent is the one I wore yesterday, and I can't wear that a second day in a row, especially after sleeping in it. I pull out a pair of black, stretchy slacks and barely manage to do them up. Just my luck, the button will pop off halfway through the day. I need new clothes, but with my height, it isn't as simple as going to the mall. I have to special order most of what I wear and have it tailored. It's a whole process, and I need something today.

A moment of inspiration strikes, and I remember an old trick of Savage Al's. Taking a hair elastic, I stick it through the buttonhole and loop both ends around the button. I can breathe! But it also means that instead of tucking in my blouse, I have to leave it hanging out.

I glance in the mirror. Ugh, I look too casual, and I hate it. Since everyone stares at me wherever I go, I like to look perfect. I want them to remember me for something other than my stature, and leave them nothing to criticize.

This will have to be good enough, especially because I'm running late.

When I reach work, Theo is already in his interview. I try to focus on my spreadsheets, but my thoughts are with him. I hope his interview is going well. I hope he gets the promotion, but I can't ignore how much I'll miss seeing him over the top of our monitors every day. It must be obvious that I'm incapable of work because Bob keeps looking over. He's usually much better at ignoring me than this.

The clock at the bottom of my computer screen has my full attention. Finally, at 10:15 Theo arrives back at the Accounting Cubby. I'm about to ask him how it went when I take in his face. There's a purple half-moon under his swollen eye and he looks like he's wearing blue eyeshadow above. I just stare, shocked that Dad did that to him.

"Do I have something on my face?" he says. He wipes under his eye, then across it. "Did I get it?"

How can he joke about my dad hitting him? I'm out of my chair and around our desk so I can get a closer look. It's horrible.

"Does it hurt?"

He shrugs. "A bit."

I feel awful. I put him in the way of my dad's fist. "What did you tell them in the interview about what happened?"

"That I got hit in the face with a basketball."

That does make me smile, just a little. I've never told him about my own basketball incident from my youth. I take in the rest of him. Instead of his usual slacks, button-down shirt, and tie, he's wearing a blue, pin-striped suit. Be still my heart. He looks like a gangster from 1930 who just got in a brawl. All he needs is a fedora. Huh, never would have thought that look was my style, but apparently, every look on Theo is my style.

"And they believed you?" I ask, hoping to cover up my staring.

"Why wouldn't they?"

I shrug. It's a plausible story, and he's a trustworthy guy. But something happened in that interview that has left him uncomfortable. He taps his finger against his leg and won't meet my eyes.

"What's wrong?" I ask. "What happened?"

He glances at Bob, then my computer, and I take the hint. I go around to my own desk and wait impatiently while Theo types out his answer.

THEO: Sandra did tell her dad that you and I are dating. He had some concerns since I can't be your boss if we're in a romantic relationship.

Shame eats me up from the inside. I can't allow the rubble of my life to ensnare Theo. He deserves so much better.

AVERY: You told him we're not dating, right? He believes you?

THEO: yeah, but it seems a rumor has started and Mr. Dickson's secretary heard it from multiple sources.

Theo keeps typing, but I close my eyes. I don't want to know. Sunday night I was a regular shy, tall girl with a mending heart and acid reflux caused by celiac. Now I'm pregnant with a mango, my parents hate me, and according to office gossip, I'm secretly dating my future boss.

With the trajectory of the week so far, by Saturday, I can expect a freak lightning strike to set my apartment building on fire.

Chapter Eight

THEO

AT THE END OF THE DAY, AVERY AND I ARE HEADING FOR THE elevator when we're once again waylaid by Sandra.

"Your eye!" Her concern is noted, but not appreciated by this point. I've had this reaction a lot by now and I'm tired of it. "What happened?"

"A basketball."

I move to go around her, but she steps in my path.

"You got a minute?" she asks.

I glance at my watch. Avery and I stayed late to finish a report, and I only have a half-hour before dinner at Michelle's, and I need to stop off at home to get Gigi on the way. I don't really have a minute, but now is as good a time as any to tell Sandra to keep out of my business. I've been stewing all day about how she meddled with my interview by telling her dad I was dating Avery.

"Yeah. Sure."

Avery passes by me and waves her fingers. "See you tomorrow."

I watch her disappear around the corner, wishing I was following. Sandra pulls open the door to the boardroom, and we go inside. She speaks before I get the chance.

"My dad said you aren't dating Avery. I need you to know that I didn't mention it to anyone else, just to him. I don't know where the rumor started."

I do. Avery and I narrowed it down to Mary. I hadn't even noticed her in the hallway yesterday, but she must have heard what I told Sandra about meeting Avery's parents and came to the same conclusion. I'm impressed by her fast work. Between 4:55 yesterday evening and 8:30 this morning, she managed to spread the word to a good portion of the office. Why anyone cares I can't understand. Still, kudos to her and her gossip network.

That doesn't let Sandra off the hook.

"I'm more concerned that you felt it necessary to tell your dad about my possible relationship at all. Who I date is none of your business, and it definitely isn't your dad's."

Her hands go to her hips. A stance I'm familiar with when she feels like she has a point to make. "It is if you're dating an employee who works for the same company."

"And if I was, then it would be my responsibility to tell HR. You don't even work here, yet still felt like you needed to get involved? You made my interview extremely awkward by telling the owner of the company about a conflict of interest that doesn't exist."

She stands ramrod straight, her lips pursed as if she's about to argue her point. But then her shoulders curl forward and her stance relaxes. "You're right. I'm sorry."

The apology doesn't do much to release the stress I've been carrying today. Between the events of last night, the interview, the pain in my eye, and worry over Avery, I'm exhausted. I don't have the energy for Sandra.

"Is that it?" I ask. "I have plans with Michelle's family tonight."

She snaps her fingers. "Right. I remember. Waffle Wednesdays." A look of regret crosses her face. We had a lot of fun on Waffle Wednesdays while we were dating.

"Okay, well." I clap my hands together in an odd attempt at finality. "Thanks for the apology."

I reach for the door handle when she places her hand on my arm. "There's one more thing."

I wait. She says nothing. I turn the knob.

"Will you go out with me?" she says in a rush. "On a date. Not a client meeting. But a real date."

This is unexpected. I've noticed her interest in me increase over the last month, but I thought it was because she missed me and wanted to remain friends. We reached a dead end on the road to romance.

"You broke up with me," I say.

"I was rash."

"You lied."

Her hands go to her hips again. "I didn't lie. I just didn't tell you the truth."

What's the difference? This is one thing I don't miss about Sandra: her need to split hairs. I rub my forehead and wince as pain shoots through my bruised eye. This isn't going to be a quick conversation.

"Let me recap," I say. "You knew from the very beginning of our relationship that I wanted kids. I never kept it a secret.

You led me to believe you wanted the same. For *a year*. Until your sister mentioned offhand that you never wanted any kids. When I asked you if this was true, you broke up with me. There was no discussion. No effort at compromise. No explanation on your part on why you lied." She's shaking her head, so I reiterate. "Yes, you lied. You perpetuated an impression that wasn't the truth. Sandra, we were talking about marriage. Starting a family. When were you planning on telling me you didn't want a family? Before our wedding vows? After? Never?"

She can't meet my gaze. The grey carpet has all of her attention. "I've never liked babies, okay? By the time my niece turned three, I loved spending time with her, but before that, I didn't enjoy her much. I've always known I didn't want motherhood."

I walk toward the window that overlooks the industrial street. It isn't pretty, but it's a whole lot better than looking at Sandra right now. "Information that would've been helpful to know when we started dating. You wasted a year of both of our lives in a relationship that had no future."

A heavy silence settles over us. My body is tense and a headache is forming in my right temple. I have nothing more to say, but I'm pretty sure Sandra does. I'd rather have it all out now than have her show up every day after work.

"I really liked you when we first met, and I didn't want to scare you away." Her voice is thick like she's crying. I keep my gaze on the traffic below. "And then I grew to love you, and I didn't want what we had to end. We were good together, just the two of us. Why add kids to the mix?"

"A better question is, why are we having this

conversation now? There isn't a point in going out on a date when our goals are so out of sync."

She comes and stands next to me. "I've changed my mind. I want to be a mom. I think."

All my fight washes away. My jaw drops as I turn my head to stare at her. "What?"

"I don't get babies. The diapers, the crying, the midnight feedings. But, if we were to have a child, and you were willing to take on a larger role when she was younger, I'm willing to compromise."

"A child?"

"I know it isn't the five you always planned on, but maybe two." She smiles, her eyes still glassy. "It's up for discussion."

"I—" Five months ago Sandra was the woman I loved. Five months ago, this conversation was all that I wanted. Five months ago, her betrayal devastated me. "I don't know what to say."

She clasps my arm and gazes up at me with pleading eyes. "Say yes to a date. Right now, that's all I want."

I'm about to say yes. All those dreams we dreamed together rebuild inside my head and heart. Two kids are a smaller family than I want, but with the right woman, I'm open to compromise. Except, I can't get the word *yes* past my lips. Once burned, twice shy, and all that. I remember how gutted I felt when she left me without explanation. I never want to feel that way again. A *no* isn't any easier to give. We were good together.

"I need to think about it."

A smile brightens her expression. "That's fair. I know this is a surprise. Maybe we can go out Saturday night and talk?"

When I raise my eyebrows, she rolls her eyes. "As friends. We'll go to Subway or somewhere super casual. Save our real date for when you're ready."

The more confident she is, the more hesitant I become. A wave of fear that she'll lie to me and then leave me again takes over my chest, tightening my ribcage. I'm relieved I have a ready excuse to put off this conversation.

"I have a date on Saturday." Petty bringing a date up, definitely, but it does irritate me that she expects me to be waiting around for her. "Give me until Baldwin-Dickson's staff picnic."

Her smile diminishes. "That's over a week away."

"Yeah, it is."

When I don't back down, she nods. "Um, okay. I'll talk to you then."

She reaches out and pulls me into a hug. She doesn't fit in my arms as well as I remember. As we walk out to our cars, we converse about her upcoming book. It's friendly and comfortable, like putting on a warm pair of socks, and by the time we part ways I'm even more confused.

I HEAD HOME TO GRAB GIGI BEFORE I HEAD TO MICHELLE'S. Waffle Wednesdays wait for no one, and I anticipate rubbery eggs and a cold waffle. Good thing syrup covers a lot.

Gigi almost escapes out of the front door when I open it, but I'm faster. I let her out the back while I feed Oscar and change clothes. We're heading out when Aaron pulls up on his Ducati. That beard makes him look like a completely different person.

"Waffle Wednesday?" he calls out.

"Yeah, you want to come?"

"Sure do. Just let me change."

Five minutes later we're on our way. Aaron studies my eye from the passenger seat.

"What really happened last night?"

I could use some perspective. By the time I finish the story, his jaw is hinged open.

"Huh. Avery's pregnant. Never saw that coming."

"Neither did she. She wouldn't talk to me about it today. I want to help, but I'm not sure how."

The memory of her parents leaving her last night still brings my anger to the surface. They don't deserve her devotion. Today she told me she's visiting them on Saturday. I'm worried enough that I offered to go with her. She declined, of course, but gave her reason as not wanting to upset her parents. Because, you know, they think I'm the father and all that.

He slaps my shoulder. "I expected you and Avery to be dating by now."

Dating Avery has crossed my mind, but I'm surprised Aaron has thought the same thing. He's never mentioned it before.

"Why would you expect us to date? We're friends."

"Yeah, you keep telling yourself that."

"I have reasons."

He laughs. "I've heard them all before, but they're just excuses. Friends make the best girlfriends."

"You date enough to know."

He puts his hand to his chest as if I've shot him. "Are you trying to wound me? You'll have to try harder. You'll also have to come up with some better excuses not to date Avery when it's obvious you two belong together. Maybe that she's having someone else's kid?"

Two days ago, that was a good reason, but now it isn't. The baby is part of Avery, and Avery is my favorite person in the world. I accept all of her.

Still, between everything she's dealing with right now and my possible promotion to her boss, our situation isn't conducive to dating. Avery and I are just friends. Forever. Why does that depress me?

"Sandra wants to get back together," I say.

Aaron whistles. "Seriously? That's gutsy after what she did to you." He studies the side of my face. "Wait, are you thinking of taking her back?"

I shrug. "Maybe?"

"No." He's shaking his head. Aaron is a low-key guy who doesn't get riled up about much, but he's surprisingly angry about this. "She threw you out like garbage, and if you go back to her, she'll do it again."

I shift in my seat uncomfortably. To hear Aaron echo my own concerns has me question even considering the option. "You think?"

"Yes. She's not malicious, but she's selfish. And what about the whole no-kid issue?"

"She's changed her mind."

"Probably for only as long as it takes to hook you again, then she'll change her mind back."

"I didn't know you disliked her."

He shrugs. "I didn't until I saw how devastated you were after she left. I don't think there's any forgiveness for that. Avery would never do that to you."

Aaron doesn't talk much about his parents' divorce or their marriages to other people. Because he doesn't appear to be affected by their failed marriages, I forget they've left their mark. We're both gun shy when it comes to a serious relationship, but for vastly different reasons. Maybe Chloe will be the one who snares him. Avery won't be the one who snares me.

I pull in front of Michelle's house and put the car into park. "You really like Avery?"

"Yeah, I do. You're happier with her as a friend than you ever were with Sandra as a girlfriend."

He jumps out of the car and heads up the walk. I'm left wondering if he's right. Maybe. I don't feel the stress of measuring up to Sandra's expectations. Avery lets me be me.

I grab Gigi's leash before I let her out of the backseat. Inside the house, it smells like IHOP. We pass through the living room into the kitchen. It's a pretty sight, all my sisters sitting around the table laughing. Naomi's boyfriend Seth is here too. The only one missing is my brother-in-law, Steve. He hates breakfast foods, but breakfast is Michelle's favorite meal. Since he's usually out of town on business for a few days during the week, she started this tradition.

Monroe sees us first. "Gigi!" She's out of her chair and sliding across the tile in her socks. Gigi sits on her haunches like the good dog she is, her tail wagging whip fast, and accepts the attention with delight. She licks Roe's face, making Roe giggle.

Kitty gasps when she sees Aaron and disappears down the hall. She's really grown up the last few months, and I can hardly believe she's started her junior year of high school.

It's Stella and Naomi, the two oldest, who notice my eye. They swarm, with Michelle on their heels.

"What happened?"

"Did you get in a fight?"

"It looks terrible!"

Aaron isn't any help when he snickers and says, "It was over a girl."

That gets them talking even more, but they don't give me a chance to explain. I wade through them toward the food-laden table, and they follow behind. I grab Aaron a folding chair from the hall closet, and everyone resituates to make room.

Kitty returns, her hair is in a ponytail, and it looks like she's put makeup on. She's changed out of her basketball shorts and t-shirt into a dress. She hates dresses, and I suspect the one she's wearing belongs to Naomi because it doesn't fit well. Her focus is wholly on Aaron. She doesn't even notice my eye, and a fight is something she would definitely be interested in. I thought she might've outgrown her crush by now, but it doesn't look like it.

"Hey." She gives a wave in our general direction before sitting back down. She almost misses the seat but catches herself before she falls on the floor.

"You okay, Kitty?" Aaron asks.

She ducks her head and looks up at him through her eyelashes. I hope she isn't trying that move on any boys at school. They wouldn't be able to resist. Aaron doesn't notice, thank heavens.

"Yep," she says in a high voice. "I'm just good. Um, fine. I'm just fine. I like your beard."

"Thanks. My mom hates it, so I like it too."

He winks. I think she might faint.

Michelle is kind enough to wait on the third degree until Aaron and I have full plates. "Now what happened to your eye?" She grimaces as she studies the mottled bruise. "Did you get into a fight over a girl?"

My sisters love nothing more than to tease me, especially when a girl is involved. I shoot Aaron a glare and he laughs.

"It wasn't a fight. Some dude misunderstood the situation and punched me. That was it."

"Who's the girl?" Naomi asks with a smirk.

Her boyfriend Seth winks at me, which is irritating. Why is a grown man winking at me like fighting over a girl is something to be proud of?

"No one you know."

"Ooooo. *So,* it was over a girl." Naomi and Stella share a look and giggle.

Roe, who's spent the last five minutes feeding Gigi chunks of scrambled egg, looks up. "Are you going to sue the guy? You should totally sue."

"I'm not going to sue."

"Are you going to marry the girl then?"

Everyone gets a big kick out of that, but it doesn't sound like a joke to me.

Time to change the subject. I turn to Stella and ask how school is going. She graduated high school a year ago but is already half way through the requirements to graduate from the University of Arizona with an English degree. She hasn't decided what she wants to do with it yet, but I'm proud of her perseverance. Her shyness crippled her in the past. She's come a long way over the last few years.

Then I listen to Naomi and Seth talk about their fall class

schedule. They both have that I-just-graduated-from-high-school, now-my-life-can-officially-begin sort of glow.

When I graduated high school, I moved to Phoenix to attend Arizona State University. It's the university my dad and mom attended, but I think the real reason I left was because I wanted to give Michelle and Steve a chance to raise their daughters without worrying about me. Stella was almost ten, Naomi eight, Kitty six, and Monroe not even two. They needed time to just be a family without their uncle hovering over them every day of the week. That didn't keep me from visiting regularly and spending every major holiday at home.

I can't say why I needed to give Michelle space, except that there's always been a part of me that felt like I didn't belong. I have nieces who call me their brother, and a sister who raised me like her own son. I think that's why Aaron and I became best friends: we both felt we didn't quite fit within our families. He has so many half- and step-siblings, I can't keep track of them all. Neither of us have the traditional family.

Not that I want a different one. I love these guys. I want my own family to be just as loud, as boisterous, and as wonderful as they are. I was an only child for the first eight years of my life. I wanted siblings. I wanted a big family. Maybe not as big and sprawling as Aaron's extended family, but at least as big as Michelle's. If I were to get back together with Sandra, I would have to give up that dream.

Above everyone else, Roe asks, "Mom, can I go see the Talbot's new puppies after dinner. Marty said they just opened their eyes." She turns toward me. "You want to come with me?"

"Oh, no," Michelle says. "Don't put him into that sort of situation. He's liable to adopt them all."

"You should!" Roe says, jumping up from the table and taking my hand, tugging me in the direction of the door. "Let's go! When you adopt them, I can come over and see them every day."

"Just don't let her name them," Kitty says. "No more Gigis."

Everyone laughs. Six-year-old Roe had me wrapped around her finger, and I let her name my dog. Gigi is not the name I expected, but my boxer hasn't minded.

My phone dings with a text.

AVERY: What did Sandra want?

I don't answer immediately. In fact, it isn't until I'm home and in bed that I respond. Avery likes Sandra, is maybe even in awe of her, and probably thinks we should get back together. I'd rather not tell her what Sandra wanted, but I can't leave her hanging and I don't want to lie.

THEO: She wants to date again

AVERY: That's great! She's amazing. I'm glad you guys could work things out

Disappointment fills my chest even though it's the response I expected. What did I want? Avery to fight for me? The image of her and Sandra duking it out in a boxing ring makes me smile. Definitely not going to happen.

THEO: I didn't give her an answer. I'm not sure I trust her enough to put myself back into the same situation as before.

AVERY: I understand. Dating can be vulnerable. I'm sure you'll figure out what you want. Good night :)

THEO: Sleep well

Chapter Nine

AVERY

I START OUT EARLY SATURDAY MORNING FOR THE TWO-HOUR drive to Thatcher.

I'm mildly excited to get out of the city for a few days. Not only will I get to stay over at Tamra's tonight, but it's been a long two days at work. I've been asked by half the women on the third floor how long Theo and I have been dating. The other half glared at me from a distance. No one believes me when I say we aren't dating, which is just as frustrating as it sounds. The problem is Theo doesn't bother telling people the same thing. He says the owners know the truth and that gossip dies down if you ignore it. He obviously did not grow up in a small town.

Yesterday after work I called Mom. I'd resisted calling for as long as I could, and apparently, two days is my limit. I need her advice. I crave her understanding. I don't know how to move forward without either of those things, and I can't hold off any longer on making plans. Each day Mango grows a little bigger. Each night he jabs me from inside, knocking up my heart rate and my worries.

As I predicted, Mom didn't answer my call. I didn't leave a message, afraid she'd avoid me if she knew I was still coming home today as I promised. I'm striving to be optimistic that this visit will fix our rift.

It's a gorgeous morning. The sun is a few inches above the horizon. The sky is pristine blue. Ladybug's AC is putting out pretty well since it's only eighty-five degrees. It's just me, my Happy Days playlist, the horizon, cacti, shrubs, and desert willows. There are a few small towns, but for almost an hour, I see no one. A smile stretches my lips as I sing along to Kelly Clarkson. I wonder how I could have stayed away from home for so long.

I wonder for about as long as it takes me to reach the outskirts of Safford, the town that borders Thatcher. With the familiarity of the streets and storefronts also comes the memories of growing up here. There's the movie theater where someone put gum in my hair. The drive-in where Billy Metcalf "accidentally" tripped and spilled his slushy down my white shirt. I pass the middle school and grimace. The worst two years of my life happened within those walls. Looking back, I think I survived because Mom wouldn't let me get a phone until I graduated from high school. Without a phone, bullying only happened at school and not at home.

I sprouted over a foot from the time I started middle school in seventh and graduated in the eighth. I had no sense of balance and was all limbs. No matter how much I hunched, I still towered over all the other students which made me an obvious target for ridicule. Being shy and hating attention, I had no idea how to respond to the verbal jabs. I don't know if my silence made the teasing better or worse. Either way, they made it clear I didn't belong.

I remind myself that it wasn't terrible growing up in Thatcher. I loved the farm. I had my parents and eventually Gavin. After Alison left, home became a haven from school. And, I had Tamra. She's the best friend I could ever wish for, and we battled out middle and high school together.

I hold onto those positives. The closer to home, the smaller I feel. It's like being away from home made me grow bigger on the inside, and now that I've returned, I need to squish back into the person I was before I left. Claustrophobia sets in as the familiar weight of expectations settle over my shoulders.

Morgan Alfalfa Farm is five minutes outside of town. I pass by the turnoff for the house without turning down the lane. I do a U-turn just to pass by it again. Finally, the third time, I force myself to turn the wheel and travel down the gravel driveway and park in front of my parent's beige rambler. Mom's truck is here. She's home.

With more conviction than I feel, I march up the steps, open the door, and step through. The lights are off, all the shades are drawn, which makes it ten degrees cooler inside than out. It takes a few seconds for my eyes to adjust. Down the hall, I hear Mom's voice from the kitchen, then Gavin's softer sounds. As I step cautiously, nervously closer, I make out their conversation.

"You have to finish your book before you can play outside."

"But I finished my homework for school." His voice is

soft, but there's an edge of a whine in there, which is more than I ever got away with growing up.

"If you want to succeed in life, you do more than what's expected. Now read. I'm waiting."

I peek around the corner. Gavin's sitting hunched over the kitchen table, a look of mutiny on his face, while Mom's at the sink behind him. Slapping the book open, he begins to read out loud. He looks just like his mom when she was a kid. The same straight, brown hair, turned-up nose, and gray eyes.

The tableau is familiar. I spent every Saturday morning, even during summer, at the kitchen table doing assignments Mom put together. When it became clear I had an aptitude for math, she bought workbooks and registered me for online courses. I didn't mind so much, but my heart goes out to Gavin. He's a lot like his mom in not only looks but in temperament and interests. He wants to be outside, playing with friends, not inside with his grandma reading books on topics he doesn't care about.

I shift my weight and the floorboard squeaks. When Gavin sees me, his whole face brightens.

"Avy!" It's the name he gave me as a toddler, and I love that he still uses it. He runs into me and wraps his arms around my waist. "You came home!"

I think I might cry. I've missed him. I've been selfish to stay away so long. He's grown since Christmas and is approaching five feet tall. At one time his only wish was to be as tall as me because I have a better view from way up here. He's only ten and hasn't started his growth spurt yet. By the looks of it, he'll probably bypass his goal.

Behind him, Mom stands with arms crossed. Her lips are

pinched, but she gives no other hint at what she's thinking. Yes, she's mad at me, but just how mad?

"I thought maybe I could take you to lunch and a movie," I tell Gavin.

He turns back to Mom. "Can I, Grandma?"

I cross my fingers.

Her lips pinch further. "It depends on if you finish that book and write a one-page report. Go to your room and let me talk to your aunt."

He turns back toward me with hope in his eyes that I'll intervene, but I'm not in her good graces right now, and I won't have any sway. I smooth down his hair and kiss the top of his head.

"Give me a few minutes and then you can tell me about the book."

His disappointment is palpable as he grabs the book and stomps down the hall.

Mom and I stare at each other. The air fills with unspoken words. It becomes apparent that they'll remain unsaid unless I begin.

"Let me explain what happened."

With a puff of air through her lips and a wave of her hand, she turns back to the dishes in the sink. "What is there to explain? I knew sending you to the city was a bad decision. I knew you weren't ready. I had two daughters, both with so much potential. Both blazed their own crooked path because of pigheadedness. Both such disappointments."

I knew this was coming, but her words still cut deep. I've failed her just like Savage Al. I've tried so hard to be the person she wants me to be, but I'm not. I'll try harder going forward.

Tears prick at my eyes. "I'm sorry. So, so sorry. I—"

She bangs a clean pot into the dish drainer. "What were you thinking? With your coworker, no less. That's very unprofessional to have a physical relationship with someone you work with."

"Theo isn't the—"

"What did I do wrong?" She adds plates to the dishwasher with a clank, her movements hard. "I tried to raise you to exceed the norm. To have a vibrant, exciting, fulfilling life. Not be tied down to a family when you're barely an adult. I didn't want you to make the same mistakes I made. I wanted better for you. Instead, you throw all my efforts back in my face, just like Alison. You've destroyed your life, despite every advantage I gave you."

It's a baby. Not a bomb. I don't know where that thought came from. I want to be more obedient, not more rebellious.

"I'm sorry. I'll try harder. I came home because I need your help figuring out what to do next."

"You have no concept of how hard raising a child is." She adds silverware to the dishwasher with a clank. "I've raised three. I know. A baby sucks away your energy and time. It will be easier to solidify your career before committing to a family. And to marry well. Single motherhood is not for the weak." She shuts the dishwasher and comes around the counter. "I have a solution for you."

Finally. This is what I need. A plan. "What is it?"

Her severe expression breaks my heart. This is how she looked at Savage Al. I don't like it, but I deserve it.

"Adoption."

The word sounds foreign. "What?"

"Gavin's almost eleven. I can't start over with another

baby. There are families that are ready for the responsibility of parenthood. You aren't. The fact that you've found yourself in this situation is proof enough."

Mom sits at the table. I collapse in the chair opposite her, too weak to stay upright.

Adoption. I'm in a daze. Over the past few days, I've grown the littlest bit attached to Mango. My hands go to my stomach of their own accord.

She clears her throat. "You and the father aren't serious, are you?"

I snort.

"Perfect. Once you've had the baby, you'll move home. Uncle Dan is still willing to take you on as his bookkeeper. In a few years, when you're a little wiser, we'll think about trying the city again. It puts you behind in your career, but it's a better option than the alternative."

The alternative of becoming a single mom at age twenty-three. She waits for me to agree with her, but the words don't come.

"Avery, I know this is hard, but you must see that this is for the best." She covers my hands with hers in what is meant to be a comforting gesture. Her pat is affectionate, loving even. Her voice is compassionate. It's a complete turnaround from five seconds before. "Gavin needs a good example in his life. His mother obviously isn't that person. You are, but not if you mess up your own life. If you're a bad example, I'll have to insist you don't visit."

My breath catches. "Wh-what?"

She nods sympathetically. "This is my home. Gavin is my priority. Everything your father and I do is with him in mind. I can't allow you to go off and ruin your life, then come home on weekends and show him how you disregard our rules."

Her ultimatum is clear: keep Mango and I lose not only my parents but Gavin as well. I only need to look as far as my sister to once again see the similarity between our situations. For the first time ever, I wonder why Savage Al was never allowed inside the house the few times she came by. Was it because she's a bad person? Or because she messed up her life and Mom was following through on her punishment? Is there a difference?

Whatever the reason, I don't want Savage Al's fate to be my fate.

Mom gets up and goes back to the sink and finishes washing the pots to give me a chance to think through my options. The idea of adoption hadn't entered my head before now, but it must be the right decision, no matter how difficult. Mom always does what's best for the family.

"Yes." I find it difficult to swallow. "All right."

She comes back and wraps her arm around my shoulder, but not before swatting my hand away from rubbing my nose. When I look up at her she smiles.

"This is for the best," she says. "There's no reason anyone will ever need to find out what happened, especially Gavin. After the adoption, we'll have you come home. Heal." She studies my face. I don't know what she sees there, but she says, "Just this once, I'll let Gavin pause on his homework. Go have fun. Be sure to have him back by three for his piano lesson."

I don't wait for her to give me any more instructions. I grab Gavin from his room, and we make our escape.

GAVIN CHOOSES THE HAWAIIAN GRILL FOR LUNCH. AS WE EAT, he tells me about his friends, his first week in fifth grade, and how he pretends he's asleep at night so he can stay up late and study the stars.

I struggle to swallow. "You sneak out at night?"

He's more like Savage Al than I thought.

"Just onto the roof. Why doesn't Grandma like me?"

His question comes as a surprise. "Grandma loves you."

He shakes his head. "No, she doesn't. She won't let me do anything that's fun. All I do is school work, even during the summer. All my friends have fun. Not me."

He looks so sad. "Love doesn't mean giving you everything you want. Sometimes love is tough. She just wants what's best for you."

He thinks on that for a minute. "Do bullies want what's best for the people they bully?"

"What do you mean?"

"In school yesterday Harry said some awful things about Maggie because she wouldn't give him her cupcake at lunch. My teacher says that's bullying. When I don't give Grandma what she wants, she's mean. She's a bully."

I open my mouth to refute his accusation, but what he says makes sense. Mom likes to get her way, and when she doesn't, she's mean. How many times have I been on the receiving end of sharp remarks or the silent treatment? Enough to do everything she demands so it doesn't happen again. She's wonderful when I'm obedient. But when I fall short, she's severe.

I glance down at my stomach. Just because Mom can be harsh doesn't mean she's wrong.

Except, maybe it does? A small wedge of doubt forms in my thoughts. Maybe what she says isn't wrong for her, but maybe it's wrong for me?

"Can we go to a movie now?" Gavin asks.

Chapter Ten

AVERY

AFTER DROPPING GAVIN OFF AT HOME FOR HIS PIANO LESSON, I go to Tamra's place. She's waiting for me when I pull up and runs out as soon as I exit the car. Her hair's a mess on top of her head, and she's wearing her standard outfit: yoga pants and a tank top.

"How have you stayed away so long?" she says as she squeezes me tight. She's five-six and her head comes to my collarbone. "You have to come home more often. Like, every six days or so."

Or maybe I'll just move back here permanently. That thought is not a happy one, though seeing Tamra and Gavin daily makes the idea a little more palatable. I miss them, and it would be nice to have a girlfriend nearby.

Tamra has never visited me because of severe motion sickness. Any time she spends over thirty minutes in a car, she loses her lunch and is unable to stand for hours afterward.

She picks up on my somber mood and pulls away. "Was it that bad with your mom?"

"No." I shake my head and try to get rid of my sadness at the same time. "It was less brutal than I expected."

"That isn't saying much," she mutters under her breath. Tamra has never been a fan of Mom, but Mom has never appreciated Tamra, either. They tolerate each other because they both love me. "Come in. I made cookies."

Even though I ate my own lunch and the last few bites of Gavin's, my stomach grumbles. I could totally go for some cookies. Especially if they have chocolate chips.

When we enter her small adobe house, it isn't cookies I smell, it's lemons and honeysuckle. We go directly to the back bedroom where her magical workshop is located. She has a successful Esty shop selling soaps, balms, sprays, lotions, and a bunch of other body care products that I can't keep track of. She dropped out of college her second year to work on her business full time, and she's never looked back.

I collapse into the wingback chair she keeps especially for me. Soft jazz music plays in the background. I've spent many afternoons in this very position as she mixes and packages her orders. Today looks like a packaging day, as one wall is stacked with boxes and envelopes of varying sizes. Printed packing slips are scattered across her workbench.

"Enough procrastination," she says with a smirk. "What is going on with Jalapeño? You've been tight lipped about him this week."

I've been tight lipped about everything, and Tamra

knows not to push, or I tend to clam up even tighter. It makes me sad that I find it so difficult to talk about what's happening inside my head, but I'm lucky she loves me anyway.

I've only given her the bare basics of the last week. I don't even know where to start. I'm afraid to tell her about my visit with Mom because I can already hear what she'll say: *Your mom isn't right.* I definitely can't mention what Gavin said about Mom being a bully. That's an idea Tamra would latch onto and never let go.

As for Jalapeño, that would be Theo. As in, hot like a jalapeño pepper. My first week at BD I snapped a picture of him incognito and sent it to her so that we could swoon over him together. Once I got to know him better and he became a friend, I stopped calling him Jalapeño. Tamra hasn't.

She thinks she's starting off easy by bringing up Theo instead of Mango, The Liar, or Mom. Except, this week, Theo is tied in with everything.

When I don't speak, she asks instead, "Is that a new dress? It's not your usual style."

It's a sleeveless sundress with a pattern of large red and orange flowers. It's brighter than I prefer, but I was desperate on Wednesday when I went shopping. I've discovered that with a human heater in my stomach, I need cooler clothes. Unfortunately, style suffers.

"It looks okay?" I ask. I had expected Mom to say something, positive or negative I couldn't guess, but when she didn't, I worried it was too awful to mention. "It needs to be hemmed. It isn't long enough to be calf-length or short enough to be knee-length. It's awkward-length."

She looks me up and down, then shakes her head. "I

don't think so. I like it. It's bold." When I grimace, she laughs. "That's a good thing."

Not when you're as tall as I am and want to disappear into the scenery. If only there was a camouflage that worked in the city.

I grab a few chocolate chocolate-chip cookies from the plate on her workbench and munch quietly while I soak in the calm atmosphere. I learned a long time ago not to bother asking if she wants help. Tamra is a control freak when it comes to her business and triple checks everything. She prefers to package all orders herself so she knows they're correct.

"You're rubbing your nose." This is Tamra's gentle nudge to remind me she's listening if I want to spill my guts.

I make myself stop and grab another cookie. "Can you guess what Gavin wants to be when he grows up?"

"I hope a farmer, or his life will be difficult."

I hate that she's right. Mom plans for him to take over the farm someday. "He wants to be an astronaut."

Tamra whistles. "When did he decide that?"

"His teacher did a unit on astronomy last year, and he can't get enough of it. Mom has him reading all these books on agriculture, and all he wants to read about are the stars. He asked for a telescope for his birthday, and I'm afraid Mom's going to give him a book about crop rotation. He'll be so disappointed."

Tamra pauses as she tapes up a box. "Do you remember in second grade when Mrs. Hargreaves gave us an assignment to write about what we wanted to be when we grew up and why?"

Mrs. Hargreaves was the mean teacher at our school so I

do remember her, vividly, but I don't remember this particular assignment. "No."

"I wrote two sentences about how I wanted to be a teacher like my dad. You wrote something like, 'I want to be a mom and have eight kids because I love babies.'"

I laugh. "I did not."

"Yeah, you did. My mom had just had Benny, and every day after school you wanted to go to my house and play with the baby. You held him and fed him, and you even wanted to change his diapers."

"Benny was the best. He still is. But I have no memory of my career aspirations being motherhood."

"True story. Mrs. Hargreaves said that motherhood wasn't a career since you didn't get paid to do it, and you needed to redo the assignment. You erased 'mom' and wrote in 'baby doctor.'" Tamra continues in a sing-song voice. "'I want to be a baby doctor and have eight kids because I love babies.' Mrs. Hargreaves wasn't happy because you technically didn't redo the assignment."

That doesn't sound like something I would do. I always did everything a teacher asked of me. "Why do you remember this, and I don't?"

She finishes with one order and moves to the next. "I don't know. It was just a part of who you were back then. Remember your dolls? They all had their own bed, and every morning you dressed and fed them, and every night you got them back in their pajamas. Didn't they all have Disney character names?"

"Aurora, Snow, Tiana, Ariel, Jasmine, Belle, Charming, and Phillip."

I loved my dolls. After watching *Toy Story*, a part of me

93

believed that they were real and came alive while I was away. I made sure they were always well taken care of, and none of them were shown more love than another. Until I came home one day from school, and they'd all been decapitated, compliments of Savage Al. I buried them in the house garden. Dad wasn't amused.

"Hey, what's that sad face for? I didn't mean to make you feel worse." Tamra comes around the workbench and sits on the chair arm. She wraps her arm behind my head and pulls me into her side. "I just meant to say that you'll be a great mother. Whatever your mom said to you this morning, just remember she isn't right about everything. You can trust yourself to make your own decisions."

"How?" I pull away and look up at her, wanting an answer to an unanswerable question. "How can I trust that I know what's right? If I had listened to you, I never would have given The Liar so much power over me. Theo met him once and in thirty seconds knew he was trouble. The Liar is proof that I *can't* trust myself. Mom only wants what's best for everyone involved."

Tamra makes a face at the last sentence. "Your mom has her own interests at heart."

"That isn't fair. She's sacrificed a lot for me and Savage Al and Gavin."

"And you've sacrificed a lot for her. When is it enough?"

Before I can come up with a reply, she stands and makes her way back over to the workbench. "No more worry. Let me finish these last few orders, and then we binge on takeout and Twizzlers. Tomorrow I've booked us a day at the spa."

I'VE NEVER SLEPT OVER AT TAMRA'S BEFORE, AND SHE IS unprepared to provide a place for my tall frame to sleep. In the end, we both campout on the living room floor, making a cocoon with every blanket, pillow, and cushion in her house. It's more comfortable than we expected and Tamra falls asleep before the movie's first kiss. I'm not so lucky. My thoughts loop on repeat, again and again. I wanted Mom to give me a solution to my situation, but the longer I think on her plan the less I like it.

Mango. *My* Mango. I didn't think I wanted a child, but now I don't want to live without him.

I also don't want to move back to Thatcher. I don't fit here any longer, even if I am safe from predatory scumbags. Even if it is for only a few years.

I love my life in the city. I love living in my own apartment and making my own decisions. It's freeing to be someone new, not defined by who I was growing up in this small town.

It doesn't matter what I want. I've already made my decision to do as Mom says, I just can't convince my heart it's the right thing to do.

The urge to talk to Theo has me staring at my phone screen. It's not yet eleven, and I know he had a date tonight. Is he home yet? Is he having a good time and would I disturb him if I sent a text? I'm about to slide my phone across the tile floor so I'll stop thinking about it, when it chimes. It's a text from Theo.

THEO: How did it go with your parents?

95

Chapter Eleven

THEO

THREE DOTS SHOW UP AS SHE TYPES. I'M SITTING OUTSIDE MY house on the bench, Gigi lying at my feet, her leash looped around my wrist. We've just gotten back from a walk around the neighborhood. My thoughts have been tangled up all day with Avery's confrontation with her parents. Each time I remember how she fell apart Tuesday after they left, the more my worry ramps up.

Also, I just really miss her. It's been months since we didn't spend at least part of a Saturday together.

AVERY: It went okay. Mom actually spoke to me, so all is not lost.

I want to drive to Thatcher right now and make things right for Avery. Tell her mom all the wonderful things about her daughter that she seems to be blind to. But Michelle tells me that women don't always want a man to come in and fix things, sometimes they just want us to listen. How can I listen when Avery won't talk to me? Text makes it twenty times harder, so I call her.

It rings a few times, then goes to voicemail. I don't know why I expected anything different. I thought we'd made progress in confiding in each other, but it appears I have yet to crack the combination to her vault. I'm about to go inside when my phone rings. It's Avery.

"Hey," I say, relieved and elated. She called me back.

"Hi. Sorry. I didn't want to wake Tamra." She's a little breathless.

"Where are you?"

"On her porch. How was your date?"

My date. She was beautiful and charismatic. Really nice and kind. She showed concern for my black eye, which is looking much better but still a little yellow, but she didn't go overboard with sympathy. Overall, a good date, except I'm not sure she can say the same about me. I was preoccupied. A few times I thought, *I wish I was with Avery.* I had to remind myself that Avery isn't interested in dating me.

"Fine."

Avery laughs. "That good, then?"

"It was nice overall, but no chemistry."

"That's too bad."

Maybe, but my date isn't what I'm concerned about right now. "Tell me how it went today with your parents?"

She sighs heavily. Then she does something unexpected: she answers using a whole paragraph instead of a short sentence.

"Mom says I'm not ready or capable of raising a child. She isn't in a position to raise a baby either. Her answer is adoption." Her voice cracks. "And since I obviously can't make good decisions on my own, she wants me to move back to the farm."

I'm left speechless. What do I tackle first: Kate's willful blindness when she looks at her highly-capable daughter, or the way my heart sputters with fear at losing Avery? Before I formulate a rebuttal, Avery continues.

"She's right."

She is not right! I want to yell, but I follow Michelle's advice and listen.

"I've watched Alison mess up her life, partly because of a guy. Even knowing how she ended up, I still fell into the same trap. I should be smarter than her. I am smarter than her, and yet I've ended up in the same place."

I literally have to bite my tongue and hold my breath so that I don't lose my temper at the wrong person. My silence allows her to keep talking.

"That gives me about four months in the city? I rescheduled my ultrasound for Monday, and they'll give me a due date. I don't know how accurate it will be because I missed the first trimester and the baby will probably be abnormally large because I'm his mother, but it's an estimate. After the baby's born, I guess I'll move back to the farm. Mom doesn't want anyone to know about the baby. I can't blame her. My situation brings back a lot of bad memories for all of us of when Alison was pregnant."

Her voice rises in pitch with each sentence. I wish I was with her so that I could offer her comfort. All I have now are words, and they seem flimsy.

"Is that what you want?" I manage to keep my voice conversational. "You love Baldwin-Dickson. You love the city." *You love that baby.* She tries to pretend otherwise, but over the past few days at work, I've caught her several times looking at her stomach with a slight smile on her face.

"I do love Tucson," she says slowly, "But not everyone is cut out to live in the city. I'm better off in the country. At least for a little while longer."

"I'm sure you really enjoy how everyone knows your business."

She snorts a laugh. "Shut up."

"I have a hard time believing this is what you want."

She changes the topic. "When you were little, what did you want to be when you grew up?"

"A firefighter. Why? What did you want to be?"

"A lawyer. My Uncle Dan is a lawyer, and he makes really good money. Well, he's not actually my uncle. He's my mom's best friend's husband, but we've always been like family. I thought I would enjoy lawyering, but as I got older, I changed my mind because I'm good at math and horrible with confrontation. And I loathe people staring at me."

What child wants to grow up to be a lawyer? I'm one hundred percent positive that she's parroting her mom's dreams for her. It's almost as if Avery is thinking the same thing I am as she continues.

"Tamra says that when I was in second grade all I wanted was to be a mom and have a bunch of kids. I don't remember that at all, but Tamra swears it's true. How do I know what I want when my mom's voice drowns out everything else?"

I don't answer right away. I don't want to be another competing voice in her head. When my sister Stella was trying to figure out what she wanted to study at college her school advisor gave her some suggestions. I offer one to Avery.

"Write down everything you love. People. Places. Activities. Experiences. Then write down everything you don't love. See if that helps you discover what you want."

"I can do that."

I imagine she's rubbing the bridge of her nose right now and the mental image makes me miss her. I wish she was sitting here with me and Gigi. But at least we're sitting underneath the same sky, just two hours apart.

"Theo, what if I can only have one thing I love, and in choosing that one thing, I lose everything else?"

"I don't understand. What do you mean?"

"What if what I choose makes my mom angry?"

And here we get to the real problem. I don't have any answers. My mom, before she died, and Michelle have always been supportive of me, in everything I've gone after.

"Whatever you decide," I say, "I will never turn my back on you. I will always support you."

"What would I do without you?"

I honestly don't know what I would do without her. Which is why I pray she decides to stay in Tucson.

———

MONDAY AFTERNOON, AVERY TAKES A LONG LUNCH FOR HER ultrasound appointment. I offered to go with her, but she refused. As she left, she looked like she was going off to the guillotine. It took all my strength to stay in my seat and not force my presence on her.

When she returns, she looks as serene as can be. She sits down, stores her purse in her squeaky drawer, and focuses on her computer. I try to catch her eye over the top of our monitors, but her attention won't be caught.

THEO: How did it go? Everything okay?

AVERY: Everything is fine.

And for the next few days, she sticks by her story.

Chapter Twelve

AVERY

THURSDAY AFTER WORK I CHANGE INTO MY RUNNING SHORTS and a tank top. Theo will be by in a few minutes to pick me up for the gym. Some of his friends are getting together for a basketball game, and I'm tagging along to go running at the indoor track.

I reach into my sock drawer, and my finger touches on The Secret Envelope. I draw back as if I'm burned. It's not like I forgot it was there. Almost every moment of every day my thoughts are drawn to the information held inside: Mango's gender. The paper inside is thick, which makes me think they might have slipped in a picture as well.

At my appointment, I insisted they tell me nothing about the baby unless there was a health risk. I closed my eyes during the ultrasound. That didn't stop me from hearing his heartbeat. I can feel myself falling in love with my baby, and

I can't afford to. I have to focus on my parents and Gavin. I can't lose them.

On the outside of The Secret Envelope is my due date: December fifth.

Mom called as soon as I left the clinic and started the countdown clock to when I come home. It feels more like a ticking time bomb. Once Mango is born, I lose my freedom, my life in the city, my baby, and Theo.

I grab my socks and slam the drawer shut, only to have my attention snagged by the list sitting on top of my dresser. One side of the paper is filled with all the things I love, at the top being my parents, Gavin...and Theo. The more confused I become, the more I hold on to his steadying presence. What if what I want the most isn't even an option?

Theo and Sandra are most likely getting back together, and once they do, I won't fit into his life anymore. One more reason it's a wise decision to move back to Thatcher. It'll be easier on me to leave than to lose him slowly.

Theo knocks on my front door, and I go to answer it.

Except it's not Theo.

It's Savage Al.

"Hey, Sis."

She raises a hand and waves awkwardly. I flinch, for one second expecting her to slap me. My response makes her grimace.

"I guess I deserve that," she says. "Can we talk?"

I slam the door in her face and flip the deadbolt. My whole body is shaking. When I reach up to rub my nose, I poke myself in the eye.

"Avery," she says through the door. "I can see you're still

upset with me. I came to apologize. I just want to talk for a few minutes."

Her voice makes me want to vomit. She wasn't always horrible, but her meanness is what I remember most about her. The ridicule and belittling she rained down on me. Unexpected pinches and punches on my arm. Basketballs to my face.

Still, my reaction to Savage Al's sudden appearance is over the top. It's been almost eleven years since I've been alone with her. After she ran away, she came by the farm occasionally and Mom and Dad were always there to talk to her at the door. I hid behind the blinds in the living room and snuck glances where she wouldn't notice.

She knocks again. I don't move. I almost expect her to try to pick the lock, but all is silent on the other side of the door for two long minutes. I begin to believe she's left, but when a knock comes a third time, I jump.

"Go away!"

The knob rattles. "Avery? Are you okay?"

It's Theo. My relief is instant. All the fight drains out of me, leaving me spent. I lean against the door and undo the bolt. When I pull it open, Theo marches inside, his fists clenched, and looks around. When no immediate danger makes itself known, he turns to me.

"Are you okay? What happened?"

He reaches out, and I collapse into his arms. I'm such a ninny for freaking out about seeing Savage Al. I'm not a child any longer. We're both adults, and I am much bigger than her. She's maybe five feet, ten inches. Probably closer to nine inches. A literal shrimp.

"I'm here," Theo murmurs. "You're safe. Nothing will harm you."

I love how tall he is and how small I feel in his embrace. I feel like we're part of a team, which is ridiculous. We're only friends. Even so, I can no longer deny that I love him. I love Theodore Decker. The realization doesn't make me euphoric, but devastates me. I'm not ready to face the heartache my feelings will bring quite yet, if ever, and push them away.

"We don't have to go out tonight," Theo offers.

I do not want to wait around for Savage Al to return. I pull out of his embrace and pick up my shoes and socks where I dropped them next to the couch.

"No, let's go."

He hesitates, but then nods. I appreciate that he doesn't push me to find out what's wrong, while at the same time I'm frustrated with myself for clamming up. Why are feelings and experiences so hard for me to vocalize?

As I tie my shoes I manage to say, "My sister stopped by. I haven't seen her in a long time, and she was always a jerk to me growing up. I freaked out a little. I'm really okay."

"You're sure?"

"I'm sure." I stand, grab my bag, and pull him toward the door. "Now let's get out of here before she comes back."

THE GYM'S RUNNING TRACK IS ON THE SECOND FLOOR ABOVE the basketball courts. The outside lanes are for runners, while the four inside lanes are reserved for walkers.

I begin with a slow jog, and speed up gradually until I'm

at a comfortable pace. While I run, I empty my mind of everything but my stride and the rhythm of my breath. With my nineties playlist filling my ears, I'm able to relax and forget everything. Mom, Savage Al, December fifth. It all disappears behind Pearl Jam.

At least for a few minutes. Savage Al has never been docile, and it isn't long before she barges through my mental defenses. I can't believe she showed up at my apartment. How does she even know where I live? Now that the panic of seeing her again has subsided, I examine the short interchange. She looked normal, just a twenty-seven-year-old woman in shorts and a t-shirt. Her dark hair was cut shoulder-length, her clothes were clean. She definitely wasn't high or drunk.

She said she wanted to apologize.

The night she ran away she snuck into my room. I pretended I was asleep, sure she only had nasty things to say if she knew I was awake. She sat on the edge of my bed for a long time before she spoke.

"I'm sorry."

Then she was gone. Since then, I've only seen her from a distance, through quick, secretive glances. Until tonight. I don't know what to make of her showing up, or of the way I reacted. In my memories, she's a monster, the very thing I've spent my life *not* becoming. Tonight, I saw she was just a person. I have a hard time meshing the two ideas together.

I'm coming around a crowded curve where the runners are all bunched up close together when a walker steps right in front of me. She's too close for me to stop, and I stumble into her shoulder. She falls forward and reaches out to the person closest, another runner, and pulls him down with her. Someone knocks into me from behind.

We're like dominos as we all tumble to the track. To prevent myself from kicking a guy in the head, I jump over him. I land on the side of my foot and stumble forward a few steps before I land on my knees. I stay where I am for a few seconds before I roll over onto my bum. The dominoes slowly pick themselves up.

Three chatting women continue on their way, unconcerned that they're blocking all the walking lanes and oblivious to the carnage they've left behind. Like my knees, both scraped up and bleeding.

When I stand one ankle revolts, and I suck in a breath. It's not a sprain, but it is sore.

One of the dominoes turns to me. "Did you get hurt?"

He casts a glare at the back of the three women. I feel the same way. They stole my bubble of peace, and I resent them. Maybe I resent their friendship with each other, too.

"Nothing serious. I'll be fine in a few minutes. You?"

"Luckily, yeah."

I limp for the hallway, and I sit down on a bench. I'm loosening the laces on my shoe when someone sits down on the same bench.

"Are you okay?" she asks kindly. "That was quite the tumble."

I noticed her walking earlier. She's about five-six and is memorable because of the two, blonde pigtails that lay low, just behind her ears.

"Yeah. I'm fine."

"I'm Jane."

"Avery."

Something I didn't notice as I passed her from behind is the fabric sling she has strapped across her chest. From inside, a little baby with wide blue eyes stares out at me. I lean closer and stare back.

"How old is he?" I ask.

"Almost two months." Jane lifts him from the sling and kisses his chubby cheeks. "Alec, this is Avery. Say hi." She moves his tiny hand in a gentle wave, and I laugh.

A peculiar feeling fills me. Is it longing? Yearning? Something that resembles those feelings. I reach out and touch his soft, smooth palm. His fist wraps around my finger. I'm mesmerized by him. Jane must notice.

"Do you want to hold him?" she asks.

I nod, unable to speak. Mango has taken control of my emotions and I think I might cry just looking at Alec's perfect nose. Mango's nose is probably even more perfect and instead of dreading December fifth, I wish it was December sixth.

I cradle him in my arms and hold him close to my chest. His warmth sinks through my skin. I run my finger over his smooth cheek, and he smiles.

At this moment I know exactly what I want. I want my Mango.

"I'm pregnant." I'm smiling, for the first time feeling a thrum of excitement at the prospect.

"Congratulations. When are you due?"

"December."

"Are you having a boy or a girl?"

I don't look away from Alec. I can't get enough of him. There's a wave of panic waiting just out of sight, but for right now I just let myself feel the anticipation.

"I don't know," I answer. "The ultrasound technician wrote the gender down and sealed it in an envelope."

"You want the surprise? Brave. I couldn't wait to find out. My husband and I had a hard time picking a name, and we needed all the lead time we could get to battle it out."

Alec yawns. His eyes crunch up. It is the cutest sight I have ever seen.

"So, um, do you come here often?" Jane asks.

"Pretty regularly. Especially during the summer. Always on Saturday morning."

"Maybe we could meet up some evening? I'm not much of a runner, but if you didn't mind my slower pace, it could be fun."

Wait. Jane wants to hang out with me? I pull my attention away from Alec and stare at her. I must have a confused look on my face because she grimaces.

"Is that too forward? My husband and I just moved here last month, and with the new baby, I don't get out much to mingle with other adults. I just thought maybe...but I get it. I really am not a runner. I'm only here because a friend talked my husband into doing a centurion bike race in October, and he's afraid he'll die if he doesn't train. I told him he's not allowed to die, so here we are."

I can't really describe how I feel about maybe making a friend. Hopeful? Fearful? Also, a little nauseous. "We don't have to run. We could walk."

Her expression breaks into a smile. "Yeah? That would be great. My sister-in-law is getting married on Saturday, so we'll be gone this weekend, but maybe when I come back we can meet up?"

"Yeah. That would be great."

"What's your number? I'll text you."

I give her my number, and a second later she sends me a text.

JANE: Thanks for ignoring my desperation :) I can tell we're going to be the best of friends.

The fear is winning out. I've never had much luck with keeping friends. Tamra and Theo are the exceptions, not the rule. Once Jane gets to know me, she might change her mind about how good of friends we'll become.

"Where did you move from?" I ask, hoping she doesn't notice how nervous I am. "I've lived here for less than a year myself."

"We moved from Fountain Park, about a half hour outside of Mesa. My husband is starting his doctorate in Musical Arts from U of A. What about you?"

Our conversation is easy, which is unusual for me. I have a hard time trusting people, but there's something about Jane, maybe her openness, that makes me hope that I can trust her. When Alec becomes fussy, I hand him back. She resituates her sling until it covers her chest and begins to breastfeed. Okay. I wasn't expecting that, but cool. Will I feel that uninhibited by the time Mango's born to do the same? I doubt it.

Just as Alec finishes his meal, a man comes up the stairs and heads in our direction.

"Are you ready to go?" he asks Jane.

"Sure thing. Come meet Avery."

I stay sitting. He's only a few inches taller than she is, maybe five-ten, and in cases like this I feel gargantuan. I prefer to appear rude rather than intimidating.

"This is my husband, Neal. Neal, this is Avery. We are

officially friends now. We're going to meet up here next week sometime and walk together."

I really like her. I hope she does contact me when she returns from her sister-in-law's wedding.

"Nice to meet you," he says. "I'm glad Jane made a friend. Just be aware, she can get a little clingy."

He winks. Jane shakes her head and rolls her eyes. I laugh. I like them both.

"See you next week!" She waves one last time before they disappear around the corner.

I call Tamra.

"What's up?"

"I think I made a friend." I sound like I'm five years old and came home from kindergarten telling my mom the news of the day. But Tamra understands.

"Oooh! That's exciting, except you sound like you're going to a funeral."

"Jane is really nice. I just can't see why she'd want to spend time with me. I mean, she is new to the area and seems lonely, so I guess I can understand, but she's the type who makes friends with everyone. Why me?"

"Stop that right now."

"Tam, you know what I mean."

"Jane isn't Becky and neither of you are thirteen. You've got to let go of what she did to you. There are trustworthy people out there."

"I wish it was that easy," I whisper. "I really like Jane. She's fun."

"I'm sure she likes you, too. You're a very likable person. Branching out and making new friends is why you moved to the city."

"And my career."

She gives me a raspberry. "And now you have Theo *and* Jane. That's a good thing."

"You're right."

"Of course, I am. I'm right a whole lot more than you give me credit for."

"Shut up." Tamra and I have texted a bit throughout the week, and she hasn't pressed me to tell her anything, but now I'm ready. I blurt out the next bit real fast. "Mom wants me to move home after the baby is born. She thinks adoption is the answer."

It shows Tamra's level of surprise that she doesn't blurt an acerbic comment about Mom.

After a few seconds of silence, she asks, "And?"

"And..." I close my eyes, wanting to block out the choice before me. "If I decide to keep the baby and stay in the city, I don't know if I'll ever be welcome home again."

"Avery." She says so much in those few syllables. Her heart is breaking right along with mine.

"Am I being selfish if I decide to keep my baby?"

"No, of course not."

"Am I more like Savage Al if I disregard my mom's concerns and keep him, or if I do exactly what Mom says and never see my baby?"

Before I moved to Tucson, my life seemed so straightforward. My decisions were already made and all I needed to do was stay the course. But when I moved here, I hadn't realized how easy it would be to screw everything up because of the thrill of freedom. Now, I have no idea what to do. I want everything: Mango, my family, my life in the city. Theo. But I have to choose and it's killing me.

Tamra surprises me by saying, "I'm coming out next week to visit."

"What? No. You'll make yourself sick."

"I don't care. I'll shut down my shop for a week and take a vacation. You finally have your own life, and I can't stand that you're contemplating giving it up. If finding a family for the baby and moving back to Thatcher is what you want, then okay. But it isn't what you want."

I look at my stomach. My tank top is snug across my belly, but I don't think I look pregnant quite yet. In a moment of bravery, I tell her the truth. "No, it's not."

"Then you're going to need someone in your corner for the coming days."

I want Tamra to come to Tucson. I saw her just last weekend, but I miss her, and I think she'd enjoy the city. Except it would come at a high cost. "Don't come. I appreciate your willingness, but I can't be responsible for you upchucking your way across Arizona. You can be in my corner from Thatcher."

"Are you sure?" She sounds relieved.

"I'm sure."

"Then promise me that whatever happens, whatever your mom threatens, you'll stick by what's right for you. If not, I will come out there and kick some sense into you."

"What about Gavin? I'm being forced to choose between him and Mango, and I can't abandon him. He needs me."

"Mango, eh? I like it."

Tamra is the only one who knows my code names for people. It started in middle school, but I never outgrew it. It would appear silly to anyone else.

113

"As for Gavin," she continues, "There are ways to get around your mom's embargo. I am here to help."

"Sorry to say this, but my mom doesn't like you."

Tamra laughs. She is very aware of how my mom feels about her. The feeling is mutual.

"True, but she does like my mom, and in this my mom will totally support you. She's all about adding branches to our family tree, not cutting them off. We'll do what we can to keep you and Gavin together."

Mom doesn't sway easily, not even for Tamra's mom, but it means so much to me that they would try. Maybe there's a chance I can keep everyone in my life without sacrificing anything. And maybe unicorns poop rainbows.

All I'm able to say through the tightness in my throat is, "Thank you."

"You're welcome. Just don't give in to your mom. And trust Jane to be a good friend. Okay?"

I'm still not sure if I can resist Mom's edict, but Tamra's given me enough faith in myself to say, "Okay."

Chapter Thirteen

AVERY

USUALLY, THEO COMES AND FINDS ME WHEN HIS GAME IS OVER, but tonight I go in search of him. As I approach the basketball court, the sound of squeaky shoes and a bouncing ball make me cringe. I have never watched a basketball game. I have a deep distrust of balls, of all sorts, but especially basketballs.

I peek inside one of the open doors into the court. The players are all men but for two women who are on the shirt team. Lucky me, Theo is on the skin team. He's easy to spot because he's three inches taller than the next tallest player. His muscles ripple and flex as he catches the ball and shoots. He's so beautiful that I hardly notice when the ball bounces off the rim. A shirted player jumps for the ball, and they all cross to the other side of the court. Theo sees me and a huge smile spreads across his face. He waves me forward before following the other players.

I don't move. There are a bunch of women standing along one side of the court watching. I could easily join them, but my feet won't budge. The hallway is safe. Inside, there are no guarantees.

The play goes on for a while. When Theo scans the watchers, I think he's looking for me. I take a step inside. No balls come flying at my face, which bodes well, and I take another step. One of the watchers notices me and walks over to where I am.

"Hey, are you Avery?"

How does she know that? I'm instantly leery. No good can ever come of a stranger knowing who I am. "Yes?"

"I'm Chloe, Aaron's girlfriend." Her enthusiasm is over the top, but things fall into place. "It's so great to finally meet you. Last week when you were so upset, I wanted to stay over, but Theo wouldn't let me. Isn't he the best? If I wasn't so in gaga over Aaron, I might make a pass at him." She laughs. "No worries. Your man is safe from me. Can't say the same for these other girls, though."

She talks so fast that it takes my mind a second to decipher her words. Why was she at my place last week? Was this the night Theo stayed over when I was so upset? I want to ask, but she doesn't give me the chance.

"Aaron says you two are *not* dating, but Theo spends so much time with you that I'm not sure I believe him."

I answer with an emphatic, "No. We're friends." Best friends, but still, not dating.

With a giggle, she says, "The lady doth protest too much." She grabs my hand and pulls me closer to the other watchers. "Come meet everyone."

"Throw the ball, Olsen!" one of the women yells. "You're on a team for a reason!"

The guy she's yelling at throws the ball to another player who's standing mere feet away from me. I physically flinch.

Chloe notices my reaction. "Are you okay?"

The play moves further down the court, and I sigh with relief. "Of course." Even so, I step back until my butt is against the wall.

Chloe rapidly fires off the names of the dozen girls. I remember one or two, but the rest I forget. Their conversation bounces between topics just as rapidly. From careers, to planning a day for pedicures, to who's dating who, to recent movie releases.

I can't keep up with their conversation because my focus is on the ball being thrown back and forth across the court. I'm not following what team has the ball or the score. It's all about self-preservation. Anytime a player gets close to where I stand, I tense and protect my stomach. My heart is getting a better workout as a spectator than running upstairs.

Finally, the game ends. My shoulders relax. I can breathe again. The players grab towels and bags from a wall of cubby holes before heading over to their admiring spectators. I try and fail to not stare at Theo's defined chest and arms. He is absolutely gorgeous. My eyes follow his movements as he runs the towel over his abs, then through his hair. Sadly, he follows that up by putting on his shirt.

His smile tells me he's happy I came to watch the game. I get lost in that smile. Why haven't I watched him before? Someone bounces the ball and the sound makes me flinch. Right, that's why. It's like nails on a chalkboard. Or the dentist's drill. Or squealing brakes. More closely, all three at once.

"We have the court for ten more minutes," he says. "Want to shoot some hoops?"

With a laugh, I shake my head. I have never touched a basketball but for the one time it hit my face, and I never will again.

"Av-er-y," Aaron says as he approaches, drawing my name out into three syllables like usual. I have no idea why he does it, but it makes me feel included, like I'm part of his group. "How's it going?"

For one second, he and Theo share a look, and I wonder how much Theo has shared about my situation. My eyes cut to Chloe. I hope she doesn't know about Mango. Aaron, though, is okay.

"Great," I answer.

"How was your run?" Theo asks.

"It was cut short." I lift my legs one at a time and study my scraped knees. My ankle already feels better. "I tripped."

Theo sucks air through his teeth. "Ouch. Do you have bandages at your place? I can guarantee I don't have any at mine."

My place. I don't want to go home. What if Savage Al comes back? Maybe she never left, but is hiding in a dark corner, ready to pounce as soon as I approach my place. I would rather not find out. No matter how human she looked, I'm not ready to see her again. What would I say to her? What does she want to say to me?

Theo and I walk out into the night. It's cooled a few degrees, but it's still too hot. It's a relief to get into his Rogue and turn up the AC. He heads in the direction of my apartment and my heart rate kicks up.

"Will you take me to a hotel?" I ask.

"A hotel? Is there something wrong with your place?"

"I'm not ready to see my sister. I don't know if she'd give up and return to wherever she crawled out of without talking to me first."

"If you don't want to go home, then you can stay at my place. I have a spare bedroom. I'm definitely not going to drop you off at a *hotel*."

I'd never heard a hotel sound so horrible before. I've never had an invitation sound so appealing.

"First stop, the store," he says. "We need to get some bandages for your knee."

"And a toothbrush." Also, something non-sweaty to sleep in. I'm not sure if I want to worry about trying to find something that fits for work tomorrow, or leave early in the morning and get ready at home. Savage Al probably wouldn't camp out overnight on my cement steps. Fingers crossed.

AN HOUR LATER WE'RE WANDERING THE AISLES OF TARGET. The cart holds hair supplies, pajamas, a flowy skirt and cotton blouse for tomorrow, bandages, and antiseptic ointment. As well as underwear and a bra. I made Theo close his eyes while I grabbed them from the rack.

I'm starving and we're on our way to the food section when we pass the baby supplies. Diapers, bottles, blankets, and toys. Cribs, rockers, changing tables, and dressers. My feet stop moving forward without express permission.

I want to walk down the rows and fill my cart with stuff for Mango. I now know what I want, which is my life in the city with my baby, but I'm still unconvinced I should grab for that future. If I start purchasing baby items, I won't be able to step back. The decision will be made, and I will never be able to follow Mom's plan.

I'm aware that Theo stands beside me. He says nothing. I love that he doesn't push or wheedle, but waits. That, more than anything, makes me speak.

"I want to stay in Tucson," I whisper, without looking away from a blue-green blanket with small white safari animals. Elephants, zebras, giraffes. I reach for it, but I have to take a step forward in order to touch it. I stay where I am. "I want to raise my baby in my small apartment. When I moved here, they only had two-room apartments available, which is more space than I need, but now I have room enough for a nursery. That means something, right?"

When Theo still says nothing, I finally turn in his direction. He's studying me.

"You're not going to give me advice?" I ask.

He shakes his head. "This is one decision you're going to have to make for yourself. Whatever you decide, I'm here."

His confidence in me is precious. Mom has never had confidence in me or my decision-making skills. Tamra is opinionated and has never shied away from telling me what she thinks. Theo... he trusts me to do what is right for me. It's all the encouragement I need to trust myself.

I take that step forward and run my fingers along the edge of the blanket. It's just as soft as it looks. An image of wrapping my mango inside of it makes my heart melt. This is my choice then. I take the blanket from the rack and slip it into my cart.

It makes no sound as it settles, but inside me there's a cataclysmic shift. A chill starts at the top of my head and travels down my body like I've just stepped into a cold shower. I shiver. My teeth chatter.

When I moved to Tucson, I did things I knew Mom wouldn't approve of, but never like this. Never have I gone against her so blatantly. I have to believe that someday I'll be forgiven and allowed home, that Mom and Dad, and especially Gavin, aren't lost to me forever. But whatever happens, this is my choice.

Theo pulls me into a hug while I'm still shaking. His embrace swallows my shivers, and I'm reminded that I'm not alone. I suddenly know that even when Theo and Sandra get back together, he won't abandon our friendship. He's a good person and my best friend. He'll be just as wonderful to Mango. If Mango can't have a father, he'll at least have a father figure.

The longer Theo holds me, the more my thoughts go in a direction I can't allow. I love him, but he could never love me. He's meant for someone better. I pull away, then step back a few paces and trip over my own feet. The torn skin on my knees pull painfully, but at least I don't fall. I'm embarrassed, awkward, and so glad that Theo isn't psychic. I grasp on to any ideas to take my mind off of him.

"I think I have a gift card from Christmas." I open my bag and take out my wallet. A cascade of change clatters to the floor. I can never seem to remember to zip my change pocket.

"I got it."

Theo gets down on his knees and picks up all the coins. I hold out my palm and he drops the change into it. His fingers along my skin make me shiver again, but for a completely different reason.

Chapter Fourteen

THEO

MY FINGERS GRAZE HER PALM AND SHE DRAWS HER HAND BACK sharply. She drops the coins into her bag without meeting my eyes, turns away, trips over her feet again, then pushes the cart toward the front of the store.

Should we talk about what happened back there when she went into shock? I bite my tongue. She'll talk to me when she's ready. I hope.

When we pass by the children's clothes on the way to the checkout, she stops at a table of baby clothes.

"Look at this one." She holds up a onesie.

Emblazoned across the front is, *Poop, there it is.* She goes around to look at the other side of the table and runs her fingers over the edge of a onesie that has a tux printed on the front.

Suddenly, she disappears behind the table. Did she trip?

Faint? I don't know and I'm panicking as I hurry around to her.

"Are you okay? What happened?" I crouch next to where she's squatting.

She looks at me with wide eyes. "Mary from HR is at the end of the aisle." She points to the other side of the clothes table from where she's hiding. "Don't let her see us."

It bothers me that she doesn't want to be seen with me. "We have nothing to hide by going out shopping together."

"We do when the whole office still believes we're dating."

I'm not ashamed of being seen with Avery, no matter the office gossip. I wish she felt the same. I try not to take it personally, but it isn't easy because it is personal. I stand and look around, but I don't see anyone familiar.

Avery grabs my hand and tries to tug me down. I don't budge.

"Theo," she says in a stage whisper. "Theo!"

"If she was ever here, she's gone now."

Slowly, Avery unbends from the ball she's in and peers over the top of the table. I glance around again, but there's no one I recognize, especially not Mary.

When Avery is completely standing, she turns in a circle.

"Well, if that was Mary," she says with a firm nod, "Then I can't imagine she would disappear like that. She'd definitely want to come over and gather the dirt. At least I think so. Come on, let's get out of here."

She pushes her cart along the aisle at jogging speed.

I lengthen my stride to catch up. "Whoa, why so fast?"

"I really don't want Mary to see us together outside of work."

"I thought we agreed it wasn't her you saw."

"I live in dread of her discovering all my secrets. She is the monster under my bed."

A little melodramatic, but who am I to fault her fears. While we wait in the check-out line, she alternately hides and scans the other shoppers. It's only after we're outside and everything is packed into the back of my SUV that she finally relaxes.

"Can you imagine what Mary would tell everyone at work if she saw us together in the baby section of Target?"

"That we were shopping for a friend? I don't think she'd jump to any conclusions about us."

"Uh...do you even know Mary? She's always jumping to conclusions, as evidenced by the current office gossip."

"You have a point."

"She'd definitely think I'm pregnant, and since we're supposedly dating, that would make you the father."

I pull out on the main street, and Avery lets out a sigh of relief.

"It's bad enough that my parents think you're the father. It would be so much worse if Mary thought the same thing. Besides, I'm not ready for anyone at work to know about my situation. I'll have to tell HR eventually, but not yet."

We swing by a drive-thru and pick up take-out before going to my place. We're greeted at the door by Gigi. Avery's a pro at blocking the door with her body so the dog can't escape, but Gigi loves Avery, so she doesn't try to get past. Once the door is closed, Avery bends over and scratches Gigi's ears until she sinks to the ground in bliss.

"I see who Gigi loves the most," I say.

I'm only half-joking. Gigi would follow Avery anywhere,

and she probably wouldn't even need a leash. Oscar saunters toward us, but doesn't get within arm's reach.

"Is Aaron here?" she asks.

"His truck was out front. He's probably asleep. He has an early meeting tomorrow. Ready for me to show you to your room?"

"Sure."

Gigi follows us down the hall, past mine and Aaron's rooms, to the guest bedroom. Without Michelle, this room would be empty, but she couldn't pass up the chance to design the space, insisting that someday I might need an extra bed. I didn't believe her, but now I'm glad I let her have her way.

Avery steps inside. Her smile grows as she looks around at all the varying shades of blue and white. I have to admit, it is a very relaxing room.

"Do you think I could take a shower?" she asks.

"Yeah, sure." I think of Aaron's bathroom down the hall. Probably best she doesn't use it because he's a slob. And in case he gets up to use it himself. "You should probably use my bathroom. I'll show you when you're ready."

She dumps everything out onto the bed and fills one of the now-empty bags with her shower supplies and pajamas, then follows me down the hall and into my bedroom. She slows, taking it in much like she did the guest bedroom. I look around myself.

My bed isn't made and there's a pile of dirty clothes in the corner. Dresser drawers are open, including the one that I stuffed my boxers into after doing laundry earlier this week. In the bathroom, my electric razor sits on the edge of the sink with the detritus of my shave this morning scattered across the counter. A wet towel lays next to the hamper.

Bringing her to my bathroom was a bad idea. She's a neat freak, and now she's seeing that I'm not. I always enjoy having her in my home, but right now awkwardness overtakes me. I quickly tidy the bathroom and place a clean towel from the cupboard on the towel rack.

"Do you need anything else?"

I leave the bathroom, and she steps inside.

"I think I'm good." She's cool and confident. Not awkward at all. "Thanks for letting me stay over."

"Not a problem. You can stay over any time."

That sounds stupid, but Avery only smiles before shutting the bathroom door between us. Once I'm alone, I quickly clean the room. I swipe dust from the top of my dresser and stuff the clothes in the drawers until the doors shut. My dirty clothes go out into the hallway for me to take to the laundry room. I tuck in my sheets and bedspread, then fluff pillows. Maybe she won't notice the dog hair that covers the carpet.

The water in the shower starts up, bringing me back to this moment. Avery is on the other side of the wall. In my shower. Naked.

I'm out of the room like a shot, into the hallway, where I trip over the pile of clothes and land sprawled on the floor.

I look up to find Gigi sitting on her haunches looking at me. She tilts her head, and I'm sure if she could laugh, she would be doing so right now.

"I'm ridiculous, you say? You won't get any argument from me. Come on, let's go outside." Her ears perk up. "Play catch." She's up and at the backdoor in two seconds. I drop my clothes in the laundry room and follow her outside.

Twenty minutes later, Gigi and I are watching the news. Oscar bats at my hair. Avery comes into the living room holding the bandages and antibacterial ointment. I don't think I've ever seen her without at least a little make-up on, even when we go to the gym together. Her wet hair hangs down her back and the scent of strawberries fills the air. Seeing her so undone undoes me. Her outer shell is completely gone, and she has never looked so perfect. My tongue sticks to the top of my mouth, and I say nothing as she sits on the opposite side of the couch.

"I'm feeling a little keyed up," she says. "Mind if I watch TV with you for a little while?"

I just nod.

She puts her legs out straight in front of her and studies her knees. There's a good chunk of skin missing on both. Before she can twist the cap on the ointment, I'm off the couch and on my knees in front of her.

"Let me do that."

I'm offering because I need to touch her, even if it's only her knees. I hold out my hand for the ointment. After a slight hesitation, she places the tube in my palm. I squeeze a little onto my finger and gently rub it onto her skin. My finger zings with the contact. She shivers.

"Sorry, did that hurt?"

"No. I'm fine."

She hands me one of the oversized bandages with the outside wrapper already removed. I place it on her knee and rub my thumb over the adhesive edges, taking my time to make sure they stick. On her second knee, I use less pressure but give just as much attention. I'm only performing simple first aid, but my pulse is racing.

When I can't prolong the contact without coming across as creepy, I move to sit back up on the couch, except Gigi's already claimed the spot next to Avery. I'm jealous of my dog, but man enough to admit it. Just not out loud.

"Do you want a treat?"

Gigi's head lifts. I'm not above bribing to get what I want. I head for the cupboard that holds the treats, and after only a slight hesitation, she follows. I hold out her favorite chew as a reward for keeping my place next to Avery warm.

When I get back to the couch, she has her legs up on the cushion next to her. It's simple enough to sit near her feet and pull them onto my lap. She gasps in surprise but doesn't move away. After the initial shock, she moves to a more comfortable position. *Score.*

"Want to watch a movie?" I ask.

"Um...sure." Is it my imagination, or is her voice especially high tonight?

I go to Netflix and pick the first thing I see that I think Avery might enjoy. My hands are impatient to touch her again, and I lift one of her feet and begin to massage her arch. Her skin is soft and warm. Her muscles stiffen, but again, she doesn't pull away. Soon enough, she relaxes. Her eyes close, and her expression softens.

What are you doing, man? You're crossing a line. Stop it.

I don't stop it. I move on to her other foot. She sighs and sinks further into the couch. A smile plays at the edge of her lips. Her very kissable lips. How have I not noticed before how full her bottom lip is?

I don't know how long I stare at her lips before I notice

her eyes are open. She studies me. Somehow, without realizing it, I've leaned in close to her. For long seconds our eyes meet. I lean in closer.

She bounds off the couch, leaving my hands empty. She's to the hallway before I've even moved.

"Good night!" she calls over her shoulder. Then she's gone.

THE NEXT MORNING AS AVERY AND I TAKE THE ELEVATOR UP TO the third floor, I struggle to keep my attention off of her. The outfit she picked out at the store last night is the most casual thing I've ever seen her wear. With her hair up in a ponytail, an anomaly, she looks like she should be on her way to the beach instead of the office. Most surprising, she's smiling at nothing. Her resting face is always serious. Some might call it severe. Not today.

My own smile won't wipe off my face.

We arrive at our desks and have time to turn on our monitors before Mr. Baldwin shows up unexpectedly. I stand so fast I jam my knee into the corner of a drawer. I hide my grimace behind a smile.

"Mr. Baldwin, what can we do for you?"

"Oh, nothing, nothing." He studies our accounting office as if he's never seen it before. Maybe he hasn't. The owners' offices are on the other side of the building next to HR. With a glance at the opening into the hallway, he asks, "We definitely need to get you all a nicer space when we move to the new building. Something with a door."

I know Avery will be excited about that.

He pats his breast coat pocket and removes a folded piece of paper, then pats his head where his glasses are perched. "Theo, I wanted to tell you in person that we were impressed with your interview and would like to meet with you again." With a look at his paper, he reads out, "Monday morning, eight o'clock. Does that work?"

This is exactly what I want, and it's all I can do not to burst out laughing with the sheer thrill of making it past the first hurdle. There were a lot of applicants, and many of them had a lot more experience than me.

"Yes, sir. Monday is perfect."

I'm a little too enthusiastic as we shake hands.

Once he's gone, Avery runs around the desks and throws herself in my arms.

"Congratulations," she says. She's laughing right along with me. "One step closer to the dream."

Bob enters while we're still hugging and rolls his eyes before making his way to his desk. We can always rely on him to help keep our heads planted in work. Avery pulls away and covers her mouth to stifle the remaining laughter. She turns toward her own desk, her skirt swishing against her legs. I don't mean to stare, but she has really gorgeous legs. Which she totally catches me checking out. I pull my attention away from her and sit down.

Since Avery and I are not meant to be, this promotion would be a pretty good consolation prize.

Chapter Fifteen

THEO

As is tradition on the day of the Baldwin-Dickson family picnic, everyone leaves work an hour early and heads to the park. Bob and I begin to pack up our things and turn off the computers at four o'clock. Avery looks up at us with her brow furrowed.

"Where are you guys going?"

"The company picnic."

"Oh. Okay. Well, have fun." She looks back at her computer.

"Oh no," I say, going around to her desk and pulling out her chair. "You're coming with us."

She ducks her head. "I wasn't planning on it."

I stagger back a step in mock horror and grab at my chest. "Not go to Baldwin-Dickson's yearly family extravaganza? It's epic. You have to come."

She's laughing at me. "Do I?"

"Yes." I hold out my hand. "There is no discussion. You must come with me."

She blows out a breath. "Well, then I guess I'm going."

"I hear Mary's brother will be there looking for his future wife."

Avery bursts out laughing. "I don't want to miss the opportunity to get in the running," she says.

I catch Bob shaking his head before he shuts his desk drawer and leaves. I pretend he secretly likes us.

Once Avery's ready to go, we head out to the parking lot together. She looks around at all the other employees leaving, and I can tell from her stiff posture, she's uncomfortable with them seeing us together.

"You really can drop me off at home," she says. "I'll grab my car and meet you there. I'm sure Alison has gone back to whatever dark hole she climbed out of."

I open the passenger door of my SUV, and she climbs in.

"I'm not sure I trust you to show up at the picnic if left to your own devices."

I shut the door before she answers. When I'm inside, she says, "I promise I will."

"Isn't it easier for us to go together? There'll be food trucks and the sooner we get there the shorter the lines will be."

She makes a face. "That's one way to look at it."

"What's another way?" I ask.

She doesn't answer until we're out of the parking lot. "The more our coworkers see us together the more validity we give to all the rumors that are going around about us. Arriving at the picnic in different cars is completely different than coming in the same car. One shows we're friends, the other makes it appear we're dating."

"The rumors will die down eventually."

I cast a glance her way, and I get the distinct feeling she wants to wring my neck.

"Aren't you worried about how this will affect your chances with the promotion?"

"Nice," I say as I drive past the street that would take us to her place. "Turn it back on me and my worries. But see, I'm just flattered everyone thinks a classy girl like you would go for a regular guy like me."

She pushes my shoulder and tries to hide her smile, but I see it.

I continue. "If we keep living our lives and ignore them, everyone will get bored with us and move on."

She makes another face but concedes. "We'll try it your way just to prove you're wrong. But if you miss out on your promotion because of these rumors, I will never forgive you."

"It won't come to that. Trust me."

When we reach the park, I pull into a space that has a view of the whole area. Avery's eyes widen as she takes in the scene. Carnival games are lined up that include a rope-ladder climb, water dunk, milk bottle throw, ring toss, and basketball. To one side are four different food trucks, too far away for me to know what they serve. There are booths with free cotton candy, ice cream, and funnel cakes. I still remember the food from last year, and my stomach rumbles in anticipation.

Many of the families of our coworkers have already arrived, but many more will be on their way. Baldwin-

Dickson takes care of their employees, and with that promotion, I could be happy working for them for years to come.

"This isn't a picnic," Avery says. "This is a party."

"And Mr. Baldwin's secretary knows how to throw a party. Now, aren't you glad you came?"

"I'll let you know after we eat. The baby is hungry, but he also likes to give me heartburn if I'm not careful."

"He? It's a boy?"

She shakes her head and fiddles with her skirt. "It's a guess."

I want to ask about her ultrasound again, but don't. "Come on then. Let's go eat."

We walk along the row of games with kids running back and forth. A booth is set up with prizes that can be exchanged with tickets won at the carnival games. It's all paid for by the company, and everyone wins something by the end of the night. There's a teddy bear I think would be a nice gift for the baby, and I plan to win it before we leave.

Avery walks close to my side and whispers, "Is it just me or is everyone staring at us?"

I glance around and see a few employees looking in our direction, but not everyone. In the office, Avery's usually sitting down so her height may be of interest. She's striking on her own and standing next to me with my height probably isn't helping. Not that I would ever say that aloud. She might take it as an invitation to ditch me.

I shake my head. "No one is staring."

"Yes, they are."

She's about to say more, but I don't get to find out what that is because we're interrupted by a basketball passing inches in front of us. I catch the ball easily, but not before Avery screams and jumps behind me where she cowers against my back.

Now, everyone is staring.

I'm at a loss as to what just happened, but I know that Avery doesn't appreciate the attention. I turn to the two teens playing Pop-A-Shot and throw them the ball.

"Hey guys, throw the balls at the hoops. Not each other."

They nod as if I have any authority, and I wrap my arm around Avery's back and lead her away as quickly as possible without looking like I'm doing so. Her face is bright red.

"That was embarrassing," she croaked. "It's time for me to leave now. Sorry, you'll have to come with me since you didn't let me grab my car."

"I'm doubly glad I drove because neither of us are leaving. But do you want to tell me what that was about?"

Before she can answer, we're interrupted once again when Sandra steps in front of us, halting our progress toward the food. She holds her niece on her hip.

"Theo! You remember my niece, Jillian."

"Of course." It's only been six months since I saw her last. "Hi, Jillian."

"Jillian, do you remember Theo?"

Jillian launches herself out of Sandra's arms and into mine. She probably doesn't remember me, but she has no fear. Her parents should teach her about stranger danger.

"My, you're getting so big," I say. "How old are you now?"

She holds up five fingers. "Four!"

Avery takes a step back as if she's intruding. Except, it's the other way around. I haven't thought of Sandra at all over the last few days. That's answer enough on where our relationship is going: nowhere.

While holding Jillian in one arm, I tug on Avery's elbow with my free hand before she distances herself too much.

"Jillian, this is my friend, Avery. Can you give her a wave?"

She puts her head onto my shoulder and waves. "Hi."

"Hello, Jillian," Avery says. "It's nice to meet you. Are you having fun?"

Jillian's head is still on my shoulder, but she nods. "I have tickets!"

"Wow!" Avery leans in a little closer. "What are you going to buy with them?"

Sandra's smile turns brittle as she looks between me, her niece, and Avery.

"Theo," she says. "We were going to talk tonight, right?"

"Yeah." I don't want to, but a promise is a promise. "Avery, are you okay if I meet you by the food trucks in a few minutes?"

Sandra's smile completely disappears.

Avery nods. "Sure."

She's brought out her business persona. Her protection. I don't want to leave her, but Sandra's staring at me with laser eyes. First things first.

Avery walks away. I hope she doesn't call a ride share and disappear on me.

Regretfully, I follow Sandra. After we drop Jillian off with her mom, and I chat with her family for a few minutes, we head away from the carnival games where we can have some privacy.

"Well?" Sandra looks up at me with hope. "What do you think? Are you up for another go?"

There's nothing to do but give her the truth. "No."

"What?" She takes a step back, completely surprised by my decision.

"I'm not in the same place I was a few months ago and getting back together seems like moving backward instead of moving forward."

Her eyes narrow, and her lips purse. It's better than crying. "Is this about Avery? You told me you two weren't dating."

"We're not dating. My decision is about you and me and how we missed our chance."

"No, Theo. No. Don't say that." She stomps her foot and shakes out her hands as if she's anxious. "We can get back to where we were before. I know we can."

"Possibly. But what if I don't want to?"

She gasps. "Did I hurt you that much?"

"I loved you. I trusted you. I wanted to marry you."

I look out in the distance. This is the closure I wanted when she left. It isn't as satisfying as I expected. I want this episode of my life to be over, so that I can move on. Sandra deserves the same.

"And now you hate me." Her hands are on her hips, and her eyes are hard. "You're throwing away everything we had, everything we could have, because of one little mistake I made?"

I take a deep breath to keep down the frustration that begins to rise.

"That's not fair to blame this on me," I say. Her mistake, if that's what she wants to call it, wasn't little. She threw my love back in my face. "It isn't fair to blame it all on you, either. We are where we are today, and I don't want to go back to where we were in January."

"What about what I want?"

"You need two to tango." It sounds stupid as it comes out of my mouth, but it's true. "I don't want to tango with you."

Her face crumples. "I'm willing to have kids. Doesn't that mean anything? I promise I'm really good with Jillian now that she's older. I can be a good mother."

"You shouldn't have to do things you don't want to do in order to make someone love you."

Now she cries. She reaches out to me for comfort, but I can't be that guy for her again. I take her hands in mine instead of wrapping her in my arms as she expects me to.

"Sandra, you are an amazing woman. Some man is going to be lucky to find you."

"That is the worst break-up line ever. I want you to be the lucky man. I don't want someone else."

"I'm sorry, but no."

Her shoulders shake from her tears. I don't feel right just leaving.

"Do you want me to go get your sister?"

"Just leave me alone."

The volume of her sobs increase, and she turns away. Does she expect to weaken my resolve because she's crying? I have four nieces. I'm capable of ignoring tears under the right circumstances. So, I do what she asks, and I leave her alone. Her cries grow louder the further away I walk, but that doesn't make me stop. I don't like making women cry, but I can't be sucked into Sandra's life.

Our chapter is closed.

I go in search of Avery and find her standing in line for tacos. I didn't realize how nervous I was that she would leave until I see her staring down at her phone, her posture stiff, her shoulders bunched up to her ears. Social situations really are not her thing, but I'm relieved she stayed anyway. I'm determined to make sure she enjoys herself tonight.

When I come up next to her, she breathes out a sigh, then looks around.

"Where's Sandra?"

I shrug. "I don't know. With her family probably."

"Why isn't she with you?"

"Why would she be?"

"Aren't you guys back together?"

"Nope. Tonight was goodbye."

Her mouth opens, then closes. Opens again. "Really?"

I nod. "Yep, really."

"Why? She's gorgeous and amazingly talented and practically perfect. You love her."

"I *loved* her. Not anymore. And nobody's perfect."

Avery has the most confused expression on her face. She's adorable. The desire to kiss her resurrects from last night. I have to look away, so my thoughts don't get carried away with what that would feel like. There are a few awkward minutes while we both stare at our phones, but we finally reach the front of the line to order.

We've barely sat down at one of the tables, me with a loaded burrito and Avery with two tacos, when Mr. Dickson's secretary stops by with her camera.

"Avery, come be in our picture. We want a picture of all the women who work on the third floor."

Avery waves her hands in front of her and grimaces. "Oh, no, I don't think so."

Mrs. Tuttle does not take no for an answer. One of the women in the marketing department comes over, and between the two of them, they get Avery to follow. Avery looks back at me with a pleading expression, as if I can save her, but what can I do against the mighty Mrs. Tuttle?

Chapter Sixteen

AVERY

I KNOW EXACTLY HOW THIS PICTURE WILL LOOK HANGING UP ON the wall of BD: head, head, head, my boobs, head, head, head, head. The story of my life. I'm about to bend my knees awkwardly to lob off five inches of height so it's my neck that's in line with everyone else's smiles, but then I see Theo staring, his expression soft.

I don't know what he sees when he looks at me, but it isn't someone who needs to hide because of her height. Besides, I have really nice boobs and a new bra. I smile big and stand straight as Mrs. Tuttle counts up to three, and all of us say "Pencils for the win!"

Once I free myself from the line, I hone in on Theo and try to make my way back toward him, as if I'm in danger of drowning in this social quagmire, and he's my life preserver. A big, orange life preserver that encircles my whole body and makes me feel safe.

I'm in shock that he doesn't want to date The Model. If she isn't good enough for him, then who is?

The women who were subjected to the same torture stand around chatting, making themselves an obstacle course to my goal. Finally, I make it back to my seat and plop down across from Theo. I went to enough dances and parties in middle school—five to be exact—to still have an active fear of social gatherings, and after the basketball fiasco and the picture, I'm ready to call it a night.

"Relax," Theo says. "This is fun. I promise. Just give it a chance."

Mango reminds me that he wants to get fed and my shredded pork tacos do smell divine. I take a bite. It tastes even better than it smells. "Well, the food is delicious."

Oh my gosh, so delicious. I waste no more time talking and practically inhale the first taco. I catch Theo staring at my lips and wipe them with my napkin.

"Do I have something on my face?" I ask.

His smile looks forced. "You got it." He shakes his head and takes a big breath. "What happened with the basketball back there? Your reaction was more than just being startled."

I was hoping he'd forget. He just turned down The Model. Doesn't he have anything more important to think about?

"Nothing. At all. It's stupid. Really. It's nothing." I stuff another bite of taco in my mouth to stop the blabbering.

"So, is it nothing, or is it something stupid?"

His tone is conversational, and I know there's no pressure to explain my bizarre fear of balls. Which is probably why I decide to.

"You have to promise not to laugh. It was really traumatic

at the time and has stuck with me." When Theo focuses all his attention on me, it's overwhelming. "I mean, it's been over fifteen years, I should be over it, but, I...um, haven't gotten over it yet."

"I promise I won't laugh."

Okay, then. I can't keep up the eye contact, so I play with my fork and stab at the tomatoes and onions that fell out of my taco. As I tell him about my black eyes and broken nose, I realize I've never told anyone about it before. In a small town like Thatcher, everyone knew what happened without me having to say a word, and as I grew older everyone else forgot. I've never been able to.

As promised, he doesn't laugh.

"Your reaction earlier makes perfect sense. Thanks for coming to my game last night. I hope it wasn't too painful."

He's taking my seven-year-old trauma seriously and I could kiss him for it. Er...hug him. Make him dinner? Absolutely no kissing. Friends do not kiss.

Imagining us kissing distracts me from what he's saying for a few seconds, but now I tune back in.

"I can't believe your sister would do that to you."

"That's Alison."

She did a lot worse, but that isn't something I want to think about. I still feel a little off-kilter from her showing up yesterday, but I was telling Theo the truth when I said I'm ready to go home. As much as I enjoyed staying over at his place, eating cold cereal for breakfast together, and driving into work this morning in his Rogue, my expectations are inching past the friend zone. Last night on the couch I thought he might kiss me. Ridiculous! I can't allow my thoughts to hang out in Imagination Land. Which means I need to put space between us and return to my apartment.

Theo points toward one of the tables nearby. "There's Bob's sister, Flora."

How does he always know when I need a topic change? He is literally the best ever.

I turn to where he's pointing and see a slender woman sitting across from Bob, talking to a woman on her right. Her hair is all gray, but it's thick and goes to her shoulders in beautiful waves. Not what I expected her to look like, as Bob is broad, has an impressive potbelly, and is at least six feet tall. His entire focus is on his plate of barbecue.

Flora notices us and her smile brightens. She stands, says something to her friend, and comes toward us carrying a bright yellow gift bag.

"You must be Avery," she says. "I'm Flora, Bob's sister. I've heard so much about you, and it's a pleasure to finally meet. This is for you."

She's always giving things to Theo and her other friends in the office. I feel a rush of joy that she's now giving something to me. I've made it into her club. I think I might die from happiness.

"Thank you."

I push the tissue paper to the side, reach in, and pull out something soft. I'm not sure what I'm holding until I unfold it. A small patchwork blanket of mint green and violet squares, just large enough for a very small human.

"It's for your baby," Flora says as if my baby is the best news ever told.

How does she know? I glance quickly at my stomach, but

Mango is well hidden. I peek at Theo. He looks just as surprised as I feel.

Flora answers my question without needing to be asked. "Mary called me this morning to tell me about your pregnancy. I'm so excited for you and Theo. You will make the best parents."

What. The. Heck.

Panic claws at my throat. Mary must have seen us in Target last night and made assumptions just like I knew she would. It's the only explanation. And if Mary knows, then everyone knows.

Three dozen coworkers have gathered, and they stare at Theo and me. If they didn't know before, they know now.

Theo opens his mouth, but nothing comes out. I know how he feels. I've been transported back to middle school. Just like then, I have no idea what to say.

Before I can figure that out, Sandra pops up behind Flora's shoulder like a deranged Jack-in-the-box. "You're pregnant?" Her voice hits a decibel dogs would find annoying. She points at Theo. "You're the father? Is this some sort of sick joke?"

My life has turned into a nightmare. I pinch my leg just to be sure I'm awake. That hurt. This is real. To make my reality even more horrifying, Gossip Girl joins the gathering crowd.

"Proposing in Target isn't something I would normally think is romantic." She speaks with her arms stretched out as if she's a circus ringmaster, and Theo and I make up her show. "But I stand corrected! It was so sweet to see you two buying the baby blanket and clothes. Then Theo dropped to one knee to ask you to be his wife! Guys," she says to her audience, "It was so sweet. I wish I had filmed it. Don't they make the cutest couple? They're both so tall. And now they're having a baby!"

I wish I could cover Gossip Girl's mouth with my fist, but I can't move. My breath is coming in strangled gasps. People I've never met before are offering us congratulations. I'm stuck in place, quietly dying inside, unable to do anything.

Gossip Girl lunges forward and grabs my hand in her vice grip. "Where's your ring? I so wanted to see it."

By this point, I'm not even breathing. The circle is growing. The story of Theo and me is spread from one person to the next. I'm not a circus sideshow. My sole reason for existing is not to entertain the masses.

It's exactly like seventh grade.

A shot of anger rips through me, enough to get me to stand, push my way through the crowd, and run as far and as fast as I can, away from the picnic and out toward the middle of the park.

I'M A LONG-DISTANCE RUNNER AND UNDER NORMAL circumstances, I'd be able to run all the way home, but this is not a normal circumstance. I struggle to breathe, and my body feels heavy. I collapse, barely registering the pain from my still raw knees as they hit the scratchy grass. Clutched in my hand is the baby blanket. It's a beautiful and thoughtful gift, but under the circumstances, I can't appreciate Flora's kindness. Gossip Girl has ruined this for me, and I throw the blanket. It's light enough that it lands three feet away.

I'm crying. My nose is running like a waterfall. I need a

GRACE J. CROY

new job. There is no way I can go back to BD and face everyone with the truth. Gossip Girl has ruined my life. I'll find out where she lives and toilet paper her house. It's what Tamra and I did in middle school to anyone who was mean to us. I'm not sure it translates the same now that I'm an adult, but I've got to do something in retribution.

Theo runs up, out of breath, and collapses down on the grass beside me. "Man, you're a fast runner. I'm sorry that I thought you were being overly sensitive about Mary's gossiping. I can't believe what just happened."

I feel instantly calmer with Theo beside me. I'm not in this alone. Then I feel terrible because I've dragged him even further into my mess. I don't know how this happened.

I use my cap-sleeve to wipe my eyes. I can't even care that I probably look frightening with smeared make-up and a red face. I'm more concerned with other matters. "Why does Mary think you proposed to me?"

He's shaking his head, his expression still one of shock, his breathing heavy. "The only thing I can figure is when you dropped the change and I picked it up?"

Seriously? I want to scream. "I expect this sort of thing from Mary, but I'm still surprised. Who would tell everyone about an engagement, and not let the actual couple do the announcement?"

"A person who loves being the center of someone else's story. After you ran, I told her off."

"You did?" My heart skips a beat at Theo standing up for me.

"I said that you weren't ready to tell everyone about the baby, and she should've talked to us about what she thought she'd seen before she blabbed about it to everyone at the

148

office. I went off on how she betrayed us and how untrustworthy she is, which is ironic since she works in HR." He puffs out air between his lips. "I feel bad about yelling at her. I was really awful. She started crying."

I could care less about Gossip Girl's feelings. It's past time she felt the effects of her loose lips. "Did you tell her that you're not the father? That we aren't dating? That she completely misconstrued the situation?"

His forehead wrinkles. "Um...no?"

"Theo!" I rub my eyes with the heels of my hands. This is worse than my worst nightmare. "You let her lies stand. You practically admitted that you're the dad, and we're engaged, we just didn't want anyone to know about it yet."

"I'm sorry. My only thought was how you probably didn't want anyone to know about Tyler. I thought I was protecting you. I didn't mean to make you feel worse."

I'm not upset with him. This is Gossip Girl's fault. For thirty seconds I curse her, but then I have to admit the truth. This is my fault. My whole life jumped off my carefully laid track the moment I accepted a date with The Liar. Since then, it's been careening down a ravine that has been getting steeper and steeper. I've finally hit bottom, and this is the resulting explosion. I'm exhausted with the weight of my stupidity.

The tears start again. *Gosh, Mango, give me a break with the emotional hijacking.*

"I don't understand why this doesn't bother you," I say.

Theo nudges my knee with his. "We're in this together, remember?"

"No." On this I'm adamant. "I am not dragging you into this mess." Except, I don't know how to untangle him. "What do we do? I can't tell everyone that this isn't your baby. Who will believe me? You practically admitted to our relationship when you didn't deny Mary's accusations. I never told anyone about dating Tyler and have no proof that he even exists. There's no way I'm tracking him down and asking him to parade around the office as my baby's daddy."

Even the thought of talking to The Liar makes me nauseous. Theo's situation is impossible, and it's all my fault.

Theo takes my hand. "Hey, it's okay. We'll let things stand the way they are. You don't have to prove anything to anyone, least of all our coworkers."

Why isn't he taking this seriously?

"What about your promotion? Your second interview is Monday. I won't be responsible for ruining your life. You can't be my boss and pretend to be the father of my baby. Conflict of interest."

"Everything is going to be okay."

He doesn't know that, but my throat is tight in my effort to hold back the tears, and I don't argue. He wraps his arm around my shoulder and pulls me close. In his arms, I can almost believe that things will be okay. Almost.

Chapter Seventeen

THEO

I PULL AVERY CLOSER. HER HANDS FIST INTO MY SHIRT, AND she holds on tight. What a mess Mary has caused. I don't mind for myself, but I care a great deal about how this affects Avery. This isn't the first time I've held her while she cried in the last two weeks.

My parents didn't choose to leave me, but after they died, I still felt abandoned. I left my home, my friends, everything that I knew, and moved to a new city with a sister I didn't know very well. I've felt alone and lost, with nowhere to belong. I can't bear to see Avery suffer in a similar way. Not if there's something I can do to help.

I want to protect her from Tyler and the situation he's left her in, and that seems easiest if I play along with the gossip. But she's not wrong. I can't be her boss if everyone believes there's a physical relationship between us. So, do I go back and tell everyone the truth about our friendship?

No. Everything inside me rebels at the idea. If I leave her to stand alone, I will regret it forever. She means more to me than anyone or anything else in the world.

Whereas walking away from the position of Chief Financial Officer leaves me unfazed. There will be other career opportunities, but there will only ever be one Avery.

Avery is everything.

How deeply I feel for her hits me hard, right in the chest. And it isn't friendship, but love. Love that's more profound and pure than what I felt for my ex-fiancée in Phoenix or Sandra. Avery is a necessary part of my every day. I want her with me every night. My future is bleak if she isn't an integral part of it.

All of my reasons for not pursuing her disappear. My attention narrows down to the contact of our bodies, where her soft curves meet my chest. Holding her will never become commonplace.

Her crying quiets to sniffles.

"Avery?"

She pulls back a few inches so she can look up at me. Tears glisten on the ends of her eyelashes. Vulnerability shines through her eyes, and the words *I love you* die on the tip of my tongue.

Telling her how I feel right now is selfish. It's what I need, but what does she need?

A friend.

I take my unruly thoughts, box them up, and store them in my mental attic. It's painful. I'm not going to be able to ignore my feelings forever. But I can for now. While I wait to tell her, I'll work to make her love me as much as I love her. Besides, I'm not even sure she'd believe me if I told her I love her tonight. She'd probably laugh in my face. Up until an hour ago, she thought I loved Sandra.

I reluctantly shuffle myself back into the friend zone. "You're my best friend," I say. "You know that, right?"

She ducks her head. "I am?"

"Yeah, you are. So, when I say that I want to help you, I mean it. But I also don't want to pressure you into doing what makes you feel uncomfortable. This is your decision, and we will do what you think best. Personally, I think we should let what everyone believes stand. No rebuttal. They don't need to know about Tyler. What's the harm in that?"

She's shaking her head. "There's a lot of harm to you. What about the Chief Financial position? You're so close to getting what you want."

Really? Because what I want is her, and that possibility seems so far away. "I'll talk to Mr. Baldwin about the situation on Monday. He'll understand."

"Even if he does understand, you're overlooking the fact that I'm pregnant. Everyone thinks this is your baby. After the baby is born, everyone will still believe that this is your baby. If we don't somehow correct this misunderstanding now, then there's no going back. They will forever see you as the father."

I take a minute to think about how to convince Avery that in my dream world, she and I build a life together, and I *am* the father of this baby. "I will be a part of your kid's life going forward, whether I'm seen as the father or not. Baldwin-Dickson is just a small part of our lives. It's a hundred people that won't know the truth."

Her shoulders droop. "I still haven't managed to tell my parents the truth."

"Okay. A hundred coworkers and your parents."

She turns in the grass so that she's facing me directly. "Theo, one person believing this lie is one person too many. I can't be responsible for destroying your chance for a promotion you've obsessed about for months. Or destroying your chance with any other woman for the foreseeable future. You deserve to be happy."

"I am happy, here with you. You and this baby are what I choose over anything or anyone else."

She blushes and ducks her head. "And what happens when we never get married?"

I shrug. I'm hoping it doesn't come to that. "We'll have a really long engagement, and everyone will eventually forget about it."

She rolls her eyes. "I doubt it. I'm tempted to take you up on your offer just to prove I'm right."

"I accept. What do you want to do for our first fake date as an engaged couple?"

Her head snaps up. "That isn't what I meant!"

"We never finished our tacos. Hungry?"

Her stomach hears my question and grumbles in response. "You're changing the topic."

I stand and hold out my hand to her. "Do you want to go back to the picnic?"

"Heck no."

"Then let's go get some dinner somewhere else."

"Theo! I'm not finished talking about this."

"You've basically moved in with me by this point. Is there really anything more to discuss?"

She bites her lip to keep from laughing. Laughing is good. Much better than the crying from ten minutes ago.

"One night in your guest bedroom is not moving in," she says.

"That isn't what Mary would say."

"Not funny." The way her eyes dance makes me believe otherwise.

"Just think about it for a few days. Fake dating will be a lot more fun than you might imagine." I'm already formulating a plan on how I'm going to win her heart. Our pretend relationship is only the first step in making it a real relationship.

She takes my hand and stands. I don't let go, but weave my fingers between hers. She lifts our hands up between us.

"Explain to me what the difference is between fake dating and dating." A smile teases the edges of her lips. "Because holding hands is something dating people would do."

I wish kissing were part of fake dating. I've become obsessed with her lips over the last twenty-four hours. I pick up the baby blanket from the grass and tuck it under my free arm. It was very thoughtful of Flora, but I wish her generosity had come about in a different way.

"Fake daters hold hands as well," I say as we walk toward the sidewalk that surrounds the park. "Especially when there's an audience. In fact, dating and fake dating are very similar. Fake daters leave work together, go out to dinner, and watch movies on the weekends while cuddling. Sometimes one of them will even spend the night in the guest bedroom when she doesn't want to go home alone."

Now she is laughing. "So essentially what we've been doing as friends, but with a fake dating label."

I pretend to think about that for a second. "Yeah, exactly.

Which means we have a lot of practice at fake dating. We're pros. It should be an easy thing to pull off."

She stops where she stands and worries her lip with her teeth. Torture, right there. I have to force myself to focus on what she's saying.

"Except they all think we're engaged, not just dating."

"Even more fun, because a fake engagement includes kisses."

Her jaw drops. "What?"

"Just kidding!" It was worth a try.

She pinches my side with her free hand. It tickles more than anything, and I sidestep her fingers.

"I'm still not sold on the idea," she says, serious once again.

"Stop thinking about it from what you believe I have to lose in the arrangement. Think about it from what *you* have to gain. Will it help you to not have to tell people about Tyler?"

She doesn't answer and we walk, hand in hand, until we're almost to the picnic. When the sounds of laughter and games reach us, Avery stops and takes a few steps back tugging on my hand. I don't let go, but follow as she walks in the opposite direction.

"I'm not ready to be seen by them," she whispers.

"Then we won't be seen. This way."

I lead her into the parking lot and make a show of hiding behind cars as if I'm a spy. It isn't an easy thing to do at almost six-and-a-half feet tall, but the point isn't to stay hidden, just to make Avery laugh. I succeed. By the time we pull out of the parking lot, Avery's laughter fills me up.

Chapter Eighteen

AVERY

I wake up once again in Theo's guest bedroom. Lying next to me is a small, stuffed penguin he won at this hole-in-the-wall Nickelcade he took me to after dinner. Every arcade game cost a nickel, but also only spit out one ticket per win. It cost him over twenty bucks worth of tickets for us to earn this one small prize, but he refused to give up. Mango's penguin isn't as grand as the stuffed bears at the BD picnic, but it means much more to me than anything else I've ever been given.

After the Nickelcade, I had a craving for homemade chocolate chip cookies, so we came back here to make a batch. By the time they came out of the oven, it was late and much easier to stay over than to make him drive me home. And honestly, I like being here. I didn't want to leave.

Last night Theo made it easy to ignore what Gossip Girl did to us, but only temporarily. Now our situation presses down upon me. If not for her, everyone at work would have eventually heard about my pregnancy, but it would've been on my terms, when I was ready. It also wouldn't have made a splash. Who would care about Shy Tall Girl's baby? No one for longer than a day or two.

Now, to fix the situation, I have to retract most of what Gossip Girl told everyone, which will prolong the gossip and make it that much more interesting. Anything that involves Theo is interesting. At this point, it's probably impossible to convince anyone that he isn't the father. Should I even try?

As much as I don't want to taint Theo by associating him with my drama, him playing the part of my fiancé frees me from so much stress. Am I really contemplating taking so much from him just to make my life easier? I don't know how this lie will age going forward. Lying now might make the future that much messier.

I glance at my phone. It's already eight o'clock. If Theo's going to make it on time to his basketball game at the gym, I need to get up. I stand and stretch with a yawn. Next to the door are my workout clothes, neatly folded. Before going to bed, Theo threw them into the wash. It's too easy to love him.

As I'm dressing, Tamra calls. I have a few minutes, so I answer on speaker phone.

"What's up?" I ask. "You don't usually call this early on a Saturday."

"Good morning. How is Jalapeño?"

"You can stop calling him that."

"No, I don't think I can."

I sit on the edge of the bed and slip on my socks. "And that's why you called? For an update on Theo?"

"Oooh, is there an update? I'm ready for it."

I do need perspective on this whole fake-dating-slash-fake-engaged situation, so I give her a quick rundown of last night. I finish with, "What should I do? Send out a company-wide memo confessing the truth so that Theo is free, or go with the flow and entangle Theo in my chaos?"

She's quiet for a few seconds. "Let me see if I understand. Instead of telling Gossip Girl that you aren't engaged or that the baby isn't his, he tells her off for sharing about the pregnancy in the first place."

"Yeah. What a mess, right?"

"Then he tells you that he's happy to play the part of the baby's father to make things easier for you. And follows that up by saying you should both pretend you're dating, and are in fact, engaged. All to explain the baby."

I lay back on the bed. "Ridiculous, right?"

"At dinner, he insists on paying for your meal."

"Apparently, that's also part of fake dating. I'm still confused on how that doesn't make it a real date."

"At the Nickelcade, he wins you a stuffed penguin. Then takes you home, where he actually has the ingredients for chocolate chip cookies and makes you a batch at ten-thirty at night."

"Yep." It's probably one of the best nights of my life, which is odd since it's also one of the worst.

"Avery, he is in love with you."

I laugh.

Tamra doesn't join in. "I wasn't joking."

"Only because you don't understand the situation. He's my friend. But only a friend."

Which is pretty amazing in and of itself because I don't have many of those. Before him, only one.

"Friends stick up for friends," Tamra says, "But they do not take on the responsibilities of a baby when it isn't their baby. He feels more for you than friendship."

"No."

"You've been swooning over him since last year. This is a good thing!"

"No, it's not."

I'm adamant. Romantic feelings would ruin everything. Yes, in my head I've dreamed about us being in love, but that is only a dream. He can't love me because...well, because I'm unlovable. My whole life has taught me that unless I become someone better, someone perfect, I'm not worthy of love. My parents, Savage Al, the kids in middle school. The Liar. They've all shown me that I'm undesirable as is.

Tamra and Theo are the only people who love me for me, and they are friends. Theo is a *friend*. If there was anything else between us, anything with love involved, he would realize that I'm not good enough. I'm not any kind of model woman. I'm a flawed, shy, tall girl. When Theo realizes that, I wouldn't be able to bear the loss.

"We are only friends," I reiterate as I slip on my running shoes.

Tamra isn't one to drop a subject. "I bet you a night at the karaoke bar that I'm right about his feelings."

"Ugh, I hate karaoke."

"But you love to sing."

"Not in front of people. It's just so awkward."

"Are you afraid that Theo might love you, and you'll have to karaoke with me?"

160

Nope. "Fine. But when you lose you can never mention karaoke again."

"It's a bet."

"I've got to go. Love ya."

"Hey wait, I called you to tell you something."

"What?" My tone is sharp, but she ignores it. I tighten the laces on my shoes as she talks.

"My mom came by this morning just before I called. She mentioned that she ran into your sister in town last week."

I freeze. "And?"

Tamra lets out a long sigh. "You know my mom, everyone is a friend. She honestly doesn't understand your family dynamic. She mentioned to Savage Al that you'd moved to Tucson and had a job as an accountant at a pencil company. I don't know if anything will come of it, but I wanted to give you a heads up in case she decides to stop by."

Too late.

After saying a quick goodbye, I stomp around the room to dislodge the effect of Tamra's words. Savage Al knows more about me than I want her to. I wonder if she's figured out that I work at BD? Will she surprise me there next? Whatever happens, she's just human. I can take her. I hope. At least I'm a faster runner than she is. That's something.

As for Theo, I feel safe with him as my friend. I will not allow anything to ruin what we have. Not even the buried hopes that he might someday love me. That can never happen because I can't lose him.

When I feel more in control of my emotions, I peek out into the hallway. Theo and Aaron's voices travel down the hallway from the kitchen. My bladder has been complaining since I climbed out of bed, so I go to Theo's bedroom and let myself in. The space smells like him, kind of musky and herbal. The overall color scheme is gray, with soft gray walls, a gray and sea green bedspread and pillows, and gray furniture. The blinds over the windows and the sliding glass doors into the backyard are fully open, filling the room with light. It's cozy. I can almost imagine sitting in here with Theo and watching a movie on the big screen hanging on the wall.

I slam that thought down quickly and hurry into the bathroom. Where I spend five minutes huffing his shampoo like I did yesterday in the shower. Why does he have to smell so good? It's really unfair when I'm committed to thinking of him as just a friend.

When I walk into the kitchen, Theo's at the counter whisking eggs. The smell of browned butter permeates the room.

Aaron's at the kitchen table eating an omelet. He lifts his fork in a salute. "Good morning, Roomie."

I blush. "Hey, Aaron."

"Want an omelet?" Theo asks.

"Yes." My stomach is already grumbling. It doesn't matter how much I eat, I can't seem to eat enough to make Mango happy.

"What would you like in it?" He waves to a cutting board with green onions, sliced mushrooms, chunks of ham, and grated cheddar cheese.

"Everything. Want some help?"

"I've got it under control. Go ahead and sit at the table. This will be done in one minute."

I need something to eat right now and grab a cookie from the bag on the counter before joining Aaron.

"You should stay over more often," he says. "I don't usually get breakfast when it's just the two of us."

I blush. "For you, anything."

"Chloe wants to know if you're coming to the game today? Or, if you want, you can join in with us."

"I don't play basketball." I like how he doesn't make a tsking sound and lament my lack of ball skills since a height like mine shouldn't be wasted. That got old around tenth grade. "But I'll come watch for a little while after I run."

"I'll let Chloe know. I'm off to get her now. See you there."

He leaves. A second later, Theo sets down two plates and sits beside me.

"You don't have to come to the game, you know."

"I want to." He was happy on Thursday when I came to watch. He does so much for me. This is something I can do to support him.

While we eat, we talk about pretty much everything except last night. I could get used to mornings like this. Except I can't, because my heart must remain protected. We will only ever be friends. Er...fake daters. Engagers? Whatever we are, we will never be anything more.

Chapter Nineteen

AVERY

FOUR HOURS LATER, AFTER A STRESS RELIEVING RUN AND AN early lunch, Theo pulls into my parking lot. I feel like I've been away for weeks and not just two nights. I sit in the car while it idles, not moving. I see no sign of Savage Al, but my real hesitation in leaving the Rogue stems not from a confrontation with my sister, but saying goodbye to Theo. We've spent every minute of the last few days together, and I'm not ready for that to end.

When I turn to face him, his attention is on my legs. Huh. That's the second time I've caught him staring. I had no idea he was a leg guy. I'm flattered he likes mine. It doesn't bother me like it does with other men because *all* they see are legs. Theo sees me. When he realizes I've caught him staring, he flushes.

"Come inside?" I ask. "I have something I want to do, but I don't want to do it alone."

He nods and together we head up to my apartment door. It's only when we're at the top step that I notice lined paper folded into thirds tucked inside the door jam. I tug it out and see my name scrawled across the outside. The script is made up of uppercase, block letters. Just like Savage Al used in high school. Strange how I'd forgotten her handwriting until now.

I've had two days to prepare myself for the possibility of seeing her, but I'm not prepared for a letter. I stuff it in my bag before I unlock the door.

"It's this way." I lead him to my bedroom where I throw my bag on the bed and turn toward my dresser. I tug open the drawer, dig through my socks, and pull out The Secret Envelope.

When I straighten, I notice Theo's attention is on the paper on top of my dresser. My list of things I love. His name is at the very top, surrounded by hearts. My body is a bonfire. I snatch the list and crumble it into a ball before tossing it toward the waste paper basket. It's only four feet away, but I'm still surprised it goes in.

"I should play basketball," I say, trying to read Theo's expression. He looks dazed. It's too late to wish he hadn't seen the list, but I'm skilled at pretending reality isn't happening. "Hole in one."

He looks toward the basket and smiles with one eyebrow quirked. "That's golf."

"Oops."

He points to The Secret Envelope. "What have you got there?"

"Let's find out."

We both sit on the end of the bed, and with a deep

breath, I break the seal. Inside are two items. On top is a card that reads, "It's a girl! Congrats!"

Mango is a girl. I've been thinking of her as a boy since I accepted her existence, and I have to wrap my mind around this new information. It's surprisingly easy. In four months, I'll have a daughter.

I slip the card behind and get the first view of her in the sonogram photo.

Theo gasps, and I clasp onto his arm. I was under the impression that it was hard to pick out the baby in one of these black and white pictures, but very distinctly I see her head in profile. Her lips are puckered. Her nose looks dainty and has a perfect slope. Her hand is floating above her as if she's giving us a wave. An overwhelming love fills me, unlike anything I've ever experienced before. My free hand presses gently into my stomach. *I see you.*

"She's beautiful," Theo says.

Lately, I cry over everything, and this is no exception. But I don't have time for tears. I need to prepare. I'm up off the end of the bed and across the hall into the second bedroom. Perfect for a nursery. I have a stuffed penguin and two blankets, but that isn't nearly enough.

It's time to go shopping.

I INSIST WE GO TO A DIFFERENT TARGET THAN THE ONE WE went to earlier this week. I'm not sure I'll ever be able to walk through those doors again, not now that I know Gossip Girl shops there. So, Theo drives us twice as far to a different store.

As we shop for furniture, Theo's really sweet. He checks reviews for everything, then gives me his own safety score. When I say he doesn't need to do that, he responds, "I need to make sure whatever you buy will hold up. Only the best for Avery, Jr."

We load two carts full and race them down the aisles until a red-shirted employee gives us the evil eye.

Once home, we remove the boxes Theo tied to his roof rack and take a few trips to transport the crib, dresser and changing table combo, glider chair, and the bags of bottles, newborn clothes, diapers, and baby wipes. Yes, I still have four months, and I went a little overboard, but I don't regret it. I'm too excited. I already know where everything will go.

We start putting together the crib first. It's one of those fancy ones that remind me of a Transformer because it converts into a bed as the baby turns into a toddler. It had the highest customer satisfaction rating online. Most important, it's Theo approved.

Theo cuts the tape with a penknife and flips open the top of the box. Soon all the crib pieces are strewn across the floor. The instructions are attached with plastic zip ties to the spring frame, and Theo cuts them off before throwing the instructions into the corner.

"I don't think we'll need those."

I roll my eyes. "They were prominent for just this reason. Is it a sign of manhood to ignore the wisdom of others more experienced than you?"

"We can figure this out on our own."

"Eventually, but let's not take any detours in the process." I pick the instructions off the floor and flip it open to step one. "We need to attach the legs to the backboard first."

I stand and grab the two legs from where they lean against the wall. I don't realize Theo stood up behind me to grab the backboard until I turn and whack him in the shoulder with the leg.

"Ouch," he says in a bid for sympathy.

I can't stop laughing at his puppy dog eyes. I didn't hit him that hard. "My family hasn't been very kind to you, have we?"

He reaches up and slips a strand of hair behind my ear. His touch is so tender that my laughter comes to an abrupt halt. It's easy, too easy, to get lost in his deep, green eyes. For one second, I lean toward him. Then drop painfully back into reality and make myself turn away. I grab the bag of hardware from the floor to hide my blush.

"I can't paint the walls since I'm just renting," I say. "What do you think about papering one wall with removable wallpaper?"

"There's actual wallpaper that isn't permanent?"

He holds one of the legs against the backboard, and I start screwing the pieces together.

"Yeah, it's like a decal or a sticker. I think I want something whimsical. Growing up I had elephant wallpaper. I loved it, and I would've kept it forever, but my mom thought it was too immature once I started middle school."

"I bet we can find an elephant pattern. I'll help you put it up."

Of course, he will. He's wonderful. He will make some lucky woman the perfect husband.

"Thanks. That would be great."

My phone rings and Mom's name pops up on the screen. My heart sinks, and my happy mood sours. I want to ignore her, but I can't. She worries when I miss her phone calls. The thrill of putting together baby furniture dies a painful death.

"Hey, Mom." I hold up a finger to Theo and head toward the living room.

"Avery, I called to remind you about the appointment with the adoption agency a week from Monday."

"I remember."

She won't let me forget. This is the third time she's called this week with information about The Adoption Appointment. But this time I know something she doesn't: I'm keeping my baby.

I don't know how to tell her. Maybe I'll just miss the appointment and put off the difficult conversation until after a week from Monday. Not an effective long-term plan, but it's the only plan I've got.

"I talked to your dad, and we think it would be a good idea for me to come down for the appointment. I'm not sure you'll remember everything they tell you, and I'll have a lot of questions you won't think to ask."

My heart lodges in my throat. No, no, no, no. There's no way for me to miss the appointment if she's with me. I have to tell her the truth. No hiding.

"Mom, don't come down. It'll be a wasted trip because—"

"Nonsense. I think I'll bring Gavin with me. I don't like his teacher this year, and I may end up homeschooling anyway. He wouldn't come to your appointment, of course, but he can stay in the car with his Chromebook and do school work."

Gavin. If I cancel this appointment, if I go against my mother, then I lose him. I know this, and I hold onto Tamra's promise to help me recover my family, but still, I'm tongue-tied. I try to speak.

"I've decided to—" Nope, I can't do it. All I can think of is Gavin.

"What? Avery, spit it out."

"Get a haircut," I finish lamely.

"Oh. Well, that's nice. Will we see it when we come up to the city?"

"Yeah, maybe." I'm screaming on the inside, but my voice is cool and calm. "Depends on when I can get an appointment. Can I talk to Gavin?"

"Now isn't a good time. He hasn't finished his book for school yet."

Mom spends five minutes catching me up on all the farm business, but I'm not listening. When we end the call, I don't move. Why am I so spineless?

Eventually, I make my way back to the nursery. The completed crib stands along one wall. It should be exciting, but now all I feel is sadness.

"What's wrong?" Theo asks. He's on his knees in the middle of the room putting together the glider chair. No instructions in sight.

I slide down the wall until I'm sitting and wrap my arms around my legs.

He sits back on his heels and looks at me as if he really sees me. It's terrifying. I want to be strong and independent and brave, but instead, I'm weak. I don't even know how he can stand to be my friend.

He taps my forehead softly. "What's going on in there? Thirty minutes ago you were practically dancing with joy. What did she say?"

"I have an appointment with an adoption agency in eight days, compliments of my mom." It's surprisingly easy to open up to Theo since he is the least scary aspect of my life right now. My feelings for him are a different matter altogether. "I couldn't tell her that I decided to keep my baby. I know that this is the right decision for me, but I'm too afraid of telling her so. Why am I so afraid of everything? I didn't tell Tyler no when I should have because I was afraid he would leave me. He did anyway. I'm still afraid of my sister, and I'm bigger than she is now. I'm afraid my parents won't love me unless I do what they say. I'm afraid of losing Gavin. I'm afraid of basketballs, Theo. *Basketballs!* What kind of adult is afraid of a ball? The spineless, jellyfish kind."

Theo moves closer until his knees are right up against my toes. My attention falls to the scabs on my own knees.

"Avery, I am amazed by your courage. You're in a difficult situation, and you aren't backing down, just taking a step back. Don't let anyone make you believe that you are anything other than remarkable. Everyone is afraid of something. All your fears are valid, and you have no reason to feel ashamed of them."

"How do I face them? I'm afraid of losing my family. How do I face that fear?"

"Maybe start by facing a smaller fear first."

"Like what?"

When he doesn't answer immediately, I look up. He has a wicked gleam in his eyes.

"Basketball."

Chapter Twenty

AVERY

WE'RE BACK AT THEO'S WHERE HE HAS A BASKETBALL HOOP and cement pad in his backyard. Gigi's chasing flies around the yard. I'd rather play her game than his, but I'm here to be brave, so basketball it is.

With my heart beating at a quick tempo, I take the ball from Theo's hand. Then I drop it immediately. The rubbery, rough plastic feels like what I imagine a lizard would feel like. Obviously, I don't like lizards, either, but I wouldn't say I'm afraid of them.

"You are brave," Theo says. "I know you can do this."

I like how he believes I can, because I have my doubts. "Let's try again."

He retrieves the ball and holds it out. I wipe my hands along my pant leg and take it once again. It's lighter than I thought it would be, but substantial, the rubber thick. I'm holding a basketball and I'm not a bloody mess. It's miraculous.

"This isn't so bad." My voice is quivering, but honestly, it isn't terrible. "Now teach me how to throw it."

"Sure, I can teach you how to *shoot* it."

He takes the ball from me and steps to the center of the cement pad. "Bend your knees. Eyes on the rim." He points from his eyes to the hoop. "Elbows pointing to the rim. Hold the ball in your right hand like so, leaving a small gap between the ball and your palm. Your left hand is on the side of the ball to guide it." As he's speaking, he points out his movements. I'm still freaking out a little that I held a basketball, so it's a struggle to focus. And, well, Theo is really hot. That's kind of distracting, too. "Then follow through. Straighten your knees and shoot in one movement."

He *shoots* the ball, and it swishes into the net. The ball bounces loudly on the cement court, and I flinch. The sound isn't as bad as on the floor at the gym, but still, not a happy sound.

He grabs the ball and holds it out to me. With only a slight hesitation this time, I take it and stand where Theo stood. I try to remember the instructions he gave me. Hold the ball with my right hand, guide with my left hand, bend knees, and throw.

I miss the hoop by four feet, but I don't care. I laugh, gleefully.

"I shot a basketball, Theo." He was right to suggest this. I feel braver than ten minutes ago. "I may have sucked at it, but I'm not wounded in any way. Let's do it again."

"Sure thing." He retrieves the ball with a bounce in his

step. "Your elbows are all over the place. Keep them pointing toward the basket. Remember, shoot the ball and straighten your legs in one movement."

With his instructions in my head, I shoot the ball again. It bounces off the rim and comes back at me. I flashback to my seven-year-old self. Not again. Before I can muster a scream, Theo's in front of me and catches the ball easily. My heart ricochets around my ribcage. I'm done for the night. It's just like a basketball to seek retribution for being thrown by bouncing back at my face.

"Shall we try again?"

Theo doesn't give me a chance to refuse. His arms wrap around me from behind. My back is flush against his chest. The tempo of my heart changes as he lifts my left hand and places it on the bottom of the ball, then puts my right hand on top. He moves my fingers until they're splayed, then places his hands softly over mine. I forget to breathe.

"Bend your knees," he says into my ear.

That's easy enough since my legs feel like pool noodles.

"Look at the hoop, not the ball."

His voice melts me from the inside out, his touch electrifies every nerve ending. I have no strength in my arms, so it's a good thing we lift the ball together. We shoot. This time it circles the rim before falling through. The vibration hums in the air.

"We make a good team." His breath on my ear causes a delicious, full-body shiver.

What is happening here? I can't even guess. Every moment I expect him to pull away and act as if the last minute doesn't mean anything. He doesn't move. Neither do I. I'm not sure I could even if I wanted to. A tiny voice in my brain is whispering, *this is a bad idea*. I don't want to ruin our friendship. I also really want him to kiss me. I can't have both.

The only part of us that touch is his chest to my back. Until his arms wrap around my middle. A perfect group hug between Theo, me, and Mango. I lean back into him and close my eyes.

He kisses my neck, just below my ear. I tremble.

"Is kissing my neck part of fake dating, too?" I only sound a little breathless.

"It is when your engagement is also fake."

The tiny voice has grown in volume. *Do not give him the chance to break your heart.* I'm terrified of what is happening, but isn't that why I'm here throwing a basketball? To overcome my fears? Sounds like a good rationalization to stay right where I am.

His hands loosen just enough to allow him to move until he stands in front of me. I'm lost in his gaze. No one has ever looked at me as if I'm precious before. Slowly, his hand comes up and cradles the back of my neck. His thumb traces along my cheek and bottom lip. He is definitely going to kiss me.

In the internal battle being waged between desire and sense, desire wins. I don't break from his loose hold as I should, but instead, run my hands up his chest. His heart is beating just as forcefully as mine.

He leans down with excruciating slowness as if he has all the patience in the world. I don't have any patience at all. No good can come of this kiss, which means he needs to hurry up before my sense overcomes my desire, and I run away.

I go on my tiptoes and cover his mouth with mine.

The moment our lips touch, my heart explodes.

His kiss is just like him. Firm, tender, perfect, and with a passion and desire I want to chase forever. He sighs into my mouth and draws me closer.

My heart knits itself back together after its explosion. From now on, it will only ever beat for Theo. This is perfection. This is heaven.

Yet, under my blissful feelings is a thread of worry. What if what I feel isn't real, but is instead far distant from reality? What if Theo is taking an opportunity and his feelings don't match my own. It's happened before.

The back sliding glass door from the kitchen slams open, and we jump apart.

"Hey guys!" It's Chloe. "It's kind of dark back here, isn't it?"

I didn't notice, but once she turns on the porch light it's obvious how dark it's become in the last half hour.

"Are you playing basketball?" she asks. "Can Aaron and I play with you?"

I flee for the house, unable to look at Theo. I allowed myself to tell him too much with that kiss. Maybe I won't be able to look at him ever again. Gigi follows me, and I lean down to pat her head. She's a comforting presence while inside I'm in turmoil. What have I done?

At least we've succeeded at one thing tonight: I will never think of basketball the same way again.

"Theo was just giving me a lesson. In fact, he's taking me home right now."

Chapter Twenty-One

THEO

THE TWENTY MINUTES IN THE CAR TO DROP AVERY OFF AT home might win the prize for the most awkward drive ever. She turns the radio up loud and sings along at the top of her voice.

It's obvious she doesn't want to talk about the kiss. I don't want to push her, but she was right there with me, every blissful second. Now, I worry I've ruined everything. What if she distances herself from me, and I lose my best friend?

I honestly didn't mean to kiss her. From the moment we shot that basketball together, my brain went offline. There was no thought involved.

I pull up in front of her apartment, and before I can turn down the radio and make sure she's okay, she's out the door and running up the stairs. Once she's inside, I head toward Michelle's place. I screwed up, and my sister is great at untangling situations that I get myself into. I don't always appreciate her insights, but right now I could sure use some.

All the lights at Michelle's house are on, and cars line the street. I forgot until now that it's Naomi's birthday party. I'm not sure I would've come if I'd remembered. I manage to find a place to park along the street, but it's a three-minute walk back to the house.

Once inside, I head to the kitchen thinking that's where Michelle might be. Half-empty pizza boxes are open on the counter, but no Michelle. I grab a slice as I pass on my way to the back door to look outside. I spot Kitty and Naomi with some of their friends next to the pool.

I catch Kitty's attention and mouth, "Where's Mom?"

"Bedroom."

I head down the hall and knock on her door. I'm not sure she heard the knock over the music, so I open the door slowly. She's sitting on her bed wearing large headphones while reading a book. Steve is beside her in much the same pose, but instead of a mystery, he's reading something about business.

They don't notice me until I jump on the end of the bed.

"Teddy!" Michelle says as she removes the headphones.

"We didn't expect to see you tonight." Steve folds down the page corner of his book before he places it on the nightstand.

"I didn't expect to see you," I say. "I thought you had a conference this weekend."

"I sent someone in my place. Naomi's birthday is tomorrow. I decided it was more important that I come home."

The house always seems like something is missing when

Steve's traveling. All of us are more grounded when he's home. I'm glad he's here. Unlike Michelle, he doesn't give advice as much as he listens and asks questions to help me find my own answers. I'm not sure which approach will help me tonight.

"What up?" Michelle asks.

I swing my legs around, so I can sit crossed-legged on the end of the bed. "I need help."

She closes her book and sits up straighter against the headboard. "You know me. I'm always willing to give advice." She speaks in her therapist's voice even though she's not a therapist. She's never taken any sort of class on psychology. She just likes giving advice.

I've mentioned Avery before, usually in the context of work or hanging out as friends, so they know who she is. I tell them the basics of the last few weeks, not going into detail because I know how important her privacy is to her, but enough to give them a good feel for the situation.

"Motherhood is hard," Michelle says. "Doing it alone is harder. She'll need friends now more than ever."

I rub my hand through my hair. "Right, except I love her."

Steve's eyebrows furrow. My sister looks pained as if she swallowed a bee.

"I know what's going on in your head, Michelle. You're worried I only *think* I love her because she needs help. Not true at all. I don't want to save her, I just want to be with her. Tonight, we kissed. It completely freaked her out, and now I don't know what to do. Up until this afternoon, I didn't think she felt anything for me beyond friendship." Seeing the list of things she loves on her dresser, with my name on top with

179

a bunch of hearts, was like the cool wash of storm clouds covering the blazing sun. "The kiss..."

The whole way here I replayed the kiss in my head. Avery did not hold back at all. She was confident and had layers of passion that peeled away with each touch of our lips. Until Chloe interrupted us. If our kissing had been allowed to come to a natural conclusion, we might have been able to talk about it before Avery freaked out. Maybe.

"I think I ruined everything. I planned to slowly convince her of my feelings while winning over hers. What should I do now? If I tell her how I feel, will that help or make her run away faster?"

Michelle's chewing on her thumbnail. "Honestly Teddy, I'm more worried about you."

"This isn't my hero complex. I know the difference between passion and compassion."

With a sigh, she leans forward. "Since you were little and Mom and Dad died, you've wanted your own family. That's been your goal. With Avery, you get two for the price of one. Are you sure you're not blinded by the promise of a ready-made family?"

Avery's dad's punch to my face didn't hurt as much as Michelle's accusation does. I stand, giving myself some space.

"It's not about the baby. It's Avery." Though I do love her baby. That ultrasound picture made her feel real for the first time. I can't wait to meet her. "It's not like I'd be willing to take on the role of a father to just anyone's baby."

Both of Michelle's eyebrows raise, and she tilts her head. She doesn't believe me but moves on. "You tend to jump into relationships quickly. The girl in Phoenix. Sandra. It hasn't even been that long since you two broke up. I don't want to see you get hurt again if you're just on the rebound."

I do tend to fall hard and fast. Still, I don't doubt my feelings, just Avery's.

I pace. "It's exactly because of my past dating experiences that I know the love I feel for Avery is real. I've never felt this much for anyone before."

Michelle clears her throat. "Okay. Then what about Avery? She's in a vulnerable spot. Can you trust her not to take advantage of you?"

Instant anger chokes me. "If you knew Avery you would never suggest such a thing."

She turns to Steve. "What do you think?"

Instead of reiterating Michelle's concerns, he clarifies mine, "You're worried about how to stay friends while moving on to something more?"

"Exactly."

"I can't imagine Avery's situation is easy. I'm sure she has a lot of concerns right now. She's also not long out of a relationship. One that probably left her emotionally scarred."

He has a point. I nod.

"Do you want a relationship that will last, or are you focused on kissing her again as soon as possible?"

Honestly? Both. "I want her forever."

"The marshmallow test."

I collapse on the end of the bed. He loves that stupid marshmallow test that Stanford did in the Seventies. The point he's making? Resist instant gratification and hold out for the bigger prize.

"You think I should wait to do something."

He shrugs. "I don't know her like you do, but if a kiss made her run, I'm guessing she isn't ready for anything serious. You both could use some time to build a firm foundation before becoming serious."

Dang it. This isn't what I wanted to hear. Keeping our relationship firmly in friendship will be difficult after that kiss. Especially if Avery decides not to fight against the rumors at work, and we pretend we're engaged. But I want the bigger prize: Her. I can be patient.

"We should meet her," Michelle says. "Invite her over for dinner tomorrow."

The image of Avery here for dinner, surrounded by my family, makes me happy. She fits. My sisters will love her. Steve, too. Michelle...eventually.

"I'll invite her, but after tonight I'm not sure she'll come."

"Tell her I'm making Kalua pork and then describe to her my pork's deliciousness. It should be an easy sell."

"I'll try."

Chapter Twenty-Two

AVERY

I CAN'T SLEEP. THE KISS KEEPS RUNNING THROUGH MY HEAD ON a delicious, torturous loop.

Delicious, because *Theo!*

Torturous, because it can never happen again.

Yes, Theo likes me. I can't pretend otherwise, not after tonight. But he deserves someone so much better than me. Someone who isn't pregnant with The Liar's baby. Who isn't shy or weak or afraid of silly balls. He deserves perfection.

But that kiss...

I throw back my covers and head for the TV in the living room. I need a distraction. In the dark, my foot hooks on a strap and I fall against my dresser. It's my gym bag from earlier today. I remember coming home and finding Savage Al's letter on my door and then I completely forgot about it. I flip on the light and take out the letter. If nothing else, it will definitely be a distraction from Theo's lips.

From between the folded pages a photograph falls and flutters to the floor. It lands right side up, and I squat to look at it. It's faded and worn, the edges rounded. I've never seen this particular photo before, but I recognize the two girls: Savage Al and me standing in front of the house, our arms around each other. We're actually smiling. I'm accustomed to seeing myself in pictures because of Mom's love of scrapbooks, so it's easy to place myself in kindergarten. I can't believe Savage Al kept it for all these years.

My curiosity is piqued, and I sit on the end of the bed while I read the letter.

Avery,

I didn't mean to freak you out by stopping by, I promise. I can see how it probably would have been better if I had called or written to you first. But you are impossible to find! I only found out you moved from the farm a few days ago when I ran into Tamra's mom at the Thatcher farmer's market. Honestly, it would've been much easier to contact you if you were on social media!

I came to say sorry for how I treated you when we were kids. I was mean and selfish. I've lived with this regret for years, and it would mean a lot to me if we could talk. I'd like to repair our relationship. I want to be the big sister I should have been from the beginning. I always loved you, I just wasn't very good at showing it.

Can we talk?

Love you, Alison

Her phone number is scrawled along the side of the paper since there's no more room on the bottom.

I honestly have no idea what to think. I reread the letter a few times and wonder why she's so insistent on talking to me now. She hasn't been by the house in years, and Gavin is the one she should be apologizing to first.

It's more proof that she isn't the monster I remember. She seems normal. Nevertheless, I'm not willing to call her. I don't want to talk to her. The memory of what she did to me as a kid is still vivid.

Mango starts up her nightly acrobatics. Her movements have become a comfort to me and I climb back into bed. No matter what, we're in this together.

Savage Al's letter has done its job. It's her I'm thinking of and not Theo when I finally drift off to sleep.

MONDAY MORNING, I LIE IN BED LONG AFTER MY ALARM GOES off. I want to call in sick and hide from everyone who might congratulate me on my fake engagement and Mango. I still haven't decided what to do about the lies Gossip Girl spread. It's so awkward!

And Theo. How do I face him after that kiss on Saturday? I pull my pillow out from under my head and use it to cover my face, then punch it a few times. A better question might be, how did I get myself into this mess?

Maybe Theo will call in sick, so he doesn't have to see me? No, he isn't a spineless jellyfish like me. He's a shark, not afraid of anything. Definitely not messy, scary feelings. As proof, he invited me to meet his family yesterday. I'm the one who faked a cough, so I had an excuse not to go.

My phone chimes with a text. Is that Theo? Calm down,

heart. He probably has important information to give me about our fake relationship that I need to know before going into the office. I sneak a peek at my phone, then wish I hadn't.

MOM: What's a good restaurant I can take Gavin to after your appointment next Monday? Nothing spicy. You know how it gives him gas.

My appointment with the adoption agency is now a week away. I have until Sunday to tell Mom I'm not going. Until then, I better practice being brave. The bravest thing I can do right now is face my coworkers.

As I dress, I sing the Sara Bareilles song, "Brave" to psych me up for the upcoming day. Mango has expanded my stomach another half inch. She won't be hidden for much longer. I suppose it's a good thing everyone already knows? I'll pretend that's the silver lining to Friday night's circus show.

Katy Perry's "Roar" is my soundtrack as I drive to BD. It gets me to the door of the building and up the elevator. By then it's too late to turn back. As I walk the hall of the third floor, I accept congratulations from a guy in the marketing department with a tip of my head. When a woman from the administrative team asks the gender of the baby, I calmly say, "A girl," and glide right past before she can start up a conversation. I'm not strong enough for that yet. Baby steps.

When I make it to the Accounting Cubby, I sigh in relief as I sink into my chair. I survived the gauntlet. It wasn't even as hard as I expected, but it's only been five minutes. The day can always get worse.

Theo isn't at his desk, but his computer is on. Bob doesn't

look up from his computer and I don't bother to ask him where Theo went. I won't get an answer.

When Theo arrives five minutes later wearing a black suit, I remember he had his second interview this morning. I am such a bad friend for forgetting. I should have sent him a good luck text, at least.

A message pops up at the bottom of my screen before I can ask him how it went.

THEO: Sorry I upset you Saturday night. We can pretend it never happened if you want.

I was ready with a bullet-point argument for why we should pretend The Kiss never happened, but he steals the wind out of my storm clouds by not allowing me to give him my reasons. Doesn't he want to remember the kiss? Am I the only one who tossed and turned the last two nights?

This is a good thing, I tell my stupid heart. *It's for your own protection. He deserves someone better.* My stupid heart doesn't listen to reason. It still remembers how wonderful it felt to be held by him. My lips remember every second of that kiss, and I bite them in punishment.

AVERY: Okay. How did your interview go?

THEO: Not the greatest. It was obvious not everyone on the interview board was interested in hiring me for the position. They have a few more interviews today. I should find out later this week, but I'm sure I'm out of the running.

My heart breaks for him. I hope that if he doesn't get the position, it has nothing to do with me. With hesitant fingers, I type out my own question.

AVERY: What did you tell them about the fiasco Friday night at the picnic?

THEO: Nothing. It never came up. What do you want to do about the fake engagement? The job is off the table.

He shouldn't be taking on the role of my baby's father or my fiancé. If I agree to let him do it, I'm taking advantage of his friendship.

AVERY: You don't know that about the job for sure

THEO: Yeah, I do.

It was difficult coming in this morning and having everyone stare, but it would've been so much harder if I hadn't known they all believe this baby is Theo's. The Liar is a part of my life that no one has a right to. If I open that door, I allow practical strangers to make judgments about me. Nightmare.

THEO: engagement or no engagement?

When I don't respond, another message pops up

THEO: I have something that will make our deception a little more believable.

He stands and approaches my desk. My focus is on my screen. Work, work, work. That's me. From the corner of my eye, I see him pull out a small ring box from his pocket and set it next to my keyboard. My resistance lasts a whole ten seconds before I flip open the top.

Inside is a white gold ring with a square setting. The center is a round diamond, surrounded by smaller diamonds. I have no idea about carats, but I would guess this one has a lot of them. Or are fewer carats better? It doesn't matter. All I know is that it's gorgeous. I'm unable to resist when Theo takes the ring and slips it on my finger. It fits perfectly. For a second, I forget that our relationship isn't real.

I look up at him, a question in my eyes. He glances

toward Bob, so I do, too. He's still ignoring us. Theo mouths, "My mom's ring."

I can't take his mom's ring. I go to remove it, but Theo's hands encircle my own.

"Keep it for now," he whispers, then goes back to his desk.

I should take it off, put it back in the box, and return it to Theo. It should be saved for the woman he loves someday, not me. Yet I find it impossible to remove. The slight weight on my finger is comforting. I feel like I'm not alone.

I get to work, but for once, Number Land isn't so easy to get lost in.

Midafternoon, my phone chirps with a text. It's probably my mom asking for an answer to her earlier question. I'm all set to respond, but the text isn't from her. It's from Jane, the woman I met at the gym last week.

JANE: We're back in town! Even better, Neal's mom is staying with us tonight which means we have a babysitter! I know this is late notice, but do you want to double date tonight? I have some certificates for crazy golf.

AVERY: Crazy golf?

JANE: Mini golf. Crazy golf is what my dad always calls it.

Besides Tamra, I haven't been invited out by a girlfriend since sixth grade. I feel like I'm *in* sixth grade again at the excitement that bubbles up. Except, its golf. I don't know how to play golf, even the crazy kind.

THEO: Why are you grimacing? Is something wrong?

AVERY: Have you ever been mini golfing?

THEO: Sure. Michelle loves it. You?

AVERY: Balls are involved. I've never been.

But I'm brave now, I remind myself. I have faced my greatest inanimate nemesis, the basketball. I can face down a golf ball. I just need a date.

I meet Theo's eyes over our monitors. I was so nervous to see him this morning, but his ease with me has calmed any fear that our kiss ruined our friendship. Friends go golfing together. I glance down at my fake-engagement ring. Fake engagers might even call it a fake date.

AVERY: Will you go mini golfing with me tonight on a double date?

The biggest grin spreads across his face. It makes my heart rate pick up.

THEO: I'd love to. Who's the other couple?

Chapter Twenty-Three

AVERY

AFTER WORK, THEO DRIVES US TO THE GOLF N' STUFF, AN outside course that I've probably passed a dozen times and never noticed. My hands are sweaty, which is gross because I can't stop rubbing my nose.

"What exactly is making you so nervous?" Theo asks. "Is it the golf balls? I promise I'll protect you if need be, but we generally don't aim them at each other so I think you'll be safe."

"No, not the golf balls."

Having a chit-chat with Jane for fifteen minutes at the gym is easy. Going out and getting to know Jane and her husband in a social setting is terrifying. Making friends is hard. Except for with Theo, but our friendship started so quickly due to shared heartbreak, we were friends before I even realized it.

"People generally don't like me," I say.

His eyebrows furrow. "That isn't true. I like you."

I blush at the conviction in his voice. "You like everyone."

"No, I don't. Mary's solidly on the 'People Theo Does Not Like' list."

I doubt that will last long. The moment she apologizes, he'll forgive her.

He takes my hand and the physical touch does two things: it calms my worry, but activates my autonomic nervous system and pushes it into hyperdrive.

"Why do you think people don't like you?" he asks. Then continues more hesitantly, "Maybe you think they don't like you because you don't give them the chance to get to know you?"

Tamra has said something similar on a few occasions, but no, that isn't the issue. I've learned from past experience that if people get to know me, they don't like me. When I keep my distance, people never get the chance to find out I'm not worth their time.

Theo's still waiting for a response. I need him to understand why I'm terrified about tonight, but also why tonight is so important to me. I unhook my seatbelt and turn in my seat to face him directly. I can't believe I'm about to tell him one of the most defining nights of my life.

"I grew a lot the summer before seventh grade. When middle school started, I was literally head and shoulders above everyone else. During the first few weeks of school there was a lot of staring and whispering, but I didn't pay much attention. I had my best friends, Tamra and Becky, and no one was outright mean. Until the back-to-school social where I asked Colby Nesbitt to dance. We were friends in elementary, even shared a half-second kiss behind the school on the last day of sixth-grade. But now that I was freakishly taller than him, he didn't want to be seen with me. His mom was a chaperone and made him say yes."

This memory still has so much power. I remember exactly how humiliated I felt when Colby's mom made him dance with me. A simple no would have been more humane. He spent four excruciating minutes pretending I didn't exist. Like he was dancing with the brick wall behind me.

"When the dance finally ended, he told his friends loud enough for half the gym to hear, 'Now I know what it's like dancing with Godzilla. Terrifying.' Everyone thought it was so funny. I think Becky laughed louder than anyone else." Her laughter hurt more than everyone else, combined. "For the rest of the school year, everyone called me Godzilla. Anytime Colby or his friends saw me coming down the hall, they scattered and screamed like I was going to bite their heads off. I became a joke."

Theo's jaw clenches. "That's awful. Avery, I'm so sorry."

"I lost Becky over it. She didn't like being known as Godzilla's friend. She stopped being my friend and told everyone my secrets."

"I'm guessing that's why you hate gossip so much."

"I'd told Becky the day before the social that I'd overheard Alison on the phone with her boyfriend and she thought she might be pregnant. Gossip spreads fast in small towns, and once Becky told someone, everyone knew. My mom found out about Alison's pregnancy from our neighbor."

"Yikes."

"You can imagine how happy Alison was when this blew

up in her face. All of our faces, really. Because I trusted the wrong people."

Theo's expression is one of sympathy, but it isn't overbearing or tinged with pity. I hate pity because it makes me feel pathetic.

"Are you afraid that Jane will turn on you like Becky did?"

"No. I'm afraid that once she gets to know me, she won't like me anymore. I don't know how to make friends. You're the first friend I've made in over ten years."

He squeezes my hand. "I like being your friend. I can't imagine anyone disliking you. You are a very likable person. Kids can be cruel."

"So can adults. Tyler ring a bell?" Before he can comment on that topic, I plow forward. "I like Jane, but why would she like me?"

My question is rhetorical. I just want him to understand. He still answers. "Because you're fun. You're kind. You have a healthy sense of humor. You're loyal. You're brave."

I snort.

"You are."

"I'm going to make a fool out of myself golfing."

"I have a secret for you." He leans close, and only when I've looked at him directly does he whisper, "You don't have to be perfect to be liked. Which is good, because perfection is impossible."

There's a message he's trying to convey through his eyes that go deeper than his words. I can't look away from him, or I may break the hold his voice has over me.

"You can miss every hole spectacularly," he continues. "Trip while doing the chicken dance down the course. Or belt out 'I'm Too Sexy' off-key and at the top of your lungs. It doesn't matter. I will still like you. I believe Jane will too."

His words expand inside my chest. I'd believe the sun set in the north if Theo told me so while looking at me like this.

"Okay?"

"Okay."

We get out of the car and head toward the building. Theo takes my hand. I can feel the ring on my finger in his loose grip and wonder if I should take it off. I don't want to lie to Jane, but I also don't want to remove my connection to Theo. The ring stays.

Jane and Neal are just inside the front door of the building. Neal is holding her tightly in an embrace.

"Sorry, guys," Jane says with a little sniffle. "I've never left Alec before, and it's harder than I anticipated." She steps back, wipes her eyes, and takes in a deep breath. "There, I'm better. We are going to have so much fun. I'm so glad you could come with us."

Tears still stream down her face, but I think she means what she says.

"This is Theo," I say. "Jane and Neal."

Neal studies Theo for a second. "I recognize you. You were on the basketball team at ASU, right?"

"Yeah, I was." Theo looks him up and down. "Were you?"

"Oh no. Mini golf is about as athletic as I get. But my roommate, Nathan Brewer, was on the team at the same time you were."

Theo laughs. "Oh, I remember Nate. Were you his roommate when he got picked up by campus police for dumpster diving in the donation bins?"

"Yeah. I was with him!"

Jane half-gasps, half-laughs. "You were arrested?"

"No. I was brought in by the *campus police*. That doesn't qualify as an arrest."

Jane snorts. "Whose definition are you going by? I doubt the campus police would agree."

"My definition. I can't have any of my students find out about my seedy past. I need to set a good example."

"Maybe you should live one first." She pokes him in the chest. "I can't believe you got arrested! We are definitely sharing the details with Alec when he gets old enough. We'll put it under the label, 'Things you should never do like your dad.'"

Everyone continues to talk as we make our way over to the golf line to pick up our balls and clubs. Turns out there's a lot of people that Neal and Theo both know from their college days. The conversation turns to more recent events in our lives. Neal was a high school choir teacher before he moved here to get his PhD. Jane is an actress.

"I tried to make it on Broadway, but I'm lucky that it didn't pan out. If it had, I wouldn't be here with Neal."

They kiss quickly. It's the sweetest.

Though I don't add much to the conversation, I feel a part of it. I've never had this sort of inclusive experience before. It's always been me and Tamra against everyone else. I love being a part of everyone else tonight.

Too soon we have our golfing gear and are back outside at hole one. Next to us is a large map that shows all eighteen (eighteen!) holes and a serpentine lake that winds through the course.

"Who wants to go first?" Neal asks.

"Not me," I say quickly, which makes everyone laugh. "I'll be last."

Jane is unlucky enough to be first. I try to take note of how she's standing and hitting the ball. She manages to get her blue ball in the hole in two hits. Theo manages the same, and Neal has a hole-in-one. Jane claps and cheers for him like he accomplished something awe inspiring.

It's my turn. I copy the stance of everyone else, but I feel awkward. Maybe because I'm so tall? No, Theo did fine. It's just me. I'm awkward.

"Is this how I hold the club?"

"Move your hands a little higher. And it's a putter," Theo tells me, then kisses me on the temple. As if kissing me is normal! After that I can't focus on anything.

I pull back, aim for the ball...and miss it. Spectacularly. The putter is at least three inches off. My face turns to fire.

"Don't pull back so far," Jane says with a kind smile. "Just a few inches."

I do as she instructs and manage to hit the ball hard enough that it bypasses the hole, skips over the side of the course, and into the lake. Did I think my face was a bonfire before? Now it's an inferno.

"I should've taken you to the driving range with that sort of swing." Theo's teasing is good-natured. "I'll go grab you another ball. Be right back."

"Sorry," I say to the other two. "I'm bad at this." Though not any worse than I expected.

"No worries," Jane responds. She loops her arm through mine. "We aren't in any hurry."

I point behind us to two groups that are waiting for us to move on. I hate feeling like a hindrance. "They might be."

197

GRACE J. CROY

She shrugs. "Then they came to the wrong place. If it really makes you uncomfortable, we can let them go before us."

Theo returns just as a third group lines up behind us. I predict they'll just keep coming, so I may as well get this over with, or we'll never finish the course.

Nine swings later I'm rethinking that decision. The stupid purple ball finally goes into the hole, and I breathe a sigh of relief. The groups behind us cheer, which heightens my embarrassment. I'm tempted to follow my first ball into the lake. Maybe never leave. Rumors will start to spread about a swamp witch who retrieves balls for free food.

Instead, I bow at their applause, as if this was my plan from the very beginning.

We head off to the next hole, and if anything, I'm worse. I hit the ball too soft or too hard, but with Jane, Neal, and Theo, instead of taking it personally, I'm able to laugh it off.

We finally, *finally,* finish the eighteenth hole. I now have a deep hate for mini golf. Still, I've enjoyed the double date, even if mine was fake, and managed to make two new friends.

It's a revelation that Theo is right: I don't have to be perfect to be liked.

Chapter Twenty-Four

AVERY

WEDNESDAY MORNING, MR. BALDWIN'S SECRETARY CALLS Theo and asks if he's available to meet with the owners. I watch him leave the Cubby, and wonder if when he comes back he'll be my boss or remain my cubby mate. I can't decide which one I'm hoping for more and make no progress on the invoices waiting to be paid.

When he returns just before lunch, he meets my gaze and shakes his head. "No promotion."

A mixture of disappointment and relief settles over me. He's still my fake fiancé. I instantly feel horrible for my selfishness. But maybe not that horrible?

AVERY: It had nothing to do with our fake engagement?

THEO: That had no bearing on their decision.

AVERY: I'm so sorry. You were the perfect candidate for that job. Their loss.

THEO: Are you up for Waffle Wednesday tonight?

My heart jumps. I hardly notice the change in subject because I've just secured an invitation to Waffle Wednesday! Ever since I first heard about his family tradition, I've wanted an invitation. I love the picture of his family on his desk, the one with Michelle and her husband Steve, and Theo's four nieces, Stella, Naomi, Kitty, and Roe. They're the perfect family.

I couldn't face them on Sunday when Theo invited me because of the basketball-shot-I-shall-never-think-about-again. But that night didn't change anything between us so I think I'm up for it now.

AVERY: Does your family believe we're friends, dating, or engaged?

THEO: BF 4 EVA

I laugh, and Bob grumbles at the noise.

THEO: No fake anything with my family.

AVERY: Yes. I would love to go

The second I hit send I wonder, *what if they hate me?* Ugh, I hate that my thoughts even go there. Jane and I have texted back and forth over the last two days. Meeting new people doesn't have to be horrible. Or even scary. Besides, I have four more days to practice being brave before facing my mom. This is a perfect opportunity. And, most importantly, I'll have Theo with me.

He sends me a winking emoji and a thumbs up. After that, I force myself into Number Land and the rest of the day flies by. Until an hour before the work day ends and Theo messages me.

THEO: Michelle sent a text. Kit broke her arm longboarding. They don't know how long they'll be at

InstaCare, so Waffle Wednesday is postponed until tomorrow.

AVERY: Is she okay?

THEO: She will be. It looks like it was a clean break. I still owe you dinner. Want to try that new Asian fusion place that just opened? I'll see if I can grab a reservation.

It's just another dinner with a friend, maybe it could classify as a fake date, but the way he looks at me makes me feel like I've just been asked out to prom.

AVERY: Can we meet there? I think I need to dress up a little bit more

What I'll dress up in I have no idea since all I have that fits are the casual flowy dresses and skirts. I never thought I would see the day I'd have to dress up *after* work.

THEO: I'll come pick you up.

Once home, I try on everything in my closet. What I settle on is the same blue jersey dress I wore when my parents visited two weeks ago. It's stretchy and comfortable, but looks elegant at the same time. The problem: it shows my baby bump. It's still small but it's obvious a baby lives inside. I take a big, deep, steadying breath and hold it. Am I ready to show Mango off? Yes. I think I am.

I'm slipping on my flats that make my feet look huge, when my eyes land on my sparkly silver heels. I've never worn them outside of my house. Tonight feels like the perfect time to break them out. I don't even care how tall they make me. Bonus, I'll still be a half inch shorter than Theo. Without another thought, I kick off the flats and slip into the heels. They make my calves look amazing.

I feel...sexy.

Even after I look in the mirror and am too tall to see the

top of my head. My reflection cuts off just below my eyes. I laugh instead of rethinking my shoe choice.

When Theo knocks at my door, I'm ready. Just as I'm reaching for the knob, I pause. What if it's not Theo, but Savage Al? I take a peek through the peephole, and it's him. He's wearing a gray suit that makes my whole body heat up. He is indecently beautiful. I open the door, and his eyes catch on my stomach. People are going to do that all night. Maybe I'm not quite as ready to show off Mango as I thought I was.

Before I can run back to my room and change, Theo steps forward and puts his hands on my hips.

"You're gorgeous," he says with such sincerity I can't doubt him. "Ready?"

His eyes are clear as he gazes straight into mine. His touch feels right, normal even. Weeks ago we were only friends, and as much as I insist that we will remain friends forever, the air zapping between us makes me wonder if that's true. This is more than friendship, but not a relationship. I suppose it's the fuzzy place called "fake engagement."

"Yes," I whisper. "I'm ready."

We hold hands as we walk to his Rogue. It's a beautiful evening. Yesterday and today's monsoon rains have left the air muggy and fresh. On the drive to the restaurant, Theo and I sing along to the radio.

I'm happy. I have Theo, Mango, and a delicious dinner waiting for me. It's a perfect evening.

The restaurant is crowded as the maître d leads us to a table in the middle of the dining area. We both scan the menu, the burble of conversation surrounds us as we discuss different meal options.

A waiter passes by, leading two other diners to their table. It's the scent that waifs toward me that makes my heart jump into my throat. Spicy and masculine. Followed by a too familiar laugh. I know, before I look up, who is also eating here tonight.

"What's wrong? Are you okay?" Theo's voice sounds far away, not from across a narrow table.

I struggle to swallow. My throat is so dry. "Tyler."

I'M HOT AND SWEATY. MY SKIN IS CLAMMY. I FORCE AIR INTO my lungs when I realize I've stopped breathing. I cannot make a scene by fainting. A perfect night has become the worst of the worst. I hide behind my menu. When open, it's large enough to cover a good portion of my upper body.

Theo scoots his chair around to my side of the table so that we're sitting next to each other. He opens his menu and hides, as well. We're spies. Awful spies that are going to get caught because we are terrible at hiding in plain sight.

"What do you want to do?" he asks.

"Leave. Just as soon as he's not looking."

I peek around the side of my menu. The waiter sat them at a corner table, with The Liar facing the dining room and his date with her back toward me. Making it impossible to leave without him noticing.

What are the chances that I'd run into him in a city as large as Tucson? I'd hoped so minuscule as to never happen. But now it has. If it's happened once, there's the possibility it will happen again. I will never be free of him. Everywhere I go, I'll be looking over my shoulder, wondering if he's somewhere nearby, ready to pounce on me.

"He can't see me," I whisper. Out of all the times to wear a dress that shows Mango. "He cannot find out about the baby."

Theo's expression turns somber as he nods. "Okay. As soon as he's distracted, we'll slip away."

By the way his foot is bouncing under the table, I surmise there's something he's not telling me.

"What are you thinking?"

He shakes his head. "Nothing. We need to focus on getting you out of here without him noticing you. I could create a distraction."

"He's met you before. He can't see you either."

"He won't recognize me. The one time we met, he was more interested in checking out Sandra."

Ouch. It shouldn't surprise me that The Model stole The Liar's attention while I held his hand, but still, ouch.

"Sorry." He grimaces. "That slipped out. It really bothered me at the time, and I guess I'm not over it."

Of course, it would bother him that some creep was checking out his girlfriend. It *shouldn't* bother me that he's thinking about Sandra right now. I have more important things to think about. Like escape from said creep.

Another peek around the menu doesn't put my mind at ease. He's still looking around at the other diners while his date talks. She leans forward as her hands move through the air. It always bothered me when he would seem more interested in watching other people than me, but he heard every word I said. I'm just not captivating to look at. Not like

The Model.

The Liar's eyes cut directly to me, and I quickly move the menu back in place. Oh gosh, did he recognize me? Or is he just curious about the two weirdos hiding behind menus?

I have to get out of here, but I'm stuck. I'm taking a wild guess that this isn't the type of restaurant that brings out cake and sings happy birthday, but if the waiter would come by, I'd give him a lot of money to create just such a distraction in the opposite direction.

I glance at Theo. His bouncing knee picks up tempo. He's peeking from behind his menu and studying The Liar. Seeing his anxiety somehow calms my own. At least a little. I place a hand on his knee and press down. He turns his attention to me.

"What's worrying you?" I ask.

"Nothing."

"Don't lie to me. I don't want you to lie to me." I've had enough with liars.

"It really is nothing to worry about now. I'll talk to you later."

That makes me all kinds of impatient. Whatever he's thinking, it has something to do with The Liar. "Tell me now."

He shakes his head. I glare. He points over his shoulder toward the door. I glare harder.

He leans forward and whispers. "Maybe it would be better in the long run if you talked to Tyler about the baby sooner rather than later. You could run into him again and secrets have a way of coming out. What if the baby has health issues and—"

I'm not listening. Fury has taken over cognitive thought.

"He *abandoned* me, Theo. I'm not telling him anything. He isn't father material."

"I agree. He's scum. I doubt he wants to be a father, and there's a good chance he'll waive his rights if given the chance. All I'm saying is it might be worth looking into."

"That creep over there professed to love me," I bite out the words through a clenched jaw. I have so much hurt, anger, and shame in my chest, I'm not sure I can say what I need to in order to make Theo understand, but I try. "He used me and then he disappeared. Do you know what I stupidly believed when he didn't respond to my texts or phone calls? That he was dying on the side of the street somewhere. I thought he needed me. Like an idiot, I called every hospital in a thirty-mile radius. I searched through every online platform for any information about him. He was nowhere, and only after a full weekend of fear and worry did I realize he left me on purpose."

I'm near tears and ready to crumble under the weight of my humiliation. Pregnancy hormones are exacerbating my emotions, and it's impossible to rein them in. I'm not sure I want to.

"And now," I say with tears running down my cheeks, "You think I should invite him back into my life? Invite him to be a part of my baby's life? No. Definitely not."

"That isn't what I'm saying at all. If you work everything out now, you don't have to live in fear that he might come after you about the baby later."

I didn't have that fear until this very second. I have to get out of here. Another peek over the menu shows a waiter standing beside The Liar's table, blocking me from his view. Now's my chance. I'm out of my chair and marching for the exit. My heels don't make it easy. I feel like I'm wearing stilts. The sob caught in my chest doesn't help either, or the overflowing tears. I turn down the hallway where a sign tells me a bathroom is located. If I'm going to fall apart, I would prefer to have something to blow my nose into that isn't my skirt.

"We have got to stop meeting like this," I mutter to the bathroom tiles. I wipe my face with a wet paper towel and grab a wad of toilet paper before braving the restaurant again. I peek around the corner of the hallway into the dining area. There isn't any way The Liar can see me from his angle.

My goal is the front door. Theo's there, waiting for me. I see nothing else, not even the man who bumps into my shoulder and makes me stumble. The fresh air of freedom is so close!

A hand catches my elbow.

"Avery?"

The sound of The Liar's voice freezes my limbs, my tears, my heart.

"I thought that was you. Wow, you look great."

I turn slowly, unwilling to face him but unable to stop myself. With the extra height of my heels, I loom over him. I'm too large in this small restaurant foyer. Like I'm Winnie-the-Pooh, stuck in the too-small-hole of Rabbit's house. All I want is freedom, and I'm caught in the one place I don't want to be.

The Liar is gorgeous, especially as he smiles with soft lips and all his perfect, white teeth on display. I trusted that smile once upon a time. He captivated me, like a Venus fly trap attracting its next meal.

Now, I'm afraid. Terrified of what he can do. I stand before him emotionally naked, a turtle without a shell. Any verbal poke or prod, and I will die. His eyes scan over my body from toes to hair. His eyes land on my stomach. *No, no, no, no. Do not notice the baby.*

His date comes into the foyer. "Tyler, what are you doing out here? You didn't even finish your order."

When she notices me, her eyes scan me up and down, much like Tyler did. From her expression, she must think I smell. Her arms wrap around his in an obvious, unspoken *mine.*

I once felt the same way. Now I wish I could dig the memories out of my brain and pretend my time with him never happened.

Theo comes up beside me and holds my hand, offering support. I grasp it, though I'm still upset at what he suggested minutes before.

"You've gained some weight," The Stupid, Horrible, Liar says. "I hope that wasn't on my account."

His date shifts uncomfortably at his remark. I want to rescue her from The Liar's smooth moves, or at least warn her that he might not be as trustworthy as he appears. I want to be brave, to stand up for myself in a way I never did when we were dating.

"You're alive," I say. My voice is soft, weak, and I hate myself for it. I swallow down the smallness I feel in The Liar's presence and dig into the bravery I hope I possess. Somewhere. "I was so sure that you were dead after you kissed me good night, and I never heard from you again." With each word my voice gains strength. "What other reason could there be for you to ghost me unless you were, in fact, a ghost?"

"Avery," he begins, his voice is smooth and cajoling. I get some satisfaction from the way his eyes dart to his date, then to Theo before landing back on me. "We had our time, but we weren't meant to last. You know that. It's been months. Time to let me go."

I think Theo's about to say something, but this is my battle. I squeeze his hand, and he remains silent.

"Rewriting history, are you?" I ask. Maybe Theo is right. Maybe the best way to keep The Liar out of my future is to tell him the truth tonight. I may have fallen for his lies for months, but I still know him. He doesn't want the responsibility of a baby. At least I hope not. "I let you go months ago when you lied about how much you loved me before abandoning me and our baby."

The color drains from his face, and he looks down at my stomach again, this time realizing the truth. I feel great satisfaction in seeing his confidence and swagger disappear.

"Wow, Avery. I am not the father of..." he waves his arm in the air between us.

His date lets go of his arm and takes two steps away into the crowd that has gathered.

Fear is lapping at my heels, but I force myself to continue. "Send me your lawyer's information. I'll have my lawyer contact yours. We have a lot to discuss about child support going forward. Eighteen years going forward. Just think how you can show off our baby's picture to all your girlfriends. Everyone loves babies."

From the look of horror on his face, I hope I'm making

the right choice. "In a few years, when the baby's old enough, we can also share visitation. You'd like to have your child fifty-percent of the time at your place. Especially over weekends, right?" When I've sufficiently horrified him, I dangle the carrot I hope he snatches up. "Or, if you'd rather, you can waive your parental rights. No child support, no visitation, no responsibility. I'm sure we can work something out."

I've never seen anyone go so pale. He's the one who looks small. I stand at my full height, plus three inches. No one will ever make me feel small again. Now, I can leave. I turn toward the door, but Theo doesn't follow.

He says, "This is from her father."

His fist knocks into The Liar's face and he crumples to the ground. Theo shakes out his hand, and together we leave the restaurant. Scattered applause follow us out the door.

My composure lasts just as long as it takes to climb into the passenger seat of Theo's Rogue. I do a full body shudder. When did it get so cold? Theo removes his suit jacket and tucks it around my body, then rubs at my arms.

"Avery, everything is going to be okay."

My teeth are chattering so loud I'm afraid I'm going to bite my tongue. I'm freaking out, and I need an answer right now. "What if he decides he wants to be a part of my baby's life? What am I going to do? I hate him. I hate him so much."

Theo pulls me into his embrace, and a smidgen of warmth soaks into my chilled body.

"I'm in awe of your bravery, Avery. You were amazing. Whatever happens going forward, we'll take it one day at a time."

We'll? Seeing The Liar for the first time since he ghosted me brings up so many painful feelings. I can't go through that again. The more I rely on Theo, the more it will hurt when he never reciprocates my feelings. That kiss on Saturday proved he likes me. But like is a distant mark from love.

I pull out of his arms and stare out the windshield. My teeth continue to chatter, and my whole body shivers even more now that I'm out of his embrace. I'm terrified for the future in a way I've never been before, but I won't show Theo.

"We aren't really a couple."

He flinches at my biting tone. Maybe I'm upset that he suggested I tell The Liar about Mango. Maybe I'm angry at myself for loving him too much. Whatever it is, I don't allow myself to regret what I say next.

"Our fake relationship is only for the office. We should stop hanging out after work."

"You're still my best friend."

He's killing me. But I can't love someone again who won't love me in return.

"Take me home. Please?"

Chapter Twenty-Five

THEO

I COLLAPSE ONTO MY PORCH SWING AT THE FRONT OF MY house. What just happened? Despite my worries, things were good between us this week. Until Tyler came along and ruined everything with his mere presence.

As I drove Avery home, I tried to convince her that I'm not going anywhere, but she has it stuck in her head that *everything* between us is now fake, not just the engagement.

She doesn't trust me anymore. I get it. She's scared. I'm scared too. Scared of losing her for good. Scared Tyler really will want to be involved with Avery and the baby going forward. I want to protect both of them, but what if I've put them in the way of harm by my suggestion? What if Tyler sees some benefit in taking from Avery what she loves the most?

Gigi whines from the other side of the front door, so I cut my worry party short and go inside. Aaron and Chloe are cuddling on the couch watching a horror movie. I don't want to disturb them. I'll take Gigi out back through the door in my bedroom. We could both benefit from playing catch for a little while.

Except Chloe sees me with the eyeballs she has in the back of her head.

"Theo!" She jumps up off the couch and approaches me like I'm dinner and she's a ravenous tiger. "I really like Avery. Aaron says you guys aren't dating, but I'm pretty sure what I interrupted last week was a kiss. What is going on?"

Aaron pauses the movie and looks over the back of the couch. "Did you kiss her?"

I haven't seen him much since last Saturday. He's been going into work early and I've gone out with Avery every night.

"You guys make the cutest couple," Chloe continues. "You're both so tall. Are you going to ask her out?"

I shake my head to her question. "She's dealing with the effects of her last relationship. Maybe in a few months."

If I get the chance.

Chloe isn't one to give up. "Whatever! I see the way she looks at you when you're playing basketball." She whistles. "Your feelings are not one-sided."

"Evidence proves otherwise."

"Tell me all about this evidence, and I'll interpret it."

She drags me toward the couch, pushes me into the love seat, then sits back down next to Aaron. Gigi believes she's a lap dog, and puts her paws on my knees. I lift her up the rest of the way and I scratch her ears.

Chloe continues. "Seriously, Avery wears her heart on her face."

I laugh at that. "She hides everything behind a pleasant smile."

"Maybe only when you're watching. Come on, spill the deets."

What do I have to lose? If Chloe thinks she has an inside track on Avery, I'd love the help.

"Avery's parents came into town a few weeks ago, and I met them. Our coworker found out and told everyone that we're dating. This week when we were out shopping this same coworker saw me kneel down to grab something from the floor and told everyone that we're engaged. In the middle of a work party."

Aaron whistles. Chloe's eyes grow large.

"Not only that, but this coworker also told everyone that Avery is pregnant and that I'm the father."

"Why would your coworker say that?" Chloe asks.

Her pregnancy is out in the open, so I'm not breaking any confidence by telling them.

"Because Avery *is* pregnant, but with her ex-boyfriend's baby. The guy who ghosted her five months ago."

Chloe's jaw hinges open. "So that's why you don't want to date her?"

"No, I want to date her. My brother-in-law suggested I wait until after the baby's born. But now, I don't know if I'll get the chance because at dinner tonight we ran into Avery's ex-boyfriend, and she confronted him about the baby. He had no idea she was pregnant until now, and she's afraid he's going to want joint-custody, and I'm suddenly the bad guy because it was my idea to tell him."

Gigi whines, and I realize I've been petting her a little rough. I take a deep breath to calm down.

"Do your coworkers still think you're the father?" Aaron asks. "Have you done anything about that situation?"

"Nope. We're faking it for now." My original plan of faking it until we make it real isn't panning out. "Avery is not happy with that plan."

"Of course, she's not happy! It's not a real engagement!" Chloe turns her head to Aaron, back to me, then to Aaron again. "Boys are so dense."

Aaron raises his hands in front of himself. "I have nothing to do with this."

"Only because I'm here to save you from doing anything stupid." She pats his chest before directing her attention back to me.

"I don't doubt that she's into you," she continues. "I think she might be afraid after being ghosted. That can mess with a girl's head big time. Still, a girl likes to know where she stands with a guy. Be honest with her, the sooner the better, but don't pressure her into a relationship. Just tell her you're interested and leave the rest up to her."

It's the opposite of what Steve suggested, but what have I got to lose? Honestly...a lot. I've been here twice before: in love with a woman who doesn't love me back.

"What if I tell her that I love her, and she doesn't feel the same way?"

I'll be alone again. That's what happens.

Chloe doesn't hear the desperation in my voice.

"You love her? Awww." She clasps her hands in front of her chest and gives Aaron a dopey smile. "Isn't that sweet?"

Aaron looks like he might laugh at me. He's shaking his head and giving me an, *I told you so* look. "Yep. Sweet."

"You have to tell her how you feel," Chloe insists. "Guys

think girls are hard to understand, but not really. All we want is upfront honesty. Faking a relationship is messing with her head. Especially because she has feelings for you, too."

"If Avery only sees me as a friend after I tell her I love her, I'm going to feel stupid." A man only has so much heart to lose. "I should soften her up a bit first, right? Show her what a good boyfriend I would make?"

If she'll let me.

Chloe doesn't agree. "Not if she thinks it's fake. Tear off that Band-Aid. If she doesn't love you back, then at least you're not left wondering. It'll be better for both of you in the long run."

"I agree," Aaron says. "You two are the perfect couple if you'd both stop being afraid. No pain, no gain."

That motto might work in the gym, but I don't think it translates well into relationships.

"I'll think about it."

That must sound like agreement to Chloe. She claps her hands, bounces on the couch, and squeals. "Do you think I can be a bridesmaid at your wedding? I feel I've been instrumental in bringing you two together."

I'm not sure if I find her enthusiasm encouraging or frightening. "Avery could very well want nothing to do with me." That seems the most probable outcome after tonight.

"Oh, I don't think so. Just bring her flowers. Roses have a way of winning over hearts."

THURSDAY MORNING, I ARRIVE AT WORK FIFTEEN MINUTES early with two dozen red roses. Avery is already sitting at her desk and doesn't look up as I enter, nor when I place the vase on her desk. Bob takes more notice of the gesture, and his response is to roll his eyes.

I sit down and try to catch her attention over our monitors. Nothing.

THEO: I'm sorry for opening my big mouth yesterday.

No response.

For hours, she ignores my instant messages. I miss us being on the same team.

At eleven, her phone chirps with a text. As she reads it, all the blood drains from her face. I'm around our desks in seconds, kneeling beside her.

"What is it? What's wrong?"

"He made an appointment for me at a lab to check paternity." She grabs my arm in a vice-like grip. "Theo, what if he wants my baby?"

Her voice is a screech. Bob can't ignore this. Nor can the group of new hires walking past, following Mary on their welcome tour. Never before have I felt this frustrated with having no privacy in our office.

Once the newbies are further down the hall, I tug Avery from her seat and lead her across the hall to the copy machine. Is now a bad time to notice that Avery's still wearing my mom's ring? Probably, but I do find it encouraging that she didn't remove it last night.

The copy room is tiny, with a counter and cabinets along one wall and just enough floor space to walk around the mammoth copier. But it's private. Once the door is shut, I take Avery into my arms. She doesn't pull away. Also encouraging.

"What exactly did his text say?"

She lifts her phone up, and I quickly scan his text.

THE LIAR: I made an appointment for you at DNA Testing Labs. I want to be sure that what you're carrying is mine before we proceed. Here's my lawyer's info.

The Liar? I like how she labels him accurately.

"I'll come with you," I say. "Do you have a lawyer? I know Steve does. I can call him."

Now she pushes out of my arms. She wipes at her face and swallows any remaining tears.

"No. Theo, stop. I'll handle this. Tyler is not your problem. You don't need to worry about me. The baby and I are going to be just fine."

She reaches for the doorknob. She's going to leave me. I am completely useless if she doesn't let me help. I want her problems to be my problems. I want to help carry her worries and concerns.

Chloe is right. Avery still sees this as a fake relationship. Why would she trust me if she doesn't believe what I feel for her is real? It's time to tell her everything and hope she wants the same as I do.

"What if I want to worry about you and the baby?" I say.

She pauses in her retreat. "You deserve so much better than this mess. I'm just holding you back." She begins to remove the ring from her finger, and I clasp her hands between my own before she can remove it completely.

Here it is. My heart is beating in my throat but I push forward.

"Avery, if I can live in such a way to deserve you, I'll be

happy."

Her brow furrows, and she takes a few steps back until she's against the wall. She doesn't take back her hand, and our arms stretch out between us.

"I love you. Nothing about the way I feel for you is fake. When I think about the future I want, it's shared with you."

It's a relief to be able to tell her how I feel...until I get no response. She stares at me without moving for an eternal fifteen seconds. I count every one of them. Her swallow is loud in the silence of the room.

When she finally speaks, it's to say, "I'm pregnant."

The tension inside of me comes out in an awkward laugh. "Yeah, I know."

"I'm a packaged deal."

"I'm always up for a good deal."

"I'm awkward and ordinary and imperfect."

"Awkward, ordinary, and imperfect is exactly what I'm looking for."

She tilts her head, unamused. "You deserve someone so much better than me. You should start your own family and not take on someone else's mistake."

She hasn't laughed in my face or told me there's no chance. Just that she doubts me because of her own doubts. That's something I can work with. I take a step closer.

"I'm not perfect either, you know. I leave wet towels on the floor and dishes sit in my sink for days at a time. I think I'm right more often than I probably am. I want to take care of you in a way that will drive you crazy if you give me a chance."

I pause. One side of her lips lifts in a half-hearted smile, but she doesn't say anything.

"Will you give me that chance?"

"I don't understand how you can love me." It's a whisper, but I hear every word.

I take another step forward. She leans toward me, but there's still a foot of space between us.

"You don't have to be perfect to be lovable." This may be the refrain I give her every day for the rest of her life. Her mom did a number on her self-worth. The kids in middle school didn't help any, either.

She leans in closer still. There's a vulnerability in her expression she doesn't often show. "Once you get to know me better, you might change your mind."

"Not gonna happen."

"Tyler said he loved me, and then he left."

"Tyler is a selfish..." I bite my tongue on what I want to say. "Jerk."

That lifts both sides of her mouth. "I..." She bites her lip. "I'm scared we'll ruin our friendship. I can't lose you."

"Aaron tells me that friends make the best girlfriends."

I close the distance between us, and she leans into me, her head on my shoulder.

"I'm scared, too, you know," I say.

"What are you scared of?"

"What if you decide you can do better than me?"

It's happened twice before. It may happen again.

She snorts softly. "There is no one better than you."

It isn't *I love you,* but it's a start.

I let go of her hand and wrap my arms around her, pulling her into my chest. She comes willingly.

"Avery Morgan, will you be my official, real girlfriend?"

I can feel her smile against my neck. "I would like that."

We stand holding each other. Nothing has ever felt so right. I could stand like this for hours. I have no desire to move. Until Avery kisses my neck. Kissing is nice, too. I turn my head and kiss her cheek, then skim my lips down to her jaw. Our lips meet, and I sigh. Kissing is more than nice. It feels necessary to life. I can't believe it's been a week since our lips last met. They should get together every day. Multiple times a day.

The door opens, and our lips break apart. Avery tries to pull away, but my arms keep her in place. One of the guys in marketing stares at us with wide eyes for two seconds before stepping back out.

"You need to get back to work," Avery says. "And I have a lab appointment."

"I'd rather stay here." She pinches my side, and I loosen my hold. "Okay, okay. Want to skip Waffle Thursday and watch a movie at your place tonight instead?" I lean closer and whisper, "That's code for making out."

She kisses my jaw before stepping out of my reach. "No way. I've been hearing about Waffle Wednesdays for a year. I want to see what it's all about."

Huh. I had no idea she wanted to eat waffles on Wednesdays. I wish I'd invited her months ago. "It's about eating waffles."

"And meeting your family." She rubs her nose. "Unless you think your sisters won't like me?"

"They'll love you. How could they resist?"

I definitely can't, and kiss her one last time before she slips out the door.

But then she turns back. "Thanks for the roses. They're beautiful."

Chapter Twenty-Six

AVERY

DNA TESTING LABS IS A FIFTEEN-MINUTE DRIVE FROM WORK. I should be running the streets instead of driving them because of the nervous energy coursing through me from Theo's declaration of love. He *loves* me. He loves *me*. One second, I'm elated. The next second, I'm giggling like I'm twelve. Then, I'm freaked out that he'll change his mind. *How* can he love me? I haven't earned the love of someone as good as Theo. All I know is that he *does* love me and I decide to trust him.

I'm exhausted.

I'm exhilarated.

And now I'm giggling again.

Luckily, Uncle Dan returns my call while I drive, interrupting my freak-out fest.

"What did you need?" he asks.

After he promises that everything I tell him is

confidential, even from my mom, I give him the quick version of the situation. If he's shocked by my predicament, he's professional enough not to show it.

"What is it you want from Mr. Vance?" he asks.

"Nothing. I don't want anything to do with him ever again."

"All right. I'll contact his lawyer and find out what kind of arrangement his client is looking for. We'll know more once the DNA results come back."

"Thanks, Uncle Dan."

"Anything for you, sweetheart."

We hang up as I pull in front of the lab. The Liar exits the front door as I park.

He has a black eye, which gives me a zing of satisfaction. That doesn't mean I want the chance to gloat. I slouch lower in the driver's seat, but at over six feet tall, there isn't much space to hide in Ladybug, and my paltry efforts fail. He sees me and veers in my direction. There is no way I'm facing him while squished in my car, and I climb out as he walks up.

My best plan of getting through this encounter is to show an emotionless exterior. I've had a lot of practice while growing up, pretending Savage Al's taunts and the bullying at school didn't hurt. I know I can do it, just as long as my pregnancy hormones agree to the plan.

"Avery."

I look at my phone to check the time. "I need to get inside. Don't want to be late."

He moves to block my way. "I paid extra to put a rush on the test. We'll know by tomorrow afternoon. If that baby isn't mine, then I'll go to small claims court and make you pay for the testing."

"This is your baby."

"I'm not so sure. I see the ring on your finger. Your boyfriend was pretty protective last night. You can bet I'm coming after him for assault. I have witnesses to back up my claim."

I'll have to talk to Uncle Dan about that, too. But for now, I move to walk past The Liar, ready to be done. He grabs my arm and holds on tight.

"I'll also sue you for slander. You humiliated me in front of the whole restaurant. My date works in the same building I do. You couldn't have at least called me on the phone to accuse me? You had to wait until you had an audience?"

So, this is my fault? He's the one who came after me at the restaurant. I tried to avoid him. Theo's right. Tyler is a selfish jerk.

I look him directly in the eye. He won't intimidate me. "If you'd done the decent thing and broke up with me instead of ignoring my phone calls, then I might have done just that. As it is, the universe brought us together, so that you can take responsibility for your actions."

He shakes his head and smiles, showing his teeth. "No, what I think is you're still in love with me. That's why I needed to disappear all those months ago. You're too clingy. And now you think you've found a way to always keep us together. You're wrong. This won't work."

I hope he doesn't notice me deflate. Was I clingy? Maybe. Would I have let him go easily if he had broken up with me like a decent human? I was a little obsessed with him near the end, but I'm not the type of person to stick around when I'm not wanted.

No! Stop! It doesn't matter. What he did was wrong. Even

if I was clingy, he's still a jerk. I pull against his hold until he lets go.

With head held high, I say, "When the test results are returned, expect to pay out of your eyeballs for the next eighteen years."

I march purposefully away and ignore whatever he yells at my retreating back.

It takes an hour to fill out the forms and have my blood taken. It's amazing that Mango is such a part of me that her DNA floats in my blood. I'd feel the majesty of it if that didn't also mean The Liar's DNA was in there, as well.

———

THEO PULLS UP IN FRONT OF MICHELLE'S HOUSE, AND MY breath catches. It's a massive home with a blue iron door, flat roof, and stucco exterior. The setting sun glints against the large, front window. The neighbors are distant enough that the house is surrounded by a natural landscape of cacti, Sweet Acacia trees, native bushes, and shrubs. It's so quiet, with just an occasional car passing, it's as if we've left the city altogether.

I take off the fake-engagement ring and slip it into my purse. It's a relief not to lie to his family, but I immediately miss the weight of it on my finger.

We walk up the long path hand-in-hand. The closer we get to the front door, the more my armpits produce sweat like its employees are afraid of losing their jobs. I hope Theo doesn't notice how I surreptitiously flap my arm like they're wings. I've dreamed about meeting his family for a long time, and now I finally am, but as Theo's *girlfriend*.

A girl comes running out the front door and throws herself into Theo's arms. I recognize her from the picture on his desk. This is the youngest niece.

"Teddy!"

Teddy? That's really cute. Can I call him Teddy?

"You didn't bring Gigi?" she asks.

"Not tonight. Avery, this is my little sister, Roe."

"Who are you calling little? I'm the tallest in my class."

If I remember correctly from Theo's stories, she would have just started middle school. I wish her well. I still have nightmares about those two years.

Theo waves me inside the house before him. I wish he wouldn't always act like a gentleman because I would like to hide behind his broad shoulders.

The front door opens into a large living space with the kitchen visible through an arch in the back. The sweet smell of cooking waffles makes my stomach wake up. Roe runs into the kitchen, her sandals echoing on the tile floor. Laughter and conversation come from where she disappeared.

The second youngest, Kitty, sits on the couch watching what looks like a documentary on motorcycles. Her broken arm, wrapped in bandages, is propped up on her lap with pillows.

"How are you feeling Kitty?" Theo asks.

"It's Kit, Teddy. How many times do I have to remind you? And how do you think I'm feeling? I broke my arm, and I'm high on pain meds."

I think that was a joke, but she says it deadpan, so I'm not completely sure.

We walk through the arch and into the kitchen. At the counter, slicing strawberries, are the two oldest girls. If I remember correctly, Stella's only a few years younger than me. She's about five-five with dark hair and a tan complexion. She and the youngest, Roe, look similar to each other except for Roe's rounder cheeks and younger features. Still, anyone would be able to tell they're siblings. If they were closer in age, they might even be mistaken for twins.

Naomi's the second oldest and just started her first year of college. She's at least three inches taller than Stella, and the differences don't stop there. She's leaner, lighter in complexion, and the only blonde in the family. Freckles scatter across her nose, cheeks, and forehead.

Roe walks by and grabs a fist full of blueberries from a bowl. Stella slaps her hand.

"Stop it. We don't want your grubby hands in our food." She peers at Roe closer. "Did you get into my make-up again? I told you to leave it alone. You're too young."

Her scowl would melt microwave-safe plastic. "I'm twelve! Everyone else at school is wearing makeup." She stomps away and plops down in a chair at the table, stuffs her fistful of blueberries into her mouth at once, and crosses her arms over her chest.

"Girls, stop arguing." This comes from Michelle, who turns from the sink and notices me and Theo before anyone else in the kitchen. She has the same smile and green eyes as her brother. Her expression is open and welcoming. Still, I feel uneasy. I want her to like me so much that my sweat production picks up another notch.

"Avery," she says as she wraps me in a hug.

"Hi." I hope I don't smell. I'm almost positive I remembered deodorant this morning.

"I'm so glad to meet you. You are so—" I expect her to say *tall* since that is the very first thing people notice about me. Instead, she says, "—beautiful. Teddy's description hardly does you justice."

Theo actually blushes. It's kind of my favorite.

"Thank you for the invitation," I manage to say. My rapidly beating heart is making my vocal cords quiver.

"Of course," Michelle continues. "These are my daughters. Stella, Naomi, Monroe, and Kitty's in the living room."

From the living room comes, "It's Kit! Not Kitty!"

Naomi studies me and Theo. "So, Teddy, this is your coworker you haven't stopped talking about for the last four months." She smiles at me. "It's nice to finally meet you."

It's an obvious dig at her brother, but this time I'm the one who blushes.

"Roe," Michelle says, "You're supposed to be getting the ice water ready. Grab the milk and orange juice from the fridge."

The front door opens and a few seconds later a young man sticks his head around the archway into the kitchen. "Am I too early?"

Naomi skips over to his side and smacks a kiss onto his lips. "Nope. Now you can help me set the table." She brings the young man over to where I'm standing. "Avery, this is my boyfriend, Seth. Avery is Teddy's girlfriend."

My heart jumps at the title of "Girlfriend." It's hard to believe it's true.

"It's nice meeting you." Seth's red hair is cut short, and it seems he's been spending time outside because his nose and cheeks are pink.

Michelle hands Theo an avocado and a fork. Without a word, he gets to work cutting and mashing. Naomi and Seth set the table together while they laugh and whisper. Stella slices peaches, and Michelle takes one waffle out of the iron and places it on a cookie sheet in the oven before adding more batter.

I stand awkwardly in the middle of the commotion. "Is there anything I can do to help?"

Michelle looks around at the food and activity. "I think we're just about ready. Why don't you go sit with Kitty for a few minutes?"

Feeling a little like I've been banished, I go where she suggests and sit down on the second couch. I don't want to jostle Kitty's—Kit's—arm.

I'm not great at idle chit-chat, especially not with teenagers, but I feel self-conscious sitting here not saying anything, so I try. "What grade are you in this year?"

She doesn't look away from the television, but she answers as if I didn't ask the lamest question ever.

"I'm a junior."

"Do you enjoy school?"

"Not really. I like shop class. This year they're teaching us how to take apart an engine, so I'm excited about that."

Oh gosh, I know nothing about cars except how to turn the key. "How's your arm?"

She sighs. "It hurts."

Right. Stupid question. Of course, it hurts.

Michelle saves me from asking another stupid question

when she calls out, "Everyone to the table. Stella, go grab your father. Let's eat."

When I reenter the kitchen, Theo takes my hand and leads me to a chair which he pulls out for me. His nieces notice his chivalry, or at least Naomi and Michelle do. They share a look. Is it a good look?

The table is covered with food. Waffles piled high, whipped cream, a gravy boat with homemade syrup, chocolate sauce, chocolate chips, berries, and peaches.

Stella and an older man come into the kitchen. His head is shaved but his dark beard is full and well-trimmed. There are gray patches on both cheeks. He looks a lot older than his wife.

"Avery, this is my husband, Steve."

He yawns. "Sorry, I just got back from a business trip and was taking a little nap. It's nice to finally meet you."

"Your leftovers are in the microwave," Michelle says.

"Thank, hon." He kisses the top of her head as he passes.

I glance at Theo. "Leftovers?" I mouth.

He leans close. "Steve doesn't like waffles."

It's a travesty. His meat loaf and veggies just do not compare to the spread before me.

Once everyone is sitting, the food is passed around in a slapdash manner. All the toppings are passed in my direction before I'm able to snag a waffle. I take a crunchy one and douse it in chocolate sauce and peaches. I notice Michelle is the only one who puts mashed avocado on her waffle. It's kind of a weird combo, but maybe good? Like avocado toast?

The conversation moves around me at lightning speed, and I try to take it all in at once. This is a lot like Tamra's large family, but lightyears away from mine. Discussions during meals at my house were usually quiet affairs that revolved around the farm, homework, and my future domination of the financial world.

Theo reaches over and runs his thumb along the bottom of my lips. He shows me the pad of his thumb, now smeared with chocolate. Our eyes lock, until Roe next to me jostles my arm as she reaches for the milk. I manage to pull my attention away from him and wipe my mouth with my napkin.

Okay, totally inappropriate physical contact for a family meal. I'll have to lecture him later about proper touching in public. And looking. We should not share hot looks like that in front of anyone. I hope none of his family noticed. I'm too flustered to look around to see.

Theo is not flustered. He leans close and whispers, "Do you want some waffle with that chocolate sauce?"

I whisper back with my trademarked eloquence, "Shut up."

He laughs and that does draw his family's attention.

"Avery," Steve says, "Theo tells me—"

—For a flash I think he's going to mention my pregnancy because Mango is always at the forefront of my thoughts and my heart jumps—

"—that you're new to Tucson within the last year. How are you enjoying it here?"

An easy question. I like easy questions. "I love it. It's very different from the farm I grew up on, but I like the pace and all the restaurant options."

All the other conversations quiet as Steve and I talk about our favorite restaurants. Soon everyone is asking me questions. My life is boring, but they don't seem to mind. Questions lead to conversation, and I'm folded into their family meal as if I've always been here.

I love Waffle Wednesday.

After dinner, I get put on dish drying duty. This is much better than being banished to the living room to make awkward stabs at conversation with a teenager. Theo wipes down counters nearby. I shake excess water from a bowl in his direction.

He quirks an eyebrow. "Really?"

Roe's washing dishes and flicks soapy dish water at him next.

He plucks a few blueberries from the bowl and launches them at us. Roe flicks more water. He throws more berries. He's a good shot, probably from all the basketball he plays. I laugh, which alerts Michelle to our shenanigans, and that puts an end to our fun.

When all the food's put away, an epic round of rock, paper, scissors takes place to decide who gets to pick the game. Stella comes out the winner and picks gin rummy. I'm good at this card game since it's my mom's favorite, but before we get started, I slip to the bathroom. I should not have drunk so much orange juice. It goes right through me, and with my bladder at half capacity, I'm sure I'll be visiting this room a few times tonight.

Before going back to the kitchen, I take a moment to relax in the silence. I really like them, and they seem to like me, too. I rub my belly. I hope they'll like Mango when they find out about her.

I open the door, then jump when Michelle is waiting just outside.

"Sorry to startle you. Can we talk for a minute?"

"Sure."

Do I have a choice? Her hiding out in the hallway doesn't bode well. My armpit factory starts working overtime again. She doesn't waste any time.

"Avery, I like you, I do. But I love my brother. He is literally like a son to me. I raised him from when he was eight years old, and I know him, and I know how he thinks. He is a superhero in disguise. Do you know what I'm saying?"

I think so, but I'd rather not guess. I shake my head.

"He's always rescuing. Pets, plants, people. He can't help it. He sees someone in need, and he does everything he can to help. I know he likes you, but I'm worried that he's getting involved with you for the wrong reasons."

I lean back against the wall, weak. Am I a rescue project?

"Family is the one sure thing Teddy's always wanted in his life. He feels like he's wasting time not having kids yet. You come as a ready-made future."

So, she already knows about Mango and isn't a fan. I cover my belly protectively with my arms. I've been worried about Theo taking on responsibility for me *and* the baby, but is the baby what he finds so appealing about me?

Michelle continues without a care for the hurt her words have caused.

"I don't want to wreck the friendship you two share. All I'm asking is that you be careful. Don't give him too many reasons to stay if he isn't in it for himself. Promise me that?"

I nod. Like her, I don't want him to stick around because he feels a compulsion to rescue me or because he wants to be a father as soon as possible.

"Thank you," Michelle says.

I follow her down the hall to the kitchen in a daze. Theo waves me to the seat next to his and once I'm sitting, he wraps his arm around my shoulders and kisses me on the temple. It calms me, but I can't deny Michelle has planted a bur in my mind that I won't easily be able to pluck out.

I'm not at the top of my game and Steve wins. He prances around the table in a wacky victory dance that leaves everyone laughing.

Chapter Twenty-Seven

AVERY

I'M IN MY PAJAMAS WHEN A KNOCK COMES AT THE DOOR. THEO dropped me off a few minutes ago, so I expect that it's him returning for one more kiss. I'm happy to oblige and don't bother looking through the peephole, which I regret the moment I open the door.

"Hey, Avery," Savage Al says.

I'm not completely surprised to see her. Still, I don't want to chat tonight. I'm on a Theo high and want to go to sleep remembering what it feels like to have his lips on mine. Before I can shut the door, she reaches out a hand.

"Can I please talk to you for a few minutes? That's all, and then if you want, I will never contact you again. Just for the record, I'm hoping that isn't what you decide."

If I get this over with now, I don't have to wonder when she'll come by again. I step back and let her inside. Mom will flip if she finds out Savage Al stopped by, which means I have another secret, and I promised myself I would stop collecting them. So no more visits.

She does a cursory look around my apartment before turning around to face me. I don't offer her a seat, and we both stand and stare at each other. She's filled out in the last ten years. She was waif thin in high school. Growing up, I was jealous of her figure, so unlike my broad, curvy, abnormally tall one. She's a solid five-nine. Oh, to be normal.

"So. What did you want?" I ask. I sound gruff and impatient, but that isn't necessarily how I feel. I'm...not sure how I feel yet. I guess it depends on what she says.

"I'm sorry for the way I treated you when we were kids. I was horrible and I am so, so sorry."

It's the sincerest apology I've ever heard, but I'm hesitant to accept it. "So, you said in your letter. But why now? You've had ten years to apologize."

"Right. Like I haven't tried." She snorts and rolls her eyes. That harks back to her teenage self. "Mom never let me talk to you. She thinks I'm bad, and she didn't want me to taint you or Gavin with my cooties." She sounds upset but then takes a deep breath and lets it out slowly. Smiles. "With Mom being your guardian, it's been impossible until now. I only found out you lived here a few weeks ago."

"Why do you care? You hate me. You always have. You threw a basketball in my face."

She grimaces. "I didn't mean to hurt you with the basketball. I thought I was helping give you a life skill."

I raise my eyebrows at that lie. "Uh huh."

"Honestly, I wanted to prove that I was better at something than you were. I was jealous of you."

That's laughable. "Jealous of me?"

She sits down on the couch without an invitation. I guess this is going to be a longer visit than I'd prefer, so I sit on the recliner opposite.

"You're so smart. You don't chafe under Mom's rules. You're the perfect daughter."

I used to be the perfect daughter. "So, you gave me a broken nose and two black eyes?"

"Again, not on purpose. Because of my dyslexia, I struggled in school. I tried, really, I did, but I never improved enough to satisfy Mom. And then you started school and were the star student from your very first day. I'm ten, and Mom is telling me to 'try harder like Avery does. Why can't you read? Avery can read and she's only six.' I could never compare. Eventually, I stopped trying to compete with you and instead tried to pull you down."

This is a revelation. I had no idea Alison had dyslexia. I've always been proud of my status as the perfect daughter. I purposefully attached my homework to the front of the fridge just so Alison would see my grades. So that I could show her I was better. Shame swallows me whole.

"That isn't an excuse for how I treated you," she continues. "I look back and wish that instead of pushing you away, I'd been a big sister you could have looked up to. Just not in academics. I would never be able to compare with you there." She looks me up and down while a smile grows. "Probably not in height, either. Anyone ever tell you you're tall?"

It's so tongue-in-cheek that I can't help but laugh. She joins in, and I believe this is the first time we've ever shared a joke. At least that I remember. Our laughter is a valve that releases tension I hadn't realized I carried.

"I live in Mesa," she says. "That's not too far away for sisters. I'd love to introduce you to my husband and daughter."

I could not feel more surprised if she told me she belonged to the circus.

"You're married? Does Mom know? Because I really think she'd forgive a lot if she knew you weren't a heroin addict living on the street."

Any lightheartedness disappears from her expression. "Is that what you thought about me?"

I nod.

She closes her eyes and scrunches up her face. "Is that what Gavin believes? That I'm a homeless drug addict?"

I nod again.

"I shouldn't be surprised. Mom doesn't forgive anyone. Why would I expect her to forgive me?" She stands and paces in front of the couch while she rubs her temples. "I don't want to tear the family apart. I just want to be a part of it. Blake, my husband, hates his job. We want to move to Thatcher, help dad on the farm, and be a part of Gavin's life. Why does that have to be so hard? But Mom won't let me near him. Her lying to my son like this is enough to convince me to call a lawyer. He's *my* son!"

I'm so confused. "And you told Mom all of this?"

She runs her fingers through her hair and pulls on the ends. "So many times. I know I failed as her daughter. I've apologized over and over again. It doesn't matter. I disappointed her, and this is her payback."

"She just wants what's best for us." I've said it so many

times that it rolls off my tongue with ease even though I'm not sure I still believe it any more.

"She isn't about what's best," Alison says in hard tones. "She's all about punishing those who don't live up to her standards. Did Dad ever tell you about her parents?"

I shake my head. "Just that they're dead."

"No, not dead. They live thirty minutes away from here. Mom just refuses to acknowledge their existence because of something that happened when she was a teenager. Dad doesn't know what happened, and Grandma and Grandpa wouldn't tell me. But whatever it was, thirty years later she still hasn't spoken to them. Why do I expect anything different in my case?"

In ten minutes, I've discovered a grandma, grandpa, brother-in-law, and niece. My family has doubled in size.

Another piece of my mom that slips into place. She bullies people to get what she wants. She lies to those she loves. And she doesn't forgive.

"Why did Dad tell you about Grandma and Grandpa and not me?" I ask.

"Maybe because you didn't need to know? I think he finds life goes along smoother if he doesn't get in Mom's way. He told me about them because I had nowhere to go after Gavin was born."

"You ran away." That's one thing I know for sure. "Weren't you with Brad?"

"Brad went to college. He wanted nothing to do with me after Gavin. I didn't want to leave home, I just didn't feel like I had a choice. Mom spent seven months telling me how I wasn't ready to be a mom, that motherhood is hard, and I was too immature to succeed. I was afraid I would ruin

Gavin's life if I stayed, so I left. I didn't know what else to do."

My whole life, everything I thought I knew, has been rewritten. I know nothing.

"I had no idea," I say.

"You were thirteen."

"I'm not sure I would have cared even if I had known the truth."

I hated the fighting that went on in the house, and I wanted her to disappear. When she was gone, all I felt was relief.

Alison's pacing stops, and she studies me. "But you care now?" There's hope in her voice.

Alison isn't Savage Al. When we were kids, she was mean and hateful. I was afraid of her. But now I understand that she was hurting and afraid herself. Does that erase the scars she left on me? No, but it does change the way I see her now.

"Yeah. I think I do care now."

She comes over and holds out a hand. I take it. Sisters. For the first time, that feels like a blessing and not a curse. I stand and wrap her in a hug. We don't hug often in our family, but Theo is a hugger, and he's rubbed off on me. Alison doesn't seem to mind.

"You're such a shrimp," I say.

"In some circles I'm considered tall."

"Not this one."

And for the second time, we laugh together as we pull apart.

"I can't believe Mom pushed you out of the house." Actually, I can. What she said to Alison matches what she's said to me since she found out about Mango. "Why would Mom tell us you're homeless?"

She starts pacing again.

"Me being homeless isn't exactly a lie. I lived with Grandma and Grandpa for a few months, but I was so depressed and angry that I ran away. It was a few years before I made it back to them, and they helped me straighten out my life. I've never taken heroin, but I was a mess with alcohol. I've been sober for five years. I got my GED. I'm a manager at a grocery store. I'm better. I waited to contact Mom again until I was sure I wouldn't be a bad influence on Gavin."

"I remember you coming by when he was a toddler."

"Yeah, those were my homeless days. When I got to missing Gavin too much, I'd come by and beg to see him. I don't blame Mom and Dad for not letting me inside. It was why it took me so long after sobriety to contact Mom again. She wasn't happy to see me, but she made me believe if I followed her timeline, I'd get to become a part of his life. But from what you've said, it doesn't seem like she's told him about me. She promised she would."

"What are you going to do?" I ask.

"I don't know. I have a stable home, and I'm his mother, so I feel like I have a solid case to fight for him, but he doesn't know me. I don't want to rip him away from his life at the farm. I want to be a part of that life. If Mom had just let up with all the school shaming when I was a kid and let me be me, I would've stayed and helped dad run the farm." She stops pacing and closes her eyes. "I'm not blaming her. At least, I try not to."

"Mom wants Gavin to take over the farm, but he wants to be an astronaut."

Her expression softens. "Really? What else can you tell me about him?"

For the next few hours, I share stories about growing up with Gavin, and she tells me about Blake and her daughter, Josie. She literally glows as she shows me pictures of her family, and I know Gavin would love to be a part of it. So would I. As we talk, I solidify my plan to drive to Thatcher this weekend and talk to Mom before my adoption appointment on Monday. It isn't just for me and Mango anymore, but for Gavin, Alison, and her family.

At one a.m. we're both yawning and half asleep.

"Do you want to stay the night? I have a king bed so there's plenty of room."

"I should probably get a few hours of sleep before I head back for work, but I'll sleep on the couch. I don't want to wake you up when I leave in the morning."

Still, it's another half hour before I make my way to bed. When I get up the next day, she's gone.

Chapter Twenty-Eight

AVERY

FRIDAY MORNING, I COME BACK TO THE ACCOUNTING CUBBY after visiting the bathroom and find Theo missing from his desk. I was only gone for a few minutes. Curiosity has me ask Bob, "Where did he go?"

He doesn't look up from his computer. I don't know why I expect anything different from him.

Theo and I were in the middle of putting together a financial report, but I do what I can on my own, inputting expenditures. When someone enters, I think it's him until I glance up.

The Model. She's studying me with narrowed eyes and pursed lips. Her hip is cocked with her hands at her waist. Neither of us speaks, but her continuing perusal makes my hands start to sweat.

After the BD picnic, I expected her to come and find me, but it's been a whole week. I hoped I'd gotten off without a confrontation. Her eyes dart to Bob before she comes closer and leans on the edge of my desk, much like Theo does.

She asks quietly, "Are you really pregnant?"

I don't want to share one iota of myself with The Model, but this isn't something I can lie about or brush aside. Mango may be well hidden today under my loose blouse, but give it another month, and the answer will be obvious.

I give Bob my own quick glance just to find him staring at his computer screen like usual. "Yes."

"It's not Theo's baby."

It isn't a question, but a statement. Here is something else I can't lie about.

"No."

Her eyes turn glassy, and she angles away from me to wipe at her eyes. When she turns back, her emotions are under control.

"I knew it. He swore to me at the picnic that you two weren't dating." Her eyes go to my hands sitting still on my keyboard and my own follow. The engagement ring winks up at us. "Yet you've found the way to make sure he'll marry you. He wants kids more than he wants me." Her voice cracks, but I can't look up at her. The guilt of lying about our engagement sits heavy on my heart, but since she doesn't ask a direct question, I let it slide. "I thought if I left first, he would come after me and give up on his dream for kids. It didn't work that way. I held out too long, and now I'm too late. He's found a new mom for his baby, and it doesn't even seem to matter if it's not his baby."

"It's not like that," I say.

But it is, isn't it? Michelle's words run through my mind. *Don't give Theo too many reasons to stay if he isn't in this*

244

relationship for himself. Without the baby, we wouldn't be as close as we are. Without what we've been through the last three weeks, he wouldn't have professed his love.

I don't want to trap him because of his need to rescue broken things. But I don't want to let him go, either.

"He gets everything he wants," Sandra says. "He has a fiancée who wants to be a mother. He has a baby on the way. He has a promotion. While I feel left behind. I love him so much I even talked myself into wanting a baby. Now he doesn't need me."

Her attention drops to my stomach. I cover Mango with my arms, even as I'm trying to decipher what she's saying. I'm confused on so many levels. So, it was her desire not to have children that broke them up? And what's that about a promotion?

"Theo didn't get the Chief Financial Officer position," I say. Maybe she hadn't heard.

"He was offered it, but he turned it down. Dad and Baldwin really like him, and there's another position coming open in the next few months. That's where Theo is now, talking to Dad about becoming a Regional Manager of Sales. He doesn't want Theo to leave, and this way Theo wouldn't be your boss, but he can still be on the executive team."

I feel nauseous and weak. Theo lied. He turned down his dream job. Because of me. Because of the baby and the responsibility he feels toward us. A manager of sales isn't what he wanted.

"You win," Sandra says.

"It was never a competition."

"Wasn't it?" She stands and walks out of the Cubby. She

gives me one more backward glance before she disappears down the hall.

I lay my head on my desk. What should I do? How do I make this right? How can I be sure that Theo wants me for me and isn't professing love to save Mango and me? Or because he wants a family ASAP?

"Don't listen to her." My head pops up. Bob is looking directly at me. "That boy loves you. I've seen it as plain as day for months now. She never even had a chance."

I quickly count and tally the total words. That takes the number he's spoken to me since I started working here up to eighty-three.

My phone rings. It's Uncle Dan. "Hello?"

I look back up at Bob, but his focus is on his computer screen. As if he hadn't just dropped a bomb in the middle of my mind. *That boy loves you... She never even had a chance.* He pays more attention than he lets on.

Dan gets straight to business. "We got the paternity test back. Mr. Vance is willing to do anything at this point not to have to bear any responsibility. We need to talk."

I sag in relief. This was just the news I needed right now. But I can't have this conversation here. I need to leave. I need to think. Somewhere Theo won't find me. I can't have him look at me or all my reservations will flee. "Can I call you back in fifteen minutes?"

"Sure thing."

I stare unblinking at the wall, thinking through my options. First, I need to untangle Theo from my life and my baby. *Don't give Theo too many reasons to stay if he isn't in this relationship for himself.* If he's really in it for himself, then nothing will change. If he's in it for anything other than me, then it's better to find that out now instead of later.

Gossip Girl passes in front of our Cubby, her attention straight ahead. She's avoided me this week, which I've appreciated, but now there's something I need her to do. I go out into the hallway and follow her into the bathroom.

When she comes out of the stall, I'm standing next to the sink, arms crossed.

"Hello, Mary."

"Sandra just told me that Theo isn't the father of your baby. Is that true?"

Sandra wastes no time. She knows exactly who to talk to in order to get this new information spread throughout the office. She doesn't know it, but she's only doing me a favor.

"Yes. It's true."

Her shoulders slouch. "Oh man, I really screwed up, didn't I?"

"Yes, you did. We're not engaged, either."

"But...your ring."

I study it on my finger for a few seconds before I slip it off. I feel bereft already, as if a part of my heart is missing. "It's fake. Theo was just trying to help me out."

Her expression perks up for half a second before they turn repentant again. "I promise I won't tell a soul. I'll keep your secret. I really am sorry. Sometimes I can't help but share good news. There's so much sad news in the world, I like making people smile. But, I promise, no more spreading gossip."

I hope she doesn't mean it. That's why I'm here.

"Oh, don't stop now. This is the juiciest bit of gossip we've had at Baldwin-Dickson in a long time. Since Friday in fact, when you told everyone Theo and I were starting a family."

She blanches, and I feel bad since she did apologize. But not that bad.

"Please activate your gossip network and tell everyone that Theo and I are not engaged and that this isn't his baby. The father is a guy I dated for a few months at the beginning of the year." I'm impressed with how strong my voice sounds. On the inside, I'm quaking. "You'd be doing both of us a huge favor if you let everyone know."

Her nose scrunches up in confusion. "You're sure?"

"Yeah, I'm sure."

I'd like to march out of the bathroom with my head held high, but I've really got to use the toilet again and I slip into a stall instead.

Chapter Twenty-Nine

THEO

I can't wait to tell Avery about the amazing position I've just been offered, but she isn't in the accounting office when I return. Probably in the bathroom again. I don't think much about it until I sit down at my desk and see the folded piece of printer paper next to my keyboard with my mom's ring box on top.

For a long moment, I don't move. I flashback to three years ago when my fiancée in Phoenix broke up with me. She didn't actually return the ring, but folded a note inside the box and left it on the seat of my car the Friday before a long weekend.

Yeah, I know how to pick winners.

I tap my fingers on the top of my desk until Bob clears his throat and gives me a pointed look. Enough procrastination. I flip open the lid. At least this time the ring's inside. I can only hope the message in the note is dissimilar as well.

Theo,

The lies have to stop. Mary's doing what she does best and spreading around the office that you aren't the father, and we aren't engaged. You're free!

I'm on my way home to tell my mom the truth. Wish me luck.

Please don't contact me for the next few days. We need time apart. Everything between us has moved so quickly over the past week. Meet me for lunch Sunday at noon at The Pit so we can talk?

PS—You should've told me the truth about turning down the promotion. I would've understood. Well, probably not. But it bothers me that you lied. No more lies, okay?

Avery.

Weariness settles into my bones. She didn't outright break up with me, but I don't know where this leaves us. The letter's vague to the point I'm not sure if I have a chance with her, or she's letting me go by degrees. Is it too much to ask for someone willing to fight for me as hard as I fight for them?

And what's this about freedom? What have I done over the past few weeks that makes Avery think I want to be free of her? I want to be tied down, shackled, grounded, whatever you want to call it. I want the two of us living in my house with rings on our fingers and our kids eating waffles on Wednesday nights.

Maybe it's time to pick a new dream.

"Your ex-girlfriend stopped by," Bob says. "Spooked Avery. I hope you're going after her. She's a good one."

Yeah, she is. The best.

Sandra's visit explains why Avery ran. It doesn't explain why Avery trusts whatever Sandra said more than she trusts me. Maybe I shouldn't be surprised. Running is what Avery does when she's cornered. Me declaring my feelings must've made her feel confused or afraid. Still, I wish she'd run *to* me instead of away.

I've never thought of Sandra as an interfering sort, but she's proving herself to be a busybody. She's working her way over to the "People Theo Does Not Like" list, right underneath Mary. Actually, I think she makes the top of the list. Mary didn't frighten Avery away.

I reread the letter looking for any clues, and this time I see the sentence my eyes skipped over the first read-through. *I'm on my way home to tell my mom the truth. Wish me luck.*

I get up and walk along the wall of our small office. She's facing her Mom, probably the hardest moment of her life, and she's alone. I feel so helpless. I need to be there with her, even if I don't say a word. Just so she knows she's not alone. Except she doesn't want me. She would rather face her demon mother solo than with me behind her.

Emily from recruitment stumbles into the accounting office and interrupts my pacing. Giggles from the hallway follow her, cluing me in to what's going on. After Sandra dumped me this sort of thing happened a few times, until they finally figured out I don't date coworkers.

Unless the coworker is Avery.

"Hi, Theo," Emily says. More giggles from the hall.

I pull out my best acting skills. "Hey, Emily. What can I help you with today?"

"I was wondering if you'd like to go out to lunch with me? Or, if you're busy now, dinner sometime?"

Avery never officially broke up with me, and I can use gossip to my advantage just as easily as she can. "I'm sorry, but I have a girlfriend. Going out to lunch would not be a good idea."

Her forehead scrunches. "Oh. I, uh, thought you and Avery weren't engaged?"

"We're not engaged, but we are dating."

"And the baby?"

"I hope to someday adopt her, but I can't claim her as mine at this time." I try not to worry about never getting the chance.

"Um, okay."

"Thanks, Emily. Have a good day."

"Oh, you too."

She leaves as if she's just seen a brown recluse spider, and I collapse back in my chair. I'm getting no work done today. I need to get out of here.

I send a quick email to HR, slip the ring box into my pocket, and head out for an early weekend.

MY HOUSE IS TOO QUIET. I STAND AT THE DOOR OF THE GUEST bedroom. If I breath deep enough, I can almost catch a hint of strawberries.

I grab Gigi and head over to Michelle's. Gigi loves car rides, and her wagging tail shakes her whole body. It makes me laugh. In the mood I'm in, that's miraculous.

The house is empty, but I wander into the backyard and find Michelle and Roe swimming in the pool.

"Gigi!" Roe jumps out of the pool and meets Gigi just as she's about to jump in.

"No dog in the pool!" Michelle calls out as she swims over to the shallow area.

"Why aren't you at school, Roe?" I ask.

"I had a temperature this morning."

"And now you're swimming? Shouldn't you be in bed?"

She sticks out her tongue and makes a face. "Swimming is cathartic. Can I take Gigi for a walk?"

I look to Michelle, and she shrugs. I say, "Sure, just make sure you keep a firm hold on her leash and don't go further than the park."

She throws on her swim coverup and runs inside with Gigi. Michelle climbs out of the pool and stretches out on one of the pool chairs. I sit down beside her and let the sun soak into me.

"Why the visit? Shouldn't you be at work?"

"Yeah, but I have a temperature and decided to come swim."

She snorts a laugh. "I'll have you know she's a very good actress. I really thought she was sick, but now I think she had a quiz fifth period, since that's when she miraculously recovered. She's on dish duty for a week as punishment. What's your excuse?"

"Too much going on. I couldn't focus."

"Tell me."

"Good news first. I was offered one of three Regional Manager of Sales positions. It isn't the job I applied for, but it's on the executive team."

"That's wonderful! Congratulations. They must really like you. When do you start?"

"Not for a few months."

"We'll have to celebrate this weekend. Have a family party on Sunday."

I have to wonder if Avery will be here with me. Why does everyone leave? Why do I keep finding myself alone?

"The bad news is about Avery. Yesterday we officially started dating. Today she fled and doesn't want me contacting her for two days."

She pats my arm. "I'm sorry, Theo."

"You don't sound sorry."

"You know I have my reservations. Besides, you said you were going to wait to do anything until after the baby."

"That was the original plan, but I couldn't wait." I failed the marshmallow test in the area of my life that matters the most. "I thought she was on the same page. She seemed happy at dinner yesterday, right? Why doesn't she believe me when I say I love her?"

Avery's enthusiastic kisses when I took her home last night confuse me now as I think back.

Michelle sighs deeply.

"What?" I ask without looking away from the blue sky.

"I might have something to do with her doubting you."

I turn my head slowly to meet her gaze. "What did you do?"

"We had a short conversation where I simply asked her not to take advantage of your kind heart. I informed her that you are focused on starting a family of your own and might not be rational when it comes to her baby."

I stare for a long time until she starts to squirm.

"I can't believe you went behind my back like that."

"How could I not? I'm worried about you. Your

relationship has developed too fast and too soon after Sandra. You like to save lost things. She is the most lost creature I've ever met."

Arguing about my feelings won't change Michelle's mind. So, I take the backdoor into this argument. "I was only a kid when you and Steve got married, but I remember Mom was not a fan of him. He was in his thirties and you were only twenty-one."

She grimaces. "So?"

"So, you argued about it a lot, but I'm positive Mom never went behind your back and told Steve to leave you."

"Hey, now. I never told her to leave you."

"You don't know her. She has a lot of scars, and you may have reopened some of them. You don't know what she's gone through, and you have no idea how your words came across."

She pursues her lips. "Do you remember when I got you that gerbil?"

It seems Michelle's using a backdoor too. "Yeah, of course I remember Hammy."

"When he died, you were devastated. For a year afterward, you'd burst into tears at random moments. It was like losing Mom and Dad all over again, and it was a *hamster*. I never allowed another pet because I couldn't bear watching you lose anyone else you loved. You have a tender heart, which I want to protect."

"You make me sound like a weakling."

"Being tender is not weak, but it does take its toll. When your fiancée in Phoenix broke off your engagement, you moved back here a shell of the man you are. Sandra started it all over again. Can you blame me when I show concern over you jumping into a new relationship so soon after your last one? A relationship with a woman who is *pregnant* from her own recently ended relationship? I just don't want to see you get hurt."

"What you don't understand is that I'm hurting right now. Avery left me. Your meddling has led to my pain. But you got what you wanted. She's out of my life. Congratulations."

Coming here was a terrible idea. I stand and go back through the house.

"Teddy, wait," Michelle calls after me.

I don't.

When I reach the front yard, Roe's running over the rock scaping in an effort to catch Gigi's trailing leash. To Gigi it's a game, and even Roe's laughing. I'm about to whistle for my dog's attention, when Roe lunges forward. Gigi jumps away, into the street just as a speeding car comes around the corner.

"Gigi!"

Chapter Thirty

AVERY

My first stop when I reach Thatcher is to meet with Uncle Dan. He doesn't have the best news. I can't do anything legally to keep The Liar out of Mango's life going forward. Sure, he doesn't want to be a father right now, but at any time in the future, he can change his mind and insert himself where I don't want him.

The only way to keep him out forever is for him to terminate his parental rights, and the only way to do that is if I'm married to someone else, and they want to adopt. This is something I don't think I can tell Theo because I'm pretty sure he'll try to convince me to elope to Vegas.

"If you allow him not to sign the birth certificate," Dan says, "Which he's refusing to do at this point, then you'll get no child support."

It's a temporary fix. "That sounds fine to me. I don't want his money."

"You're sure? We have the paternity test. You can get him to sign the certificate and pay child support even if he doesn't want any visitation rights."

I want him to disappear. And I'm afraid if I take any money from him, even money he owes to care for his offspring, he'll expect something in return. "I want nothing from him. Except for him to not sue Theo for the assault."

He shakes his head as if he doesn't agree with my decision. Doesn't matter, it's my choice.

"Okay. I'll talk to his lawyer."

Once I leave, I drive slowly to the farm, composing what I want to say to Mom. The moment I pull up in front of the house, my brain empties. I might be sick. I'm sweating through my clothes. I definitely need a new car with a better AC, but for now, I have to face my mom looking like a wet handkerchief. The desire to drive back to Tucson right now is overwhelming, but I have to do this. For me and Mango, for Alison and Gavin.

I climb out of my car, march up the steps, and bang the front door open. Mom and Gavin are in the front room, him at the piano, and her sitting in an armchair reading a book.

Gavin's up and in my arms in seconds. "Avy, did you come to save me? I hate the piano."

I kiss his forehead. He hasn't yet discovered that it's gross to be kissed by his aunt, and I love it.

"I came to speak with Grandma, so you have a break at least."

Mom closes her book. "Gavin, go to your room while I talk to Avery."

He cuddles closer into my side. "I want to stay. I never get to talk to Avy anymore."

"Gavin, go. It's my turn to talk to her."

"It's always your turn."

He stomps out of the room. Mom doesn't seem any happier than him as she closes the book and places it on the end table.

"What was so important that missed a day of work? I'm sure it could've waited until tomorrow. We need you to get a good recommendation from your little pencil company. Eventually, you'll return to the city, and you'll need all the help you can get to find a new, better job."

I can't put this off a second longer, but I'm not sure how to start this conversation.

"Do you remember when I failed a spelling test in second grade?"

She shakes her head and stares at the ceiling. "A second-grade spelling test?"

"I spelled all twenty words correctly, but I put them in the wrong order on my paper. Mrs. Hargreaves marked them all wrong because I needed to pay more attention. You were angry at me for a silly mistake."

"I don't have time for this."

She stands and heads toward the kitchen. I follow.

"I begged you to read to me that night like usual, and you couldn't even look at me."

She sits at the table. Her scrapbook supplies are laid out in front of her. There are pictures of Gavin at the piano, fishing down at Roper Lake, and helping Dad in the fields. She loves him, but for how long? He has a rebellious streak, and I can't imagine him not fighting back harder as he gets older. As hard as this is for me to face Mom, for Gavin, I make myself continue.

"How do you think it made me feel to realize that you only loved me when I was perfect?"

"Don't be ridiculous." She lays pictures on colored cardstock and moves them around to try and find what she likes best. "Of course, I love you always. You're not a mother, so you don't understand the responsibility of motherhood. It's my job to teach you to be your best. When you fall short, what am I supposed to do? Let you get away with it?"

"You could hug me? Comfort me? Definitely not make me feel stupid and small."

"It was just a spelling test."

"It wasn't just one test. All growing up I never felt like I was enough to make you happy. I had to earn your love, and every little mistake brought down your displeasure."

"Psh. You take things too seriously."

"I wonder where I got that from."

"Your father." She laughs as if it's a joke.

Speaking of the devil, Dad comes in through the back door and heads toward the kitchen sink.

"Little Owl. What a surprise. Were we expecting you for the weekend?"

"I'm staying over at Tamra's tonight."

"But we get you for dinner?" He starts scrubbing his hands at the kitchen sink.

"Maybe." It depends on Mom. She won't listen to me like I'm an equal. She isn't hearing what I'm trying to say. Maybe I'll surprise understanding out of her. "Alison stopped by my place yesterday."

Mom's hands pause over the embellishments. She doesn't look up. "Did she?"

"You lied to me about her for years. You lied to Gavin.

Alison wants to be a part of the family and you won't let her."

Dad doesn't look surprised at what I say. He's in on the lie. Is that because it's easier to let Mom have her way, or does he really not care about never seeing his daughter again?

"Dad? Why didn't you tell me the truth?"

He turns off the faucet and wipes his hands on a dishtowel. "I've always left the decisions on raising you girls to your mother. She knows best what to do."

I hate that line. It's blatantly not true. "Did you know Mom threatened to cut me out of the family if I didn't give my baby up for adoption?"

Mom rolls her eyes and raises her hands theatrically. "Now really, Avery. That's going a little far. I never said that."

"You did imply it. You haven't let me speak to Gavin on the phone since you found out about my pregnancy. A reminder of what was coming if I didn't keep in line with your dictates. Right?"

Dad's furrowed brow tells me he hasn't been informed about this. Even if he had, would it make any difference?

"Kate, is that true?"

Mom stacks her paper into a neat pile. "Avery is being ridiculous. I should probably get dinner on." She looks up at me. "I think you should go. I don't want you upsetting Gavin by mentioning his mother. She's best not spoken about in this house."

"He has a right to know she loves him. She wants to be a part of his life."

"No!" She stands and leans across the table, her finger pointed at me. "This is my house, and I decide what happens here. Not you, not Alison. If you want to live here, you follow my rules."

"I'm not moving home," I blurt out. "I'm keeping my baby."

She shakes her head in disgust. "You and Alison are peas in a pod. Exactly alike. I had such hopes for you. But no, Alison comes and tells some sob story, and now you want to follow her example? I've only had your best interest at heart. Always. And this is how you repay me?"

At one time, comparing me to Alison hurt more than any other criticism, but not anymore.

"I respect what Alison has made of her life. She didn't have the support of her parents, but she managed to overcome a lot."

Mom points toward the front of the house without looking at me. "Just go. But know once you leave, you aren't welcome back."

Her words hurt just as much as I knew they would. Tears prick my eyes.

"Kate!" Dad steps forward. "Avery is our daughter. We can't just cut her out of our lives."

I'm amazed that he's sticking up for me. Why didn't he do the same for Alison all those years ago when she was seventeen? Or even more recently, when she wanted to see her son?

"Jim, there are consequences to every decision. This is Avery's consequence. We tried to help her fix the mess she made with her coworker, and she refused."

"Theo isn't the father of my baby," I say. Both of my parents swivel their attention to me. It's a relief to finally be honest about this. "In January I met a guy, and we started dating. He made me believe he loved me, and then he left."

"That's even worse," Mom says. "At least your coworker has a job and seems respectable." She turns back to Dad. "We must think of what's best for Gavin. He doesn't need to know about any of this."

"I'm his aunt. What's best for him is knowing I love him and support him no matter what mistakes he makes." My voice grows louder with every word. "What's best for him is having his mom be a part of his life."

"I can't listen to this." Mom covers her ears. "Ruin your life. Make your decisions based on emotions instead of smarts. But I won't watch, and neither will Gavin."

"Mom, you've already banished Alison and her family. Now you're banishing me and my family. Soon enough Gavin is going to want his freedom to pursue a life he chooses. What will you do if he decides to become an astronaut instead of a farmer? Cut him out of the family too?"

She snorts. "Becoming an astronaut is a childish dream."

"And he's a child. As he grows, he may find a different dream, but I doubt it will be to stay here. All my life you told me to live out my desires. Only recently have I realized that what you were really saying was to live out *your* desires. I don't want to be the head financial advisor to some company. I'm not ambitious. I love my little desk in a cubby off from the main hallway where I can focus on numbers all day. That's my dream, and I'm not sacrificing it for yours."

"Such a disappointment," she mutters just loud enough for me to hear. "Jim, you're on your own for dinner tonight. I need to lie down. I have a headache."

Mom heads for the hallway. Dad calls out her name. She stops but doesn't turn.

"We're a family," he says. "This is the time to come together, not tear apart."

Mom doesn't say a word as she disappears into her bedroom.

Dad lays his hands on my shoulders and tenderly wipes a thumb across my wet cheeks. "I'll talk to her, Owl. We love you. You're not banished from this family."

"And Alison?"

He clicks his tongue. "I don't know if your mom will soften on her. I'm not sure I'm ready to, either. She hurt us both when she was a teenager. She ran away a few times, the alcohol, the verbal abuse. It's hard to trust she's changed. It's hard to forget."

I get it, I do. So much of my childhood was influenced because of her abuse, but I don't want to hold on to the fear and anger any long. It's an amazing feeling to forgive.

"You can't keep her son away from her," I say. "She'll go through the courts if she has to."

"Well, I don't think it needs to come to that."

"If you two don't relent, it will."

More clicks of his tongue. He looks to his bedroom door. "I'll try to talk to her. Don't expect anything soon. It may take a while."

That's about all I can hope for right now. "Can I take Gavin out for the evening? When I visited Unc—" Um, I don't want to mention my visit to Uncle Dan right now. "— When I visited town, I noticed a flier about a star party tonight at the college."

He hems and haws. "He would like that, yeah? He loves the stars."

"Please?" I don't know how long it will be until Mom lets me see him again.

Dad looks one last time to his bedroom door and grimaces. "Okay, but have him back by nine."

I TAP MY KNUCKLE SOFTLY ON GAVIN'S BEDROOM DOOR SO THAT Mom doesn't hear. It opens instantly. Gavin has his backpack on and takes my hand. We tiptoe from the house and load into Ladybug.

I take a second to accept what I just did. I stood up for myself. I didn't back down. I want to call Theo right now and tell him about it, but I can't. I told him no contact until Sunday.

"Do you want to go to a star party at the college?" I ask.

He shakes his head. "I want to go see my mom."

I choke on nothing. "What? Were you listening to my conversation with Grandma?"

"Yep," he says matter of factly. "But I hear a lot of things Grandma and Grandpa don't want me to hear."

What a sneaky kid. "Huh. Like what?"

"I know you're pregnant. I know about my sister, Josie."

How? I just found out a few days ago. "How long have you known?"

He shrugs. "A while. They talk about her at night when they think I'm asleep."

"Why didn't you tell me?"

"Because I didn't think you'd listen. You don't like my mom."

"I..." That was true until this week. "I do now."

"Great. Let's go see her. I brought Monte to give to Josie. Do you think she'll like him?"

Monte is a stuffed gorilla that Gavin still sleeps with every night. His wanting to give it to his little sister is sweet. But it's not like I can take him to Mesa for the weekend.

"I can't take you to see your mom right now. Maybe eventually."

He gives me his puppy dog eyes. "Please?"

How do I say no to that face?

I've climbed into a pickle jar and have no idea how to escape. I pull over to the side of the road and try to think my way out of this. Alison should have a role in her son's life. Gavin should know his step-dad and sister. *But,* if I go behind Mom's back, she will dig her heels in deeper to keep Gavin completely hers.

Unless Mom never finds out? I take out my phone and stare at the screen. Can I take another step in the direction away from Mom?

"You can obviously keep a secret," I say, "So if you don't tell anyone, not even your friends at school, we can call your mom."

He perks up. "Really?"

Yeah, really? Am I going to do this? Yes, I am. I pull up the number Alison gave me last night and FaceTime her.

"Avery. This is a surprise." She looks confused but not unhappy. The sound of grocery cart wheels over asphalt and cars driving past her come through. "I'm just leaving work. Is everything okay?"

"I'm in Thatcher for the night, and there's someone who wants to meet you."

I pass the phone to Gavin. "Hi, Mom."

Alison bursts into tears. It takes a minute for her to get control. "Hey, baby. Wow, you're so big."

"I'm not actually that big. I wish I was tall like Avy. Then everyone would want me on their basketball team."

She gives a wet laugh. "Not all of us are lucky enough to be like Avy. What else do you like to do besides basketball?"

As they talk, I pull back onto the road and head for the direction of the college. We can get dinner on the way.

Chapter Thirty-One

THEO

I PACE DOWN THE MIDDLE OF THE ANIMAL ER WAITING ROOM. Gigi has a broken leg and internal bleeding. It could've been a lot worse. The driver of the car saw her with enough time to slow, but not to avoid her completely. Since the vet took her into surgery an hour ago, I haven't heard any news on how she's doing.

I can't shake the sound Gigi made when the car collided with her. Or her whimpers as I drove to the vet emergency clinic. It's tearing me up inside.

A bawling woman comes out of an exam room with an empty cat carrier. My anxiety grows.

Aaron waits with me. I called to let him know what happened as soon as they took her back. She means a lot to him, too. She's our family. I appreciate him being here, but I wish he would stop staring at me like that.

If I'm making wishes, I wish Avery were here. I want to

call her and tell her about Gigi, but I also need to respect her decision to have no contact.

Michelle arrives.

"Any news?" she asks.

"Not yet. How's Roe?"

Roe was inconsolable after Gigi was hit. She feels guilty for letting go of the leash. It isn't her fault. Gigi loves to run, and sometimes when a lizard catches her attention, she gets away from me too. I shouldn't have let them go off alone. Roe's only twelve, not strong enough to hold on.

This is my fault.

"Steve came home to stay with her." Michelle squeezes my wrist. "You hold on so tightly to those you love. Sometimes you have to let them go."

This is her way to prepare me for the possible outcome that Gigi isn't coming home. She's probably right. It seems that the things I love the most leave me. I sink into myself, and Michelle pulls me into a hug.

No more Gigi. No more Avery. Chloe might actually be the one who keeps Aaron's attention, and he'll move on, as well. I'll bang around my big, empty house for the next fifty years and die a bitter old man.

The mental image of me as a lonely old man puttering around in baggy sweats and slippers breaks me out of my spiraling grief. That is not my future. It isn't in me to give up.

Michelle's words ultimately have the opposite effect than intended. I hold on harder to my hope.

Gigi's still here, and until I hear otherwise, I'm focusing on that fact. Maybe it will hurt more later, but for now I'm holding on.

Avery ran, but that doesn't mean I need to give up on her.

She might not be strong enough to fight for us, but I am. If she decides she doesn't want to be with me, there will be someone else.

But man, I hope with my whole soul there's no one else.

I won't allow myself to fear the pain of a broken heart. Whatever happens here and on Sunday, it won't change me. I'll keep giving my whole heart to those I love and bear the grief that might follow.

I pull away from Michelle.

"Thanks for coming," I say.

"Of course."

We sit next to Aaron. I can't keep my knee from bouncing, and though that usually irritates my sister, she doesn't say a word about it.

After an eternal ten minutes, she leans close and whispers, "I'm sorry for what I said to Avery. I was out of line."

"Yeah. You were."

"I thought I was helping, but I can see that what I said was hurtful, to you both."

It means a lot that she's apologized. Hopefully I get the chance to tell Avery.

"Thanks. Just so you know, I'm hoping she's going to be a part of my life going forward."

"I hope so too. Just maybe not too quickly."

I don't bother bringing up how long she knew Steve before they got married. Seven months, for the record.

"I'm proud of you, you know?" she says. "You are a remarkable young man and I'm lucky to have you as a brother-son."

It's an old joke, but it brings a small smile. "I'm lucky to have you as a mom-sister."

A vet tech comes out of the back. "Theo Decker?"

"Yeah." I walk over to her. Michelle and Aaron follow behind. "How is she?"

"We were able to stop the internal bleeding, and she has a few pins in her leg. Overall, the surgery went well and we expect a full recovery."

I lean into the wall. All the anxiety and stress drain away. Gigi is okay.

The tech continues. "We'll keep her here for the next few days for observation. Would you like to see her?"

"Yes. I want to see her."

"Follow me."

Michelle pats my arm. "I need to call Steve. Roe will be so relieved."

Aaron and I follow the tech back to an exam room. They've put a blanket over her so only her head is visible. Her eyes flutter open, then closed. I pet her neck and she licks my wrist.

"You're going to be okay, girl."

We both will.

Chapter Thirty-Two

AVERY

GAVIN HAS A BLAST PEPPERING THE STAFF AT THE STAR PARTY with a million questions about stars, planets, black holes, nebulas, and a bunch of other stuff I've never heard of before. I love seeing him this happy. I hate that I have to drag him away at 8:40. It isn't even dark enough to see the stars and planets properly, but I don't want to get him home late. Mom will probably be livid I took him out at all, and I'm not sure how effective Dad will be in calming her wrath.

When we pull up in front of the house, Mom and Dad are waiting for us on the porch.

"Can I go home with you?" Gavin asks.

I wish he could!

"No, you need to stay with Grandma and Grandpa. But maybe I can convince them to let you come visit me for the weekend sometime."

That is a big maybe, but I'll try to make it happen. Mom

coming out on the porch to meet us is encouraging. Normally, she would ignore us. She looks angry, but not as angry as I expected.

We both get out of the car and approach slowly.

"Did you have fun?" she asks Gavin.

He nods.

"I'm glad. Go inside and get ready for bed."

Her dismissal is stern and unemotional, but not unkind. He hugs me quickly before running up the steps and into the house.

"I still think adoption is the best solution," she says.

"I know."

"I don't think you understand what kind of situation you're getting into."

"Probably not."

"But," she pauses and takes a few deep breaths. "I...We miss you. We want you to come home more often than you have so far this year."

She walks stiffly back into the house. I'm astounded. This is much more than I expected from her. I get to keep Mango *and* my family.

Dad approaches.

"Did that really just happen?" I ask.

"We had a talk. What you said about losing her whole family really shook her up. She's stubborn, but she isn't heartless. She does what she thinks is best for the family."

"That doesn't mean it's right."

"I know. Or at least, I'm starting to know a little better. Don't give up on us, okay?"

"As long as you don't give up on me."

"Never, Little Owl. Never."

I'VE LEFT TAMRA SPEECHLESS.

We're once again on her living room floor, sitting in a nest made of blankets and pillows. I've caught her up on all the news.

"Your mom," she finally says. "That was almost an apology."

"I know. I'm still in shock."

"I was totally right about Theo."

"You were."

"The Liar." She growls.

"Yeah, but at least he's out of my life. Next time he sees me in a restaurant, I can almost guarantee he'll run in the opposite direction."

"You're a walking soap opera. I really need to move to the city. I could use more excitement in my life."

"I don't think it's this kind of excitement you're looking for."

"No, probably not. But Theo loves you!" She takes my hand and bounces up and down.

Theo. Wonderful, patient, Theo.

"I shouldn't have left him like I did," I say regretfully.

Tamra's enthusiasm dissipates. "No, you shouldn't have."

It would be nice if she didn't agree with me so quickly.

"I let Sandra and Michelle's words convince me that Theo might not have pure intentions. What if he loves me because I'm a damsel in distress, and he feels compelled to rescue me? Or because I can make him a father by Christmas?"

"Do you really doubt him?"

I'm aware that I'm rubbing my nose, but I don't even bother stopping. "What if I'm just as clingy as The Liar says I am, and Theo's too kind to tell me to get lost?"

"The Liar is called The Liar for a reason. Anything that comes out of his mouth should not be trusted. Theo, however, has proven himself trustworthy."

Tamra's right. She usually is. I wrap my arm around her shoulder and pull her into my side.

"We need to find a tranquilizer strong enough to whisk you away without any side effects. Somewhere you can meet a wonderful man who will fall madly in love with you."

She blushes.

"What?" I ask.

"I downloaded a dating app last month."

"And you didn't tell me! Did you meet someone?"

"A bunch of someones, but no one special. It's been fun, though."

"Get out your phone. I want to see these guys."

We send messages to a few matches. We scroll through dozens of profiles. Some of them are worthy of screenshots before swiping left. Much giggling is involved.

Then we pull out the iTunes and sing and dance around her living room until we're hoarse.

It's midnight when she falls asleep, but I can't sleep.

Theo.

Thursday in the copier room was like my perfect dream come to life. He professed his love, combatted all my concerns, and then kissed me like he never wanted to stop. Those were fifteen perfect minutes. Except for one thing: I never told him that I love him in return. Instead, I ran away to the lab for the DNA test.

Earlier today, instead of waiting for Theo so we could talk about my concerns, I ran again. I ran toward something infinitely scarier, and I told myself I was doing it for him, but I should've stayed and told him so instead of leaving a note.

What if all of my running has changed his mind about me?

Then too bad for him. I'm not ready for him to give up on me. I will do everything to prove my love. Whatever it takes, I want us to be a team.

I can't wait until tomorrow to tell him so. And this is definitely not a conversation to be had over the phone.

I shake Tamra awake.

"What?" she groans, then yawns and stretches her arms over her head.

"I need to leave. I have to talk to Theo. Right now."

She smiles sleepily. "Go get your man."

Chapter Thirty-Three

THEO

I'm in bed, but I can't sleep, so I turn on the TV and channel surf for a while. Aaron must be wearing headphones because Oscar the Grouch is walking up and down the hallway meowing loudly. I'm not the only one who misses Gigi.

Gigi is only part of my sleeping problem. I blame most of it on my worry over Avery.

How did things go with her mom? Will she let me love her, or more immediately, let me hold her hand again? I want to call. All evening, my finger hovered over her name in my phone, but I managed to resist. Barely. Now it's the early hours of the morning, and I'm counting down until I can get away with a text. There is no way I'm making it until Sunday.

A knock comes at the bedroom door that leads to the backyard. Strange. It's almost three in the morning. Maybe someone has an emergency and noticed the light from the

TV? Um, probably not when I'm at the back of the house. More likely, it's a guy trying to get me to open the door so he can knock me out and rob me. I grab the fire bat from under my bed and peek out through the side of the blinds.

I can barely make out the dark shadow, but from the silhouette, I know it's Avery. She's rubbing her nose. I drop the bat. In seconds, the door is open and I pull her into my arms. Then the worry sets in again.

"Are you okay? What's wrong?"

She pulls back far enough to look at me. The only light is from the TV inside. It flickers across her face.

"I'm sorry for leaving you that note and running. I promise I will never run from you again."

Relief overwhelms me. Not a breakup letter. A smile stretches across my cheeks. "Yeah?"

"Yeah. From now on, anytime I'm spooked, I'll talk to you about it. Will you forgive me?"

"Of course."

I lean in to kiss her, but she puts her hand up between us. Okay, so we're not back to where we were. I respect that. I loosen my arms to lead her inside, but she doesn't let go of me. We stay where we are.

"Theo, when you say you love me, do you love me, or do you love the idea of rescuing me?"

Michelle. I mentally shake a fist in her direction for casting doubt.

I shake my head. "You don't need to be rescued from anything. I simply want to be with you. I love you."

"You're not just desperate for a family?"

Was that what Sandra said to her? "I want a family, but

I'm not desperate. Definitely not desperate enough to lie about loving you."

She studies my face. "I trust you. I trust that you love me, but sometimes I might wonder if you've changed your mind. Will you tell me you love me every day?"

"I'll do better. Every day, I'll *show* you I love you."

She presses her lips to mine. That's all the invitation I need to kiss her with all the love I have in my heart. I wasn't sure I'd get the privilege to kiss her again, and I feel lightheaded. Or maybe that's because I don't want to take my lips back even to breathe. No matter, I lean into the doorframe and pull her closer. It's Avery that pulls away for breath.

"I love you," she whispers. "You have no idea how much."

She *loves* me. She loves *me*. I've just won the lotto. No one is luckier than me.

"I love you."

Before I can kiss her again, she pokes my shoulder.

"You should've told me about turning down Chief Financial Officer. You shouldn't have done that for me."

Not to be deterred, I give her a quick peck before answering. "I would do it over again if needed. Besides, I was offered a different promotion."

"Sandra stopped by and told me at the office yesterday. But it's not what you really wanted."

"*You* are what I really want. And working with the sales team is exciting. I think it'll be a better fit overall."

"Really?"

"Really."

She yawns. "Can I stay in your guest bedroom again. I'm too tired to drive home."

"Yes."

I take her hand and pull her inside my bedroom, then flick on my bedside lamp. It isn't any cleaner than the last time she saw it, but she isn't looking at the mess. She's looking at me.

I can't hold in my question a second longer. "Tell me about how things went with your mom? I've been worried."

"My mom's upset," Avery says, "But I think I got through to her. She almost apologized and didn't kick me out of the family. She wants me to come home more often."

She barely finishes her sentence before she yawns again. I'm not ready to say good night. The only place to sit is on the bed, so that's where we sit. I put my arm around her shoulder and she leans into me.

"Can I come with you next time?" I ask.

"Yes. I want you to meet Gavin, and my parents need to know that we're a packaged deal going forward." She turns her head to look at me. "Right?"

"Definitely."

"What's up with Oscar? He wasn't meowing like this the last time I was here. And where's Gigi?"

It's hard to tell her what happened. The sound of Gigi in pain will probably never leave me. At least the story has a happy ending.

"I feel terrible," she says, once I finish. "I left you to deal with that all on your own."

"She's okay now. That's all that matters."

"I should've been here."

I wish she had been here, but at least she didn't spend the afternoon worrying. "We'll go visit her tomorrow."

"Before or after basketball?"

I can't help but kiss her again. "Maybe skip basketball? There's some furniture at your place we haven't finished putting together."

She grimaces. "Were you able to finish the financial report without any problems? Sorry for leaving you with it."

Huh. The financial report. "Well, I kind of forgot about the report. I left work early, too."

Her eyes go wide. "Do you think Mrs. Tuttle is going to kill us?"

She whips out her phone and checks her work email. "There's only one email from her, so maybe she isn't too upset? We'll have to go in early on Monday and get it done first thing. Wait. Mary sent me an email. Maybe we got fired." She's joking. I think. When she looks up, I can't tell if she's shocked or horrified. "Theo, did you tell everyone at work that you plan to adopt my baby?"

I scratch my cheek. Right. I forgot about that. It was a little rash to say out loud without talking to Avery first. She's isn't storming out of here furious, so maybe she'll forgive me.

"Um, yeah. I did. It isn't a secret that I love you. I love her. I loved seeing my mom's ring on your finger, and I want to put it back. For forever."

She pulls away. I can't read her expression. Confused? Hesitant? "Are you asking me to marry you?"

"Not right now, but I will. As for adoption, I want to, but that depends on what you want."

A large smile blossoms, and she kisses me. Crisis averted.

"Spoiler alert. I'll say yes. To marriage and adoption. Mango is going to love you so much."

Mango? I must've heard her wrong. "Margot?"

She looks off into the distance for a second. "Yes, Margot. We're both lucky to have you. Oh!"

She grabs my hand and presses it into her stomach. "This is her telling you so herself."

It's surreal to feel Margot push back against my hand. We sit in silence and enjoy the moment. Nothing has ever felt so right as the three of us together.

Avery lays her head on my shoulder, but we keep our hands where they are. Margot has quite the press for being so small.

Avery sighs happily. "I never believed I could be this happy."

That makes two of us.

Epilogue

AVERY

"You're beautiful," Tamra says. She leans in so that both of our reflections fill the full-length mirror.

"I want in, too." Alison comes in under my arm and makes a face. Tamra and I burst out laughing.

"You really are a beautiful bride." Tamra sighs. "Theo is going to faint when he sees you walking down the aisle."

"I hope not. I want to marry him without any delay."

"It might be romantic." Jane's sitting on the bed in her slip doing her best to remove a sticky handprint from the bodice of her dress. "You can kiss him awake with a true love's kiss. We'll call him Sleeping Handsome."

I like it. Tamra winks.

We're in my old bedroom at the farm. It's strange being back just long enough to say goodbye. I'll visit, but it isn't my home any longer. Home is now with Theo.

Music waifs through the open window from the

283

backyard. Family and friends have already begun to gather at the farmhouse. Grandma and Grandpa are out there. They're the sweetest, most supportive grandparents a girl could ask for, and I'm blessed they get to be part of today. Even if Mom isn't thrilled.

Jane shakes out her dress and holds it up. "What do you think? Did I get it all?"

"Hard to tell," Alison says. "There's a wet patch on your bust, but I don't see a handprint any more. I suppose that's an improvement."

"A definite improvement," Tamra offers.

I'm so lucky to have these women here with me, but it makes me miss Mom. It's been a rough few months as we work out our relationship. She's vocal in her opinions, but she's also learning that I have a voice and am no longer easily manipulated. It's hard to turn off the part of me that wants to make her happy.

She's softened enough that she's in attendance today even though she still disapproves of me getting married so young. She might even have helped me get ready if Alison wasn't here. There's still a lot of resentment between them, but Alison and her family moved to Thatcher a few months ago and have started to get involved with the farm. Dad is now their biggest supporter and has a soft spot for little Josie.

Next month Gavin is moving in with his parents. He can't wait. He spoils his little sister. Josie follows him around like he's her hero. They're the cutest family. Second only to mine.

All these changes haven't been easy for Mom, but I remain hopeful she'll come around.

Then, as if I've willed Mom into being, she walks

through the door. Her face is pinched, but she tries to smile when we all turn to face her.

She holds up her camera. "I thought I would take some pictures for the scrapbook."

The official wedding photographer has already taken pictures of the wedding preparations, but there isn't any way I will say so.

Tamra steps forward. "Why don't you get into the picture? I'll take it."

Mom doesn't object. Alison, Mom, and I stand together and smile. I think Savage Al, Zealous Mama, and Shy Tall Girl might have a chance at complete forgiveness. It's the best wedding gift I could imagine.

KIT

Avery's niece, Josie, is the flower girl. She shyly walks down the grassy hill toward the altar, dropping a rose petal here and there. When she reaches the front, most of the petals are still in her basket.

Gavin and Gigi follow. He doesn't have a shy bone in his body and marches forward enjoying the oohs and ahhs that come as he passes with the dog. Attached to Gigi's halter is a pillow with the rings.

Next up is Tamra and Aaron, the Best Man and Maid of Honor. Tamra's definitely enjoying herself as she glides past the assembled guests. She dyed her hair lavender to match the wedding color, and it looks really good. Aaron smiles at her, and a flash of jealousy erupts inside me.

I lobbied Avery to let me be her Maid of Honor, but she laughed as if I was joking. I would've done anything, even plan her bachelorette party, in order to walk down the aisle on the arm of Aaron Ledger.

They reach the front and separate, but Tamra gives Aaron a flirtatious smirk. He broke up with his girlfriend a few months ago when she moved to California, and I haven't heard that he's started dating anyone new. Tamra looks like she wants to throw her name into the ring of possibilities. With her dimples on display, she has a chance, darn her.

The wedding march begins and we all stand as the bride and her father make their way to the front. Avery is beautiful in a simple sheath dress with embroidered purple forget-me-nots along the hem. Her eyes are trained on Teddy. A glance up toward the front and he's wearing the exact same dopey grin. Avery reaches him, they clasp hands, and he kisses her cheek.

"Everyone be seated," the officiant says. We obediently do as he says. "On this day, we gather together to celebrate Theodore Decker and Avery Anne Morgan's everlasting love. They will begin by sharing vows they've written themselves."

Teddy smiles at Avery. My eyes cut back to Aaron. I want someone to look at me like that. Someone in particular.

Teddy clears his throat. "I have searched for you my whole life—"

Margot, Avery's daughter, has been distracted by Stella for the last half hour, but at the sound of Teddy's voice, she turns her head as if she recognizes it.

"—You have surpassed the woman of my dreams. My imagination could never conjure up a woman of such beauty, compassion, and—"

Margot's face screws up in her pre-cry expression. Stella tries to distract her with a tummy tickle and an ugly stuffed penguin Avery insists is her favorite toy. I don't think four-month-olds have favorite toys.

"I promise to be your sidekick to all of life's adventures. I promise—"

Margot begins to cry. In three seconds, her decibel output goes from twenty to sixty. Everyone looks over at the family row. Stella blushes while she bounces Margot on her lap, but the baby will not be comforted.

"—To cherish, honor, and—"

Nor will she be ignored. Her cries reach eighty decibels. Teddy looks over his shoulder and shakes his head before walking to Stella and taking Margot into his arms. She instantly calms.

There's a wave of whispers from the wedding guests, as they all sigh over how cute the three of them look together under the wedding arch. The photographer goes crazy with the photos, as does Avery's Mom. I've seen the bookshelf full of scrapbook binders inside, and I imagine this event will be just as well-documented.

The rest of the ceremony is quick and within ten minutes the officiant says, "I now pronounce you man and wife. You may kiss the bride."

They enthusiastically comply while everyone applauds. Teddy has one arm holding Margot and the other wrapped around Avery's waist. They keep kissing. We all keep clapping. Oh my goodness, save something for the honeymoon.

It's Margot who makes them stop when she starts to fuss again. She's my hero.

We cheer as the couple walks back down the aisle. It's all rather romantic, but I don't watch them. No, my attention is on Tamra and Aaron. Is it my imagination, or does he wink at me as he passes?

Everyone follows the bride and groom to the big tent set up in a field. I sit at a table near the front with my sisters and a few cousins, while the main table has Avery, Theo, my parents, her parents, Aaron, and Tamra.

If I ever needed proof that life isn't fair, it's Aaron and Tamra talking and laughing throughout the meal.

The time for toasts arrives and while my dad and Avery's dad say their bit, Aaron grows increasingly uncomfortable. When it's his turn, he stands, swallows a few times, then says, "Theo, you're my brother in every sense but the biological one. Thanks for everything, man. Avery, welcome to the family."

Tamra squeezes his elbow as she takes the microphone. Generally, I like her, but tonight I really just hate her.

"Theo, you are one lucky man. Avery is the best person to have in your corner. I saw this day coming long before she did. We made a little bet, and it is now time for her to pay up."

The melody to Christina Perri's "A Thousand Years" begins to play over the sound system. Avery takes the microphone from Tamra and stands in the middle of the dancing floor, facing Theo. She begins to sing in a strong, sure, and beautiful voice. I don't think I'm the only one shocked to see this performance.

She sings the first two verses, then the music abruptly changes to Bruno Mars' "Marry You." Tamra and Jane run out and join her. They've put together a choreographed dance to the upbeat rhythm, and everyone starts to laugh and clap. Theo's loving the show, and clapping along loudest of all.

When they finish the song, Theo comes out and meets Avery. They kiss. Again.

When dancing begins I'm up out of my seat, but Tamra's closer and beats me to Aaron. It's too depressing to watch, and I sit back down. My sisters and cousins disappear except for Stella. I know exactly what she's going to say before she says it. Anyone outside the family might believe she never speaks, but with her sisters, she's bossy, bossy, bossy.

She leans near and says, "You're only seventeen. He's twenty-eight."

"I won't always be seventeen," I mutter.

She shrugs. "You will always be eleven years younger."

"Mom and dad are ten years apart."

"All I'm saying is maybe it's time to let this crush go. He'll always see you as Teddy's kid sister."

Except I'm not a kid. I don't expect anything to happen while I'm in high school, but maybe in a few years. That is, unless he decides to settle down with Tamra. A new song begins, and they continue to dance together. We should institute Regency rules and say no one can spend more than two dances with the same partner.

Finally, after their third dance, a guy asks Tamra for the next one. Now is my chance. Aaron's almost back to his table when I catch up to him.

"Hey, Kitty. Having fun?"

"Wannnadancewithme?" I say quickly, before I lose my nerve.

He looks around. "Um, sure."

We go back to the dance floor, and he takes me into his arms. There's enough space between us to put two bibles. This isn't exactly how I envisioned this going, and I didn't plan very well since the song is almost half over.

"I liked your toast."

He smiles. "Thanks. I had a longer one memorized, but once I stood up, I forgot it all. It wasn't stupid?"

"No. It was really sweet."

He grimaces. "Okay, I guess that's good." He looks over to where Avery and Theo are dancing together. "It's going to be hard to leave next week. Theo and I have done almost everything together since we were nine. But now he has Avery, so it's a good time to make my own way."

Leave? "Where are you going?"

"I have a new job in Connecticut."

"You're moving?" My voice comes out in a screech, and a few people nearby glance over.

"Yeah. It's a good opportunity. And my mom just got remarried. That's my cue to get away before I'm pulled into her drama."

I have not wasted the last five years of my life pining after a guy to have him leave when I'm on the cusp of adulthood.

"Are you ever coming back?"

He shrugs. "Probably when my mom gets a divorce. Someone has to pick up the pieces. Again." He mutters the last word.

I'm at a loss. "Will I ever see you again?"

"Sure." The song ends and his arms drop from my waist. "Thanks for the dance, Kitty. See ya next time."

Except I won't see him next time. He's Teddy's friend, not mine.

"Goodbye," I whisper.

*Find out what happens **seven years later** when Aaron comes home in* It's Not Like It's Fate.

Thank you for reading *It's Not Like It's a Secret!* If you'd like to be notified when the next book in the series releases, sign up for my MVR (Most Valuable Reader) mailing list through my website, gracejcroy.com. Use the QR code below for easy access.

When you sign up, you'll get a free novella, *Kiss Me, Jane,* all about Avery's friends, Jane and Neal.

If you enjoyed *It's Not Like It's a Secret,* please let other readers know by leaving a review on Amazon, Goodreads, or BookBub. A star rating is enough to make a difference!

Thanks for your support!

About the Author

Grace's favorite things include reading, writing, traveling, her cats, and potatoes.

She lives in Utah, in a little house at the bottom of a little mountain, where the snow piles high in the winter.

When she isn't writing, she works as a librarian, planning awesome community events and advising readers on what book to try next.

Her favorite places to travel are New Zealand, California, and Paris. No matter how long she's away, she always loves coming home.

She authored two books in the multiple author *Magical Regency* series, as well as *The Lonely Lips Club, It's Not Like It's a Secret,* and *Her Christmas Rescue.*

Made in the USA
Las Vegas, NV
29 October 2021